My Boy Is Home

The Story of LCpl. Hunter D. Hogan

Pat Sovern

Illustration by Nick Walden

ISBN: 1722906359
ISBN-13: 978-1722906351

DEDICATION

Some men are born to be a cowboy. They yearn for the freedom of riding their horse on the open range and the thrill of jumping on a bucking bronc or bull in the rodeo. They do it, not because of the money, but because of their love for the sport. The rodeo cowboy is as American as you can get. They value the traditions of family, love, and religion. There are still such young men and women today who keep the rodeo alive, but fewer are willing to take such risks.

Other men are born to be a soldier. They may come from a long line of military service or desire to be a part of something bigger than themselves. They also don't do it for the money, because they certainly don't get paid enough. They do it because they want to serve their country and are willing to lay down their life for their family, country, and band of brothers.

Then, there are those few rare breeds of men who are both a cowboy and a soldier. This story is about one such young man. He loved the rodeo and everything it entailed. He was not afraid to get hurt and challenged himself to go farther. Then, he put aside his rodeo career and joined the U.S. Marine Corps, pushing himself to be stronger and braver each day.

I dedicate this book to Hunter "H.D." Hogan as a tribute to him, the American cowboys, and the Marines. These young men and women are the finest resources our country has to offer. They are why I am proud to be an American. H.D. taught me to push myself out of my comfort zone and not be afraid to take risks. He is an example for us all. Semper Fidelis, H.D.!

Pat Sovern

CONTENTS

PREFACE

I was born in Heilbronn, Germany and grew up as an "army brat". My dad was a hard-core drill sergeant. I felt like for most of my childhood, I was in boot camp. MSgt. Neville's character is modeled after him. My mom is a sweet-natured German who gave me the love and support I needed growing up.

I struggled with my own path in life and eventually earned my BA in education. I chose to stay in my hometown: Brownstown, Indiana. I worked in the elementary school for twelve years and was transferred to the middle school to work with special needs students in their language arts classes.

Sitting in the classrooms of Corey Lanier and Brandon Allman and listening to their lessons on grammar and improving writing actually helped me relearn skills to improve my own writing. I am thankful I was given that experience and enjoyed working with those two outstanding teachers. I'm not sure I could have written this book without their knowledge.

I got married and raised my two daughters in rural Norman, Indiana. That is where I met Steve Hogan and his son, Hunter, best as I can figure in 1997. They were neighbors of mine. Our families spent many evenings grilling out and drinking wine. I will always cherish those memories.

Steve told me endless stories about H.D. He shared how he got injured in some of the rodeos. He also told me how H.D. got injured in boot camp and more. The stories were so interesting and humorous, I kept thinking, *This could be a great book!* The idea kept nagging at me. A voice inside my head told me over and over, "You need to write this book!"

Finally, after months of agonizing, *Can I do it?* I decided I would. I picked up the phone one weekend in February 2015 and called Steve. I asked him if anyone had offered to write a book about H.D. He told me, "No." I said, "Well, I want to do it!" There was silence on the other end. I added, "You think about it for a while and let me know." He told me, "No, I don't need to think about it. Let's do this!"

I was overcome with excitement and nervousness at the same time. I still questioned myself if I was capable of writing an entire book. I had written research papers in college and always earned good grades, but this was different.

This book has been a labor of love. Steve and I would go back and forth texting or calling until I got the answers for my questions. I learned more about him and about his son. They both have my eternal admiration and respect. Numerous hours were spent on research. I learned all I could about the rodeo, and I watched several live junior rodeo events and pro rodeo events. I had always had an interest in the rodeo growing up and had ridden horses a few times. My research gave me a new appreciation of the hard work those cowboys and cowgirls put into it and their dedication to the sport.

After I completed the first ten chapters, I spent many more hours researching the Marine Corps to help me learn more about boot camp, the Crucible, and fighting in Afghanistan. I talked to other Marines about their experience to get personal stories. One of those times was sitting on Steve's deck at midnight with one of H.D.'s fellow Marines. We talked for three hours!

This research also made me appreciate the sacrifice Steve, H.D., and other Marines gave to serve our country. The same could be said for all those who serve in the military. Words just aren't enough. This book is my way of thanking them.

To be clear, this story is fiction. Most of the events in the story are true and based on Hunter Hogan's life. Some of the events happened to other Marines. With the exception of H.D. and Gino Mills, I changed the names of the other Marines in the book to protect their identity. Some are still in service today. I added or changed dialogue and details to recreate the events and for reader interest.

The medal of honor citations read during the Crucible were shortened to reduce the length of the chapter, but the full citations are worth reading at the CMOHS.org website. I am honored to have had the privilege to write this book and hope those who read it feel the sense of faith, honor, courage, and commitment that is portrayed throughout it. Thank you for reading this!

Pat Sovern

ACKNOWLEDGMENTS

I would like to thank God for putting me on the path that led me to write this incredible story. I am grateful for my parents who raised me to be strong and value education. My family has been a huge support for me during this endeavor. My two daughters, Amanda and Christina, are the greatest gifts I have been blessed with. I love them dearly.

I would also like to thank those who took their time to answer my questions and share stories about H.D.: Betty Hogan, Scott Hogan, Karah Joyner, Chase Plumer, Laura Plumer, Kyle Mails, Clinton Luttrell, and the outstanding Marines.

I want to thank my brother, Marty, for sharing what it was like for him going to fight in Iraq and Echo Sharkey for writing her beautiful poem and letting me share it. Thank you, Amy Hartley, for sharing your experience as a teacher on the unforgettable day of September 11, 2001. Nick Walden, thank you for your artistic talents illustrating the cover of the book for me.

Thank you, Brandon Allman and Corey Lanier, for imparting your expertise on improving writing to your students and to myself. Finally, and most importantly, I want to thank Steve Hogan and Brittney Hogan for sharing your personal and emotional memories of H.D. Without you two, this story wouldn't have been possible.

Sincerely,
Pat Sovern

1 LIFE IS A HIGHWAY

Letting go of pain and bitterness is not an easy task, but necessary to move forward and embrace the life for which you are destined. This truth most definitely applied to Steve Hogan's life, and the road to that revelation would be a long and bumpy one. In the spring of 2009, Steve's son, Hunter Dalton "H.D.", turned down four full-ride scholarships for rodeo and joined the United States Marine Corps shortly after graduating high school. He was not expecting H.D. to follow his footsteps in the military, but eventually accepted his son's decision.

After suffering from a difficult divorce and scarce jobs in Jackson County, Indiana, Steve knew it was time for a change, not only for himself, but for H.D.'s future. Consequently, before H.D. left for boot camp, father and son made plans to move from Indiana back to Steve's hometown: York, Nebraska. They were going to go into business together working rodeos after H.D. served his four-year tour. Steve found a house near York and sold his property in Norman during the fall of 2010.

While H.D. was stationed at the Marine Corps Recruit Depot (MCRD) in San Diego, California, Steve had made several trips across the country moving his and H.D.'s possessions to the new home. Packing and unpacking the horse trailer while trying to work was wearing him thin. On the second Sunday of November, the

1

last day of moving finally came and none too soon.

Steve woke up early in the morning just before dawn to prepare for the last of the packing. After slipping on his blue jeans, t-shirt, and socks, he drank a cup of hot, black coffee and ate the last piece of biscotti he had made. The house was empty except for the cot and sleeping bag he used to rest in. Steve rolled up the sleeping bag and folded up the cot. He pulled on his cowboy boots and black leather jacket, grabbed his belongings, and headed for the front door.

His boots hitting the hardwood floor echoed throughout the house, mimicking the hollowness of his heart. The house once held the sound of laughter but now was only a constant reminder of what was gone. Steve approached the door, stopped for a moment to check his back pocket for his wallet, and glanced around the room for any remaining items. Deciding he had everything he needed, Steve switched off the light, turned the doorknob, and locked the door as he went out.

The crisp, refreshing autumn air smacked Steve directly in the face as he stepped out onto the front porch of his country home. He breathed in the fresh air and exhaled it slowly out, feeling relieved he was almost done loading the remaining items into the horse trailer hitched to his truck. He walked into the front yard and surveyed the beautiful morning portrait mother nature created for him.

Just peeping over the horizon, the yellow sun splashed brilliant colors of red and pink onto the wispy, white clouds against a dark blue sky. As far as the eye could see beyond the perimeter of his ground, frost provided a thin, sparkling blanket of cover for the remaining corn husks left lying in the fields. The wind whispered, "It is time."

The last of the orange, yellow, and brown maple, oak, and sycamore leaves were strewn around his yard crunching as he stepped upon them. After putting away the cot and sleeping bag, he loaded the rest of his and H.D.'s hunting gear into the horse trailer. Then, he proceeded to gather the saddles, horse tack, and

tools, placing those into the rear of the trailer as well. Steve looked around the dilapidated barn that once held so many relics of past rodeos and reminders of time spent with H.D. He gave a sigh and said, "Guess that's it, Hank. Ready to say goodbye?" A miniature red and white Australian Cattle Dog nuzzled his leg and emitted a *"Rumpf?"*

Steve remembered the day he got Hank like it was yesterday. While in the junior rodeo, H.D. spent a lot of time with a boy whose mom bred the Australian Cattle Dogs. One day, H.D. asked his dad if he could have one. Steve had told him maybe, but later asked Cody's mom about getting a pup for H.D. She said there was a litter due to be born in November. Steve told her to save one for him, but not tell H.D.

When the puppy was six weeks old, he was given to H.D. as a Christmas present the year he was in seventh grade. H.D. was so surprised when he woke up Christmas morning to find the puppy decorated with a big red bow in a basket by the Christmas tree. H.D. decided to name him Hank. Boy and dog hit it off immediately! H.D. loved Hank and Hank loved H.D. The two were inseparable until H.D. left for the U.S. Marines.

"Woof?" barked Hank, snapping Steve back to the present moment and task at hand. He looked at his red brick, split-level ranch house one last time, tipped the front of his black Stetson, and said, "So long, can't say I'll miss you, and I sure as hell won't be back!"

He opened the passenger door and summoned for Hank to hop into the truck. Hank looked back at the house forlornly with a look that said, "Where is H.D.?" Steve instinctively replied, "It's okay, Hank, you'll see H.D. at our new home later."

Hank seemed to acknowledge what his master uttered and obediently hoisted himself into the black 2005 Dodge four-wheel-drive dually diesel. Steve closed the passenger side door. He went around to the back, checked to be sure the trailer latch was locked, and strolled slowly around to the driver's side of the truck with a limp affirming his wounds earned as a Marine and rodeo cowboy.

His tall, lanky frame displayed the strength and contention he still held despite his age and limp. He looked into the large side mirror and smoothed his handlebar mustache before entering the truck. Satisfied, he climbed in and closed the door.

The slam of the door jolted Hank for a moment, but he settled quickly into his horizontal position on the passenger seat. He knew it would be a much longer ride today than their usual Sunday outing. After placing his sunglasses on, Steve reached for a small tin can, placed a pinch of Copenhagen into his cheek, closed the lid, and sat it on the dashboard. Then, he backed the trailer onto the country road and pulled forward to start the journey to Nebraska.

He put in a Chris LeDoux CD and hummed to "Life is a Highway". A slow smile crossed his face as he listened to one of his favorite country songs. He would miss his friends, but he couldn't wait to finally begin this new chapter in his life. His job planning rodeo events with Diamond E Bucking Bulls was a perfect fit for him. Steve was excited to finally return to the place he was born and raised and spend more time with his family. He knew he was doing the right thing for both himself and his son.

The truck seemed to be on autopilot as it cruised down Highway 50 and headed east. He would travel through Jackson County, head north toward Indianapolis, and then west to Nebraska. His truck and horse trailer had traveled this route numerous times with H.D. to participate in rodeos out West. He loved those trips with his son, despite the long drives.

As he was traveling down the scenic, winding roads of Jackson County, Steve was entranced by the words to "Simple as Dirt". He had just entered Seymour when he saw the sign indicating the direction of Cortland. Seeing the sign reminded him of all the rodeos H.D. had participated in that tiny town and weekends spent with the Plumers.

Gary and Laura Plumer were the gracious hosts of the Jackson County High School Rodeo held every August in an arena set up on an enormous field of their family farm. The rodeo was becoming quite the social event in the county and growing each year as more people heard about it. High school students from all over Indiana, Kentucky, and Ohio came to participate in the competitive junior rodeo.

Leaving Jackson County and all those familiar people and places felt bittersweet. He pictured his son riding a bronc in the Plumer Arena. Steve thought, *Damn, where'd the time go? Those were some great times, H.D!* Cruising on down the road, fond memories hit him like a flash flood.

2 THE WILD AND WOOLLY RODEO

One lazy, rainy Sunday afternoon, Steve was watching ESPN on
television. The 1995 National Finals Rodeo in Las Vegas was
airing. In an excited voice, the announcer boomed, "This is going
to be *one phenomenal rodeo competition!*"

All of a sudden, Hunter came thundering down the stairs from
his bedroom, jumped off the last couple of steps, ran into the den,
and pounced on the couch beside his father. "Are they showin' the
rodeo comtition?" Hunter inquired. Steve smiled at his young son
and replied, "Yep, they are. It's beginning to start."

The two enjoyed watching either hunting or rodeo events
together, bonding as father and son. It was their "man time".
Hunter especially loved the bull riding events. Five-year-old Hunter
was a miniature replica of his father. He had dark brown hair,
intense brown eyes, a square jaw, and was *all arms and legs* as his dad
would often say. Ever since he could begin walking, Hunter loved
the outdoors and action going one hundred and ten miles an hour,
full throttle!

Hunter settled down beside his dad, propped his feet out (not
quite reaching the coffee table) and stuck his thumbs in his jeans
pockets imitating his dad. They watched the bareback bronc riding
first. The next events were the steer wrestling, team roping, saddle

bronc riding, tie down, and the barrel racing. Hunter especially liked the second-place winner of the barrel racing, Fallon Taylor, who was just thirteen making her one of the youngest qualifiers ever. He said, "I like her. She's real purdy!" Steve nodded in agreement of his son's good taste.

After those events were completed and a couple of commercials shown, the announcer came on and said, "Folks, hang onto the edge of your seat! The bull riding is about to begin. We have with us one brave cowboy who will attempt to ride Bodacious: the meanest, most audacious bull in the West. Give a hand for Tuff Hedeman- three-time world champion!" The camera panned to Tuff from the sidelines as he waved to the crowd.

"This is going to be good!" Steve said.

"Yeah!" replied Hunter, nodding enthusiastically.

When the bull riding showdown began, Hunter sat straight up on the couch and was entranced with the action. He was watching the rodeo as if for the first time he truly understood what was happening and the element of danger. A spark began to flicker inside him that grew with each minute of the competition. The light in his eyes could almost illuminate a dark room. His interest peaked and he could barely keep seated on the couch! Steve was just as excited as his son to see what was going to happen with Tuff and Bodacious.

Finally, it came to round seven and Tuff's turn to ride. The announcer stated in a serious tone, "As you rodeo fans know, Tuff suffered massive facial injuries after riding Bodacious earlier in the year, and few men have the testicular fortitude to climb on top of that bull again after taking that kind of beating. Good luck, Tuff!"

Tuff climbed over the railing and straddled the yellow, 1,900-pound bull in the chute; but as soon as the gate opened, he hung onto the back railing and let the bull run out from under him. The enormous audience rose at once and gave Tuff a standing ovation. As Bodacious left the arena on the other side, Tuff took off his cowboy hat and saluted him. Shortly afterwards, a reporter asked Tuff, "Why didn't you ride Bodacious?"

Tuff said, "I promised my son, Lane, that I would not ride Bodacious again if I drew him." He kept his promise even though it meant he was out of the finals. The audience could be heard saying, "Awww!" in unison as Tuff left the arena. The reporter explained to the viewers on the television, "Lane is Tuff's three-year-old son named after his best friend, Lane Frost, who was tragically struck by a bull in the rodeo a few years ago. You have to admire him for keeping his promise to his son. Now back to the rodeo."

Hunter turned in his seat, looked at his dad, and asked, "Dad, is that true about Lane Frost?"

"Yes, it is. In fact, I have the movie, *Eight Seconds*, that is about Lane Frost," explained Steve glancing sideways at his son.

"Can we watch it sometime? I want to see it!" urged Hunter with pleading eyes.

"Sure, maybe next weekend," promised Steve.

Hunter was satisfied that he would be able to see the movie and settled back in his seat to watch the rest of the rodeo with his dad. Two rounds later, Scott Breding also drew Bodacious to ride. The announcer said, "We have Scott Breding riding the bull we call Dodge Bodacious. This is a world-title bull and one of the hottest bull riders in the world. Take a look at chute number four!" The camera panned to the chute where Scott was preparing to ride the bull.

Scott climbed on top of Bodacious and strapped his hand in the rope. The announcer continued, "Ladies and gentlemen, this bull is a disabler. He has jerked a lot of guys down. Tonight, Scott has a mask on and I don't blame him!" Scott had borrowed a wire mask from a friend to wear for protection.

The chute opened and Scott hung onto Bodacious as he bucked forward. High into the air, the bull kicked his back hooves with a thrust so strong causing Scott to lean forward just as it reared its broad head back, hitting him in the face. The impact knocked Scott off, and he fell like a rag doll onto the ground with a *thud!* Steve and Hunter jumped off the couch simultaneously and shouted,

"Woah!" as they watched Scott lying there unconscious.

The rodeo clowns instantly jumped forward steering Bodacious through the gate just beside the chute he exited. Immediately, a team of men came to Scott's rescue and checked him over. Scott managed to get up and limped away with a broken cheekbone and a cracked eye socket. His mask was mangled and completely useless. An ambulance took him to the hospital to get medical attention. Later, it was announced in the tenth round that Bodacious would be retired from the rodeo arena "for the safety of the cowboys".

Hunter and Steve sat back down and watched the end of the bull riding competition with Jerome Davis sticking on top of his bull, scoring an 89 to take the lead in the final go-round. Steve was stunned at what had unfolded before them on TV and looked at his son. Hunter had an ardent look on his face and with a *serious as a heart attack* voice said, "Dad, I wanna do that!"

"Do what, Son?" asked Steve, glancing at his boy.

"Ride in the rodeo like them guys," replied Hunter, looking directly in his dad's eyes.

"You do?" Steve questioned in disbelief.

"Yep....Yep, I surely do," stated Hunter, holding a steady gaze at his dad.

Steve looked at his son square in the eye and could tell Hunter meant exactly what he said. He remembered his own passion for the sport when he was young and knew Hunter would keep pestering him about it if he didn't let him try participating in the rodeo. He thought about it a minute and said, "You saw what can happen when you're riding broncs and bulls. It's not a matter of *if* you'll get hurt, but when and how bad."

"I know, Dad, but I want to try it...*real* bad," pleaded Hunter, not giving in.

"You're sure?"

"I'm sure," nodded Hunter solemnly. Steve conceded, nodding his head, "Okay, Son, I'll see what I can do to get you in the rodeo."

Hunter grabbed his dad around the neck nearly choking him and shouted, "This is the bestest day of my life!" Steve grinned and gave him a big hug back.

The following week, while working at the Big Blue store in Seymour, Steve talked to Terry Haller who mentioned he was just establishing the Southern Indiana Junior Rodeo Association (SIJRA) and told him to call him at home to get Hunter enrolled. He called Terry the next day and inquired about the age requirements, types of events for Hunter's age, and cost. Steve was satisfied with the information he was given and enrolled Hunter in the next rodeo event in April.

Early in the morning, the day of the SIJRA rodeo, Steve helped Hunter dress properly for the competition. Hunter wore slightly worn Wrangler blue jeans that fit him just right, a belt, and a Western shirt tucked in- nothing too flashy since this was his first rodeo and Steve knew he would take a dive to the ground. Hunter put on his brown cowboy boots and tan cowboy hat as a finishing touch.

He was eager to go to the rodeo. "Come on, Dad, I'm ready to go!" he commanded. Steve looked him over and said, "I reckon you are." The two went outside, climbed into the truck, and rode to the junior rodeo taking place on Haller's farm near Georgetown, Indiana.

A large metal arena was set up on a plowed cornfield. On one side of the arena, horse trailers were parked and the owners were unloading their horses and gear. On the opposite side was parking for vehicles by the food stand and visitor seating. Steve pulled into the parking section and they got out of the truck.

He went to the registration booth and checked Hunter in for his events: steer head roping and mutton busting. Hunter was given a laminated tag with his number and name on it. "Now be sure to keep this and use it every time you come to the rodeo competitions," said the female volunteer. "The steer head roping is right over there. Just line up behind the other kids," she directed, pointing straight ahead.

"Okay," replied Hunter, nodding his head.

After his dad pinned the tag on the back of his shirt, Hunter walked over to the graveled area chained off for the preschool to first grade age kids to practice roping before they competed. Different kinds of goat and steer dummies were available for them to practice on. Hunter got in the line with the steer head with horns. When it was his turn, he stood on the chalk line three feet from the head. He practiced twirling his lariat and flinging it toward the head. Points were given for roping both horns, half a head, or the neck. The youngsters had one minute to get as many points as they could.

The judge keeping the stopwatch said, "Okay, kids, practice is over. It's time for the competition to begin. Everyone, get in your line." The children moved into rows and waited for their turn. When it was Hunter's time to go, he missed the first couple of flings but managed to lasso the neck once. On the last fling, he got his rope around one horn when he pulled the slack out of the loop. The judge yelled, "Time's up!"

He wrote down Hunter's points as he stepped over to the side to watch the other contestants. Many of them tried but were not as successful as he was. However, at the end of the competition, he was beaten by a boy slightly older than him who managed to rope both horns. He went back to his dad frowning.

"Dad, I really need to practice my ropin'."

"Don't feel so bad. You're just getting started. You'll do better next time," said Steve, patting him on the back.

"Can we set up a head like that for me to practice with?"

"Good idea! We can do that," said Steve.

"Yay!" yelled Hunter, feeling much better.

"For now, let's get a drink and watch the goat tying and calf roping. Then, it will be your turn to do the mutton busting," suggested Steve.

The two walked over to the food stand and ordered two cold waters. Steve set up a folding chair for himself and one for Hunter to sit in to watch the other events and drink their water. It was beginning to warm up, but the clouds kept it at a comfortable temperature. Other families were also setting up chairs and awnings to give shade, in case it got too hot, along the front side of the arena.

Before the calf roping began, the rodeo announcer said, "Everyone, please stand up as we sing the National Anthem and say a prayer." Steve stood up and removed his cowboy hat and said, "Son, take off your hat, too." Hunter did what he was told, placing his cowboy hat over his heart like his father did. He sang the words he could remember of "The Star-Spangled Banner" that he learned in kindergarten. After the prayer was said for the safety of the contestants and families traveling home, they put their cowboy hats back on and sat down.

As they watched the calf roping, Hunter admired the way a couple of boys rode on their horse and roped the calf in less than a minute. He imagined himself riding his own horse and roping a calf. When the calf roping was almost done, the rodeo announcer said, "All contestants in the mutton busting event need to go to the south end of the arena at this time!"

"That's me, Dad!" shouted Hunter as he jumped up from his chair.

"Okay, Son, you ready for this?"

"Yes, I am!" assured Hunter with a big grin on his face.

The two walked over to the end of the arena and waited for Hunter's name to be called. Hunter stood and watched the first boys his age attempt to ride a sheep, paying attention to how they did it. His dad slid a padded vest on him to protect him from injuries and told him to put the mouth guard in. Next, he placed a helmet with a face guard on his head and a glove on his right hand. Then, he boosted him up to climb over the wooden rails and lower himself onto the sheep that entered the chute. A volunteer inside the chute helped Hunter straddle the sheep while another volunteer held onto the front of the wiggly animal. "Lay your gloved hand down, palm up, and we'll tie the rope around it," said the man. "When you're ready, nod your head."

Hunter began to feel very nervous at that moment but was intent on completing his first riding event in the rodeo. The man made sure his hand was secure and asked, "Are you ready?"

Hunter mumbled, "Yeah," nodding his head.

The gate was opened and the wild, woolly sheep tore out of there as fast as its hooves could run. Hunter jiggled like a bowl full of jelly. A young volunteer watching along the rails yelled, "Squeeze! Squeeze!" Hunter held onto the rope with all his might and dug his legs into its sides like he saw the others do.

Once he felt himself slipping off the side of the sheep, there was nothing he could do but let go. He fell to the ground with an *"Umph!"* Two volunteers ran over to help him, but Hunter got up on his own. He dusted his pants off, exited the arena through the center gate, and walked over to his dad who was beaming with pride.

"Are you alright?" asked Steve. Hunter nodded.

"Close your eyes," commanded Steve. Hunter closed his eyes.

His dad removed the helmet and dusted the dirt off his face. "You can open your eyes now and take out the mouth guard." Hunter did what he was told and spat out the dirt from his mouth after he took out the mouth guard.

"Good job, buddy!" praised Steve as he smiled down at his son.

"Dad, how long did I stay on?" asked Hunter, looking up at his dad.

"Four seconds, Son. Not bad for your first time. How did it feel?"

"I was *real* nervous, thought I might pee my pants!" Hunter replied with a straight face.

"Yeah, that's normal," said Steve, nodding his head and grinning. "Even grown men piss their pants a little on a scary ride, but you get used to it."

"I sure hope so. I wanna practice some more. When can I do it again?"

"I'll see if I can find someone with sheep for you to practice. Your next rodeo is in a month."

"Cool!" said Hunter finally smiling and relieved he made it through his first rodeo.

Hunter and Steve watched the rest of the kids try to ride the sheep and had a few laughs at the entertainment. A couple of boys cried. "Look at those babies," said Hunter pointing at them. His dad chuckled, knowing they were the same age as his son. When the mutton busting was over, Steve suggested, "Let's grab a hotdog and drink and watch the rest of the rodeo."

"Yeah, I'm one starvin' cowboy!" shouted Hunter.

Steve laughed and took his son to the food stand to get lunch. Then, they sat in their lawn chairs to watch the rest of the rodeo and eat their food. Hunter liked watching the goat tying and flanking. He definitely wanted to compete in those events after he practiced. Steve talked to Terry Haller when he walked up to them about the goat events. "You really will want to get a goat of your own for Hunter to practice. It's the only way he will get the hang of it," suggested Terry.

"Do you know where I can get one?" inquired Steve.

"I have a momma goat with some babies now. I'll call you when you can take one home."

"Great, thanks Terry!"

"You're welcome," said Terry as he walked away to talk to some of the other parents.

Steve and Hunter watched most of the rodeo until it was getting close to dark. Then, they packed up their chairs and left. After stopping for a bite to eat on the truck ride home, Hunter fell sound asleep. When they pulled up into the driveway, he never stirred a muscle. Even the slam of the truck door couldn't wake him. Steve had to carry him inside, up the stairs, and put him to bed. Looking at his son, he grinned from ear to ear. He finally found an activity that matched his son's exuberant energy. He didn't think such a thing existed!

3 LET SLEEPING DOGS LIE

Hunter was anxious to get his goat in order to practice for his next rodeo. He asked his dad every day if Terry had called. Every day, his dad told him, "No." Finally, two and a half weeks after his first rodeo, Haller called his dad shortly after he arrived home from work and told him the goat was ready to be picked up. "Are you going to be home today?" asked Steve.

"As a matter of fact, I am," replied Terry over the phone. "We'll be there in just over an hour."

"Okay, see ya later!"

Steve hung up the phone and immediately called his friend, Zach. He invited him to join them on the ride to get a goat. Zach said he'd be right over.

"Hunter, we're going to get your goat now!" yelled Steve up the stairs.

"Awesome!" yelled Hunter back at him. He bolted down the stairs, pulled his cowboy boots on, and grabbed a jacket to wear. Steve told him, "You'd better go use the restroom. It's going to be a long ride." Hunter used the toilet and washed his hands. When he came back into the living room, he saw Zach pulling into the driveway. "Is Zach going with us?" he asked his dad.

"Yes, he is."

"Great!" yelled Hunter.

They went outside to greet Zach. Steve retrieved a rope from the barn to use to tie up the goat, and the three got into Steve's truck. They drove over an hour south to Haller's farm in Southern Indiana.

When they pulled in the driveway, Terry greeted them and invited them in to chat and have a drink. The men talked and made jokes for almost an hour when Hunter began to get restless. "Dad, when are we going to get the goat?" he inquired. Terry spoke up, "We can go out to the barn and look at them now." He got up and the others followed him.

They went out to an old, red barn where a mother goat was in a pen with three kids. The one with floppy ears came up to Hunter, peeked through the rails, and bleated. Hunter began petting him, noticing how soft he was. "Can I have this one, Terry?" asked Hunter.

"Yes, if that's the one you want," replied Terry.

"It is," nodded Hunter.

"Alrighty, that's settled," said Terry, smiling.

Steve paid Terry for the goat and told him, "We need to head home now. It's getting late. Thanks for the goat. We'll see you in a couple of weeks at the rodeo."

"You're welcome. Have fun practicing, Hunter, and take good care of that goat!" said Terry, looking at Hunter as he shook Steve's hand.

"I will," promised Hunter, nodding his head to Terry.

Steve tied one end of the rope around the goat's neck, making sure it was loose enough so the goat wouldn't choke, but tight enough he couldn't get loose. Next, he took him to the truck and lifted him up into the truck bed. Then, he tied the other end of the rope to the storage box hook to keep him from jumping out of the truck. The goat pulled on the rope and bleated loudly. Ignoring the goat, the three fellows climbed into the truck and headed north.

"Are you hungry, Hunter?" asked Steve as he drove toward home.

"I'm hungry!" shouted Zach.

Hunter and Steve laughed out loud at Zach. Steve spotted a Dairy Queen ahead and pulled into the drive-through to order food for them. The blonde teenage cashier was surprised when she saw the goat in the back and asked what its name was. Hunter was peering at her through the open window in the backseat behind his dad. "Flop," he answered with a straight face.

"That's an interesting name. Why Flop?" inquired the cashier, looking at Hunter.

"He has floppy ears and he's going to flop on the ground a lot," he answered, maintaining his poker face.

Steve was taking a drink of his Pepsi and burst out laughing, spewing it out of his mouth onto the dashboard. They all had a hearty laugh at that. The girl handed Steve some more napkins and shook her head with a puzzled expression as they drove away. *Why is that goat going to flop on the ground?* she wondered.

Steve pulled up, wiped off the dashboard, and continued the journey north. It was just after eleven o'clock when they arrived back home. They got out of the truck, and Zach headed to his own vehicle. Hunter went to see his goat in the back and found a pile of poop and stream of pee in the bed. "Dad, look what Flop did!" he shouted.

"Well, I guess you'd better get started cleaning it up," ordered his dad.

"What?"

"You heard me. He's your pet! You have to feed it *and* clean up after it."

"Aww, man!" moaned Hunter, shaking his head and frowning.

Steve handed him a trash bag and paper towels as he untied the goat from the truck and took it to the barn in the backyard. "Bye, Zach! See you later!" he yelled to his friend. Zach waved goodbye back at him as he left in his truck. Disgusted by the smell and feeling of warmth permeating through the paper towel, Hunter wiped up the excrement and threw it into the trashcan by the barn. Then, the two called it a night and went to bed.

After school that week, Hunter came home and checked on his

goat, giving him water and food along with his dogs. He had two dogs: one was a grey Blue Heeler named Rudy, and the other was a red Australian Cattle Dog with yellow eyes named Bear. The pair were very adept at herding Flop, keeping him from leaving the grounds.

Flop began to get used to Hunter and his new home. He even took a liking to Hunter's dogs, following them wherever they went. It wasn't unusual to see all three drinking out of the same water pail, eating the same food, or lying on the back deck together. Hunter began practicing for his upcoming rodeo.

One evening, Steve heard a horrendous sound coming from the backyard as he was trying to cook supper. He darted out the sliding door to see what in the world was going on. Behind the barn, he found his son tying Flop's legs together. The goat was on its back and bleating pitifully while the dogs were running in a circle around them barking. The animals were extremely annoyed at Hunter for disturbing their slumber and chasing them around the barn with his lasso. Hunter looked up at his dad nonchalantly and said, "Hi, Dad!"

"I could have sworn you were strangling that goat with all that noise!"

"Naw, just practicin'," said Hunter as he finished tying Flop's legs.

"Okay, carry on. I'll let you know when supper is done."

"Alright," Hunter replied as he waited for a few seconds to see if Flop stayed tied before he released the rope.

Steve walked back into the house, ignoring the noise in the backyard. He was surprised the neighbors didn't call the police, complaining about the racket. But, then again, most of them had farm animals themselves and wouldn't think the noise was unusual.

The following weekend, Steve had a cookout and invited his brother's family and friends to come. While Steve was preparing the grill on the deck, Hunter was showing the guests his new goat and demonstrating how to flank the goat by reaching over it, grabbing the flap of skin on the underside, and flipping it over.

Then, he showed them how to tie the legs together using piggin' string (a short nylon rope used to tie small animals). They were very impressed with how quick he could do it. The children clapped and patted Flop, which seemed to help appease the goat.

While the children were all standing there, Steve warned them, "Kids, stay away from the field over there. There are snakes and some of them could be rattlesnakes!" They all said, "Okay, we will." Steve returned to cooking and talking with his brother, Scott. The children continued playing with Flop and the dogs.

Steve was just about done with the hamburgers when he suddenly realized Hunter wasn't around. He asked, "Where's Hunter?" Nobody knew where he was. Steve and Scott went behind the barn and across the field of grass to search for Hunter. They saw him at the edge of the cornfield, stomping something on the ground with his cowboy boots.

When he got closer, Steve saw a listless black snake on the ground beneath Hunter's cowboy boot. He sprinted over to him, grabbed him by the shoulders, shook him, and yelled, "What did I tell you to do!"

"But, Dad, someone has to save the children!" replied Hunter earnestly.

"You're damn lucky that was a kingsnake and not a rattlesnake! Now get back to the house and don't leave my sight!" yelled his father.

Hunter walked sullenly back to the house, kicking his feet in the ground and muttering to himself. Steve looked at Scott and said, "Can you believe him? *Save the children?*" They both broke out into laughter, trying not to let Hunter hear them as they walked back to the house.

Finally, the day of Hunter's second rodeo came. He was very excited he would get to ride his own horse for the goat tying. He had an Appaloosa pony named Allie. She was brown with white mottled skin and her hooves had the colorful stripes unique to the breed. She was an even-tempered pony and easy for Hunter to ride.

Today, they had to get up early to get the horse and saddle

ready and loaded into the trailer. Hunter was glad to help his dad. They fed Allie some hay and gave her some water. Then, they went inside to eat themselves. After they had a hearty breakfast of scrambled eggs, bacon, and toast, they were ready to leave.

"You got your rope and name tag?" asked Steve, looking at his son as they stood in the kitchen.

"Yep, they're in the truck," assured Hunter, nodding to his dad.

"Okay, let's do this!" commanded Steve.

Father and son went back outside to the barn. Steve put the bridle onto Allie and guided her into the trailer. He made sure all the supplies they needed were in the back before he latched it closed. The two, once again, climbed into the truck and headed to Haller's farm for the junior rodeo.

The arena was set up the same way as before. This time, they pulled to the left side of the arena where the other horse trailers were and parked. They unloaded Allie and tied her to the side of the trailer. Hunter brushed Allie which helped calm her down after being cooped up in the trailer during the long drive. His dad helped him put on the saddle pad, saddle, and tighten the straps.

Then, he pinned the number tag on the back of Hunter's Western shirt, and they walked over to the other side of the arena to register for his events. They noticed there were more kids signed up to participate. What started as thirteen had grown to twenty members in a month.

Hunter again tried the steer head roping. He only missed the first time and was able to rope the head around the neck twice. On his last twirl of the lasso, he roped both horns giving him more points. He was proud of his improvement and walked over to his dad, grinning. "Nice job, buddy!" said his dad, nodding in approvement.

"Thanks!" beamed Hunter.

Hunter tried the mutton busting again. He managed to hang on for five seconds this time and was happy with that. When he walked up to his dad, Steve stated, "We need to go get Allie warmed up for your next event."

"Okay, Dad," said Hunter after he took off his helmet and spat out his mouth guard.

They walked back to the trailer and untied Allie. Hunter put his left boot into the stirrup, grabbed the saddle horn, and hoisted his right leg over her back, placing his right boot in the other stirrup. He guided her into the open field of freshly cut, green grass where some of the other riders were also warming up their horses.

He rode Allie around for twenty-five minutes when his dad hollered at him to come to him. After he guided the horse up to his dad, Steve took the reins and walked Allie with Hunter on top to the side of the arena where the horse riders were gathered for the goat tying. Hunter was the third rider listed for the event.

"Remember how we practiced, Son. You can do this!" encouraged Steve.

"I remember. I got this, Dad," replied Hunter with a confident nod.

They watched the first two riders compete. Then, Hunter's name was called to get into place. He trotted Allie up to the spot shown by the man volunteering and waited. He put one end of the piggin' string used to rope the goat in his mouth while he held onto the rest of the five-and-a-half-foot loop with his right hand on the saddle horn.

The signal was given and he shook the reins commanding Allie to move forward. She gave a loud, "*Neigh!*" and shot out into the arena. Hunter jerked in the saddle and his cowboy hat flew off with the lunge forward. A volunteer picked it up for him and handed it to his dad.

The crowd clapped and yelled, "Go Hunter!" He steered his horse toward the goat tied with a ten-foot rope on a stake over halfway down the arena- one hundred feet from the starting line. When he got to where he thought he should stop, he pulled the reins back hard. Allie stopped abruptly and Hunter quickly dismounted. He began running toward the goat, slipping on the dirt in his boots. Then, he ran alongside the rope, leaned down, and grabbed the goat by reaching over its back to grab the flank, lifted it off the ground a few inches, and flipped it over in one quick sweep.

With his right hand, he grabbed the goat's front left leg, took the piggin' string out of his mouth, and made a loop around the goat's hoof. Then, he grabbed the goat's back legs and wrapped the string around the three hooves several times. The goat lay on its back passively watching the boy tie him up. After he got the legs secure, Hunter stood up and raised both of his hands into the air, signaling he was done. The cowboy keeping time made sure the goat stayed tied for six seconds and gave the announcer Hunter's time.

"Ten point four seconds! Great job, Hunter. That moves you into first place!" the announcer said over the speaker.

Hunter jumped for joy and went to his dad who had retrieved Allie when she came back to where he was waiting by the gate. "Very good, Son," he said as he handed Hunter back his cowboy hat and patted him on the back.

"I can't believe I got first place!" yelled Hunter, shaking his head in disbelief.

"Don't get too sure of yourself. We have to see if the rest of the contestants beat your time."

"I know," he replied, feeling the wind leave his sails.

They watched while the remaining three contestants tried to tie their goat. One boy attempted to lift the goat but couldn't get it turned over and timed out. Another boy got his goat tied, but it shook loose. The last boy came close to Hunter's time but fell on the ground when he dismounted his horse which cost him a couple of seconds. Hunter ended up winning the event. He jumped up and down with joy and asked his dad, "Can we go to the Dairy Queen to celebrate my victory?"

"Of course, we can," promised his dad.

When the junior rodeo was over, they removed the saddle from Allie, brushed her down again, and made sure she relieved herself of the hay and water given to her before they put her into the trailer. They packed away the saddle and the rest of the equipment, latched the trailer, and got into the truck.

They drove to the same Dairy Queen they went to before and

parked the truck and horse trailer in the bus parking area. The two got out and went inside to get ice cream. Hunter grinned from ear to ear while eating his chocolate sundae. He looked like a cat who just swallowed a canary. In the truck on the way home, he told his dad, "I don't want to do the mutton busting anymore. That's for little kids. I like the riding and roping events."

"That's alright. Whatever you want to do, Son. It's your choice."

"Thanks, Dad," said Hunter, smiling.

Hunter continued practicing his roping, goat flanking, and tying his first year in the junior rodeo. The year ended in the fall with a big celebration and awards given for points earned in each event. Hunter was proud of his trophy for goat tying and even improved his time to just under ten seconds. He displayed his trophy in the living room for everyone to see when they came to their house to visit.

4 COWBOY UP!

Shortly after Hunter turned seven years old in September 1997, he and his dad were watching the Western movie *My Heroes Have Always Been Cowboys* with Scott Glenn playing the character H.D. Dalton, a champion rodeo cowboy. Father and son thoroughly enjoyed watching the movie together. When it was over, Hunter turned to his dad and said, "Dad, I don't want to be called Hunter anymore. I like the name H.D. It's a *real* cowboy name."

"H.D., hunh?" nodded Steve, contemplating the name.

"Yep, it's H.D. Hogan now, okay?"

"H.D. does fit you. That's what you want me to call you?" asked Steve.

"It is," assured H.D.

"Well, H.D., if you're going to be a real cowboy, you're going to need to look the part. We need to get you fitted for chaps and pick out an outfit to wear in the rodeo."

H.D. jumped off the couch and yelled, "Whoopee!" Steve laughed at his son and said, "I'll call Tonto Rim and get a time set up for you to get fitted."

The following Saturday, the two went into the Tonto Rim Trading Company, a Western outfitters store in Seymour, Indiana. Steve greeted the owner, Denny, and said, "My son, H.D., is here to get fitted for some chaps for the rodeo this year."

"Glad to help you out, pardner," Denny said to H.D. "Let's get you measured and you can pick out your colors."

He took H.D. back to the dressing area and measured his arm length, leg length, waist, and inseam to get an accurate fit. H.D. just stood there patiently while he measured him. When he was done writing down the measurements, Denny asked, "Okay, son, what color of chaps do you want?"

"I want black leather chaps with red fringe and red triangles on the side," responded H.D. without hesitating.

"That's some kinda detail you have there, boy," said Denny. "Let me see, I think I have a catalog with some chaps like that in there." Denny walked over to a table with magazines and a catalog to order supplies, picked up the catalog, flipped a few pages, and pointed out the picture to H.D.

"Yep, that's them. That's what I want," said H.D., nodding his head.

"Okay, what color of shirt do you want?"

"I want a blue Wrangler shirt with a black leather vest," responded H.D. promptly.

"You don't say!" said Denny surprised at the precise details H.D. was providing him. He flipped through the catalog and pointed to the items H.D. described.

"Yes, sir, that's them," assured H.D.

Steve was standing near them not paying a whole lot of attention to what his son was ordering. When H.D. was finished, he asked, "You're sure that's how you want 'em, 'cause once you've ordered them, that's it."

"Yes, Dad, that's how I want 'em."

"Okay, Denny, go ahead and order them. He also needs some spurs to go with his boots," said Steve, looking at Denny.

Denny nodded, turned to H.D., and asked, "H.D., why does that outfit sound so familiar to me? Where did you get the idea for those colors?"

"I saw it on *Eight Seconds*. I wanna look just like Lane Frost," the boy said wholeheartedly.

Both men's mouths dropped open and they stared at H.D. speechless. After a few seconds, Denny said, "Well I'll be darned, that is exactly what Lane wore!" He looked at Steve and asked, "So, how many times has he seen that movie?"

"Too many to count. He wore out one tape, so I had to order another one," chuckled Steve.

"Never seen anything like it in all my years ordering outfits. Whatta kid you have there!"

"You have *no idea*!" said Steve. "Thanks for your help. Let me know when they come in."

"Will do!" replied Denny.

Steve and H.D. left the store. Patting his son on the head, he said, "Great taste, Son. Lane Frost, hunh?"

"Yep, he was an awesome cowboy. I wanna be the best- just like him!" replied H.D.

Father and son climbed into the truck and headed home. Steve returned to Tonto Rim three weeks later to get his son's outfit when he got off work. It arrived just in time for H.D.'s next rodeo. Denny handed the package to him and shook his head, still in disbelief. "That is some outfit your son has. He's going to look pretty sharp!"

"Yes, he will!" said Steve.

"If you need anything else, you bring that boy of yours in here anytime," smiled Denny.

"Sure will," said Steve as he walked out the door.

H.D. had practiced riding bull calves the past year in the junior rodeo. From the moment he hopped on a bull, he was hooked! The feeling of nervousness and excitement simultaneously made him long for the next ride. He knew he didn't want to stop at the young calves, he wanted more.

Sticking on top of the bull was a challenge; but each time he did it, he got a little better and rode a little longer. By his third and fourth ride on a calf, he was beginning to get pretty good. Steve signed him up to ride at a pro rodeo event in Clarksville, Indiana.

The day came for the pro rodeo. H.D. had his new rodeo outfit

on and was ready to show it off. "How do I look, Dad?" asked
H.D. modeling his brand-new chaps he wore over his blue jeans.

"You look like a cowboy. You ready for the big-time rodeo?"
asked Steve with a smile.

"Do cows crap? Of course, I am!" quipped H.D.

Steve laughed, slapped him on the back, and said, "Let's git to
it!"

Before they got in the truck, he snapped a picture of H.D. in his
outfit. H.D. posed for the picture, placing one boot on the deck to
show the chaps off. He wore a polished silver buckle on his belt
and had spurs on his cowboy boots- just as the real cowboys do.

They drove to Clarksville and Steve registered H.D. for the bull
calf riding event. While his dad was attaching his number tag to the
back of his vest, H.D. looked around at the arena. He was
awestruck when he saw the huge crowd in the stands, the bright
lights, and the professional rodeo cowboys all decked out in their
gear.

They wore silver buckles and spurs that glimmered brightly
when the lights hit them. Their vibrant Western shirts and chaps
were a kaleidoscope of color tantalizing the young girls and women
in the audience. Instead of the usual black or brown cowboy boots
H.D. was used to seeing, they had on colorful, expensive leather
boots with intricate designs reflecting their bold personalities.

He could smell their leather mixed with dirt, sweat, and cologne.
It was the distinct musky, masculine smell of the American
cowboy. He wanted it to be *his* smell. The sound of the bulls and
calves snorting, stomping, and bellowing could be heard over the
noise of the crowd. There was also a menagerie of sheep, goats,
and horses kept in pens and corrals adding to the cacophony of
animal noise.

H.D. caught a whiff of the pork barbecue coming from a
smoker by the food stand. The smell made him hungry, but he was
way too nervous to eat anything before his ride. His dad took him
over to the side of the arena to watch the opening ceremony and
the first events.

Horse riders entered the arena carrying different flags: the American flag was first followed by the Professional Rodeo Cowboys Association (PRCA) flag, the Confederate flag, the Professional Bull Riders (PBR) flag, as well as sponsor flags. As they began parading around the arena, the announcer said over the speaker, "Ladies and gentlemen, let me introduce you to a beautiful lady...I give you Old Glory. She has stood tall through our battles and continues to stand strong today. Who isn't proud to live in the greatest country of the world...the land of the brave and the free...the United States of America. Put away all your differences and beliefs. Here at the rodeo, we are free to pray. I ask you to stand now and remove your hats as Father Murphy says the prayer."

The audience and cowboys stood at once, removed their hats, and bowed their heads in prayer. A hush fell over the crowd. Young and old honored the flag and the Father. Even the animals seemed to sense the sanctity of the moment and stood still.

"Our heavenly father, we ask you to send a guardian angel to watch over these brave cowboys and cowgirls. Climb onto the bull with them to protect them. Ride shotgun with them as they travel home. Lord, somewhere tonight our military are fighting overseas. Please bring them safely home, amen," prayed Father Murphy.

After the prayer, an attractive, young woman sang the National Anthem as everyone held their right hand over their hearts. The audience and contestants stood steadfast staring at the American Flag with many mouthing the words along with her.

When the song was over, the announcer introduced the rodeo clown. The clown performed some rope tricks and told jokes with the announcer while the first contestants were getting ready for their events. H.D. laughed at the clown and was feeling a little less nervous.

The mutton busting event was first, goat flanking and tying next, and then it was time for H.D. to go to the chute for the calf riding. Steve walked him over to the chute, helped him put on his padded vest, and handed him the mouth guard and a helmet. After making sure his helmet was secured tight, he told him, "Good luck, Son."

H.D. nodded his head and climbed over the rail. A stout, brown bull calf entered the chute. H.D. handed the cowboy assisting the riders his bull rope with a cowbell on it. "Great outfit, H.D.!" said the cowboy to him as he wrapped the rope around the calf while the bell jingled loudly underneath it. Loving the compliment, H.D. grinned back at him.

The calf began to stomp and bellow, banging against the side of the chute. H.D. lowered himself down slowly onto its back as the cowboy stood watch over him. He helped him secure his right hand in the rope, palm up. When he was finished, the cowboy asked, "You ready, H.D.?"

H.D. nodded and the chute was opened, releasing the calf and rider. The calf shot out forward and began kicking its rear legs up. He raised his left arm up to balance himself and hung on for dear life. The calf made a quick turn causing H.D. to slip slightly to the side, but he still tried to hold on. However, the tension in the rope came loose and it suddenly fell off the calf along with H.D. He hit the dirt hard, heard the bell clang as it hit the ground and bounced several times, and felt a sudden hard blow to his groin.

The calf's stomp was a square shot. "*Ugh!*" groaned H.D. as he lay curled up on the ground. He was *knocked into a cocked hat* as the cowboys would say. The pain was nothing like he had ever felt before, and he couldn't move without causing more pain. Darting out into the arena, the rodeo clown steered the calf away from him through the corral.

Steve came running through the gate to help his boy. "Are you okay, Son?" he asked. H.D. had the wind knocked out of him but managed to say under his breath, "Just get me on my feet...Just get me on my feet! Cowboys walk out of the arena."

Taking hold of one of H.D.'s arms, Steve helped him limp out of the arena. The audience rose to their feet and clapped loudly for H.D. One pro rodeo cowboy said, "I like how you hung on there, bud! You took a hard hit!" H.D. nodded at him but couldn't talk just yet.

Steve went to the medics standing by the gate and asked for an ice pack. One said, "Sir, does he need us to look at his injury?" Steve told him, "Naw, he'll be alright once he has some ice to cool the pain." He took H.D. to the truck and let him lie down in the back, removed his chaps, unzipped his jeans, pulled them down slightly, and applied the ice pack on his underwear. H.D. lay there moaning for a while until the ice began to bring some of the swelling down. "You think you can make it home now, Son?" asked Steve.

"Yeah," whispered H.D.

Steve helped him pull his jeans back up, leaving the zipper undone, and get into the passenger seat of the truck. H.D. moved slowly and groaned loudly when he raised his leg to get into the vehicle. He got in place, sitting on his vest for extra padding, and Steve latched his seat belt for him.

The ride home was excruciating, but H.D. held up. Feeling every crack and bump on Interstate 65, he was never so glad to finally see his house when they pulled into the driveway. His dad assisted him out of the truck, walked him up the stairs, and helped him undress for bed.

"Can I have another ice pack?" whispered H.D., lying on his bed.

"Sure, Son."

Steve went downstairs, prepared a small bag with ice in it, and brought it up to his son. H.D. was completely motionless. Steve wasn't sure if he was still awake or passed out until he said, "Thanks, Dad." He paused for a minute and continued, "You know what, Daddy? I've been thinkin'.... All them townies I go to school with, they'd still be on the ground cryin' for their mommas." Steve laughed so hard tears came to his eyes, and he handed H.D. the ice pack.

"You're right about that, Son," he replied. "You keep the ice on there for a few minutes and I'll come back to check on you." Steve went downstairs, got a drink, locked the doors, and turned off the lights. When he returned to the bedroom, H.D. was sound asleep. He removed the ice pack and covered him up.

"Goodnight, cowboy," he whispered. He was very proud of his son for taking his pounding like a man.

5 WALKING TALL

The up-close-and-personal experience with the calf did not deter H.D. from continuing in the rodeo; in fact, it did quite the opposite. He was determined to master the art of bull riding and threw himself into practicing on his makeshift bull for the next competition in the spring. The following Saturday while eating breakfast with his dad, H.D. asked, "Dad, can you work with me on my form and dismount on the bucking barrel?"

"Sure, Son, let me finish up a couple of things and we'll git to it."

"Thanks. I wanna be good and ready for my next rodeo."

When Steve was finished with his chores, he went with H.D. to their small red barn in the backyard where they had suspended a barrel with ropes to three wooden beams earlier in the month. They hung a fifty-five-gallon drum by welding three holes: two in the front on opposite sides and one in the back through the bottom of the drum. They sanded down the edges of the holes to keep the rope from rubbing through. Then, they rigged the barrel three feet off the ground and placed a mound of hay underneath to protect H.D. when he falls. Lastly, they attached a piece of beige Berber carpet on top to simulate a real bull ride.

H.D. climbed onto the barrel and his dad secured his right hand using a rope with a cowbell on it. He commanded, "Ready, Dad!"

Steve grabbed the two front ropes and began swinging the barrel forward. Raising his left arm straight up to balance himself, he leaned forward and backward with the swaying motion. Just as his dad quickly swung the front down, H.D. let his arm drop forward, lost his balance, and fell off the barrel onto the hay below. Steve laughed at him as he stood back up and brushed the hay off his jeans.

"That's not funny, Dad!" objected H.D.

"Okay, climb back on and we'll try it again," Steve replied, grinning.

H.D. remounted the bucking barrel and his dad resumed swaying him back and forth. "Be sure to swing your arm the opposite direction the bull's head is moving to keep your balance," directed Steve. H.D. stuck his arm up and swung it the way his dad said.

"Keep your head down, lean forward, and bend your arm a little at the elbow keeping it flexible, so you can change direction easier," suggested Steve. Following his dad's instructions, H.D. noticed the difference it made in his balance. Thinking H.D. wasn't paying attention after a few swings, Steve jerked the ropes sideways to the left to throw him off, but it didn't work. H.D. squeezed his legs into the sides of the barrel and hung on, using his arm to balance.

"Good catch, Son. You're getting the hang of balancing on the bull. Now, when I pull it to the side and you feel the rope come loose, you need to jump off landing on your feet; or if you fall, roll out of the way- away from the bull, okay?"

"Yeah, Dad."

Steve jerked the rope to the right and H.D. hung on. His dad laughed and quickly reversed the direction back to the left. This time, the tension on the bull rope came loose and H.D. fell to the ground. Remembering what his dad said, he rolled over and jumped to his feet to move out of the way.

"Now that's how you do it, H.D.!" Steve shouted.

H.D. grinned and replied, "Ain't no bull gonna stomp me again!"

"I hope not. Made me hurt watching it!"

The two burst into laughter together as they walked back toward the house.

The spring of 1998 brought a new year of competition to the Southern Indiana Junior Rodeo Association. H.D. signed up for the roping events and bull riding. The rodeo used young bulls or steers for the youth to practice on until they moved onto larger, mature bulls in the high school rodeo. After practicing his roping and riding on his bucking barrel in the barn, H.D. gained more confidence and strength. By the time he began his 1999 rodeo season, he had plenty of practice bull riding and was one of the top three bull riders in the SIJRA, which had tripled in membership since it began.

At the seven points rodeo (last competition of the year) in October, three bull riders were close in points. H.D. was determined to win. He didn't care that the other two boys were two years older than him; he was going to give his all and beat them. The first boy, Jake, stuck on his bull six seconds and scored sixty-eight points.

The next boy, Alan, hung on top of his bull seven seconds. It appeared as if he was going to make it; but just before the eight second buzzer, the bull bucked hard knocking him off. He scored seventy-two points. H.D. began to get nervous but didn't let it rattle him. When his name was called, his dad said, "It's do or die time, Son. You show 'em what you're made of."

"You bet I will!" shouted H.D.

He put on his protective equipment, pulled his glove on his right hand, and grabbed his bull rope. Scrambling over the wooden rails like a monkey, he stood on the platform as the steer came through the corral, scraping its horns on the sides and snorting. When it entered the chute, the gate was narrowed behind the steer closing him in.

One cowboy took H.D.'s bull rope and dangled it down one side of the steer as the cowboy on the other side used a hook to bring it underneath and wrap it around its chest. H.D. descended quickly upon the animal. The cowboy near H.D. helped secure his hand in the rope as the steer tried to shake him off. It didn't like him on its back one bit and began grunting, squirting diarrhea everywhere, and splattering it onto H.D.'s back as it stomped repeatedly.

"Yuck!" muttered H.D., repulsed by the smell.

The steer looked back at H.D., the orneriness oozing out of him, and snorted. It began to stomp, then swayed, and banged H.D.'s leg against the side of the chute. H.D. felt a drip of perspiration dribble slowly down the back of his neck, and his palms began to sweat. He shook away the nerves, decided he was ready, and mumbled, "Now!" as he nodded his head.

One cowboy unlocked the gate as another in the arena swung it open with a rope. The steer shot forward into the ring. H.D. raised his left arm up and swung it back and forth just as he had practiced so many times. The beautiful dance of boy and bull began.

The steer began a series of back kicks and leaps in an effort to thwart the boy to no avail. When the bucking didn't work, it ran along the arena rail to shake its rider, but H.D. hung on. It was an equal match of strong will between the steer and H.D.

Whack! went his right leg against the steel panels. H.D. winced in pain but didn't let it distract him from staying on. *Whack!* went his leg against the panels again. "Damn you, bull!" cursed H.D., still hanging on.

The steer realized that plan wasn't working and began to twist in a circle. H.D. continued to hang on squeezing his legs even tighter into the sides of the steer. The seconds seemed to go on forever until he heard the eight second buzzer. Just as the steer straightened to begin another throw tactic, H.D. swung his left leg over its back and jumped down onto his feet. The steer turned right around and came directly at him; but luckily two rodeo clowns intercepted, shouted at it waving their arms, and guided it into the corral.

H.D. was ecstatic and felt the adrenaline rushing through him. He jumped up and down shouting deliriously. The crowd rose to their feet and clapped for the young bull rider. The announcer shouted, "What a ride, H.D.! You got eighty-five points!"

Standing in the middle of the arena, he spread his legs apart and raised both of his arms up giving the touchdown sign. The crowd roared with laughter, clapped even louder, and chanted, "H.D., H.D.!" He ate the attention up!

"*Whoop, Whoop, Whoop!*" he yelled, shaking his right fist in the air. Turning his head, he saw his dad standing by the exit gate inside the arena, sprinted to him, and slapped him a high five. Steve grabbed him and hugged him tightly. "I'm so proud of you. That was a heck of a ride!"

H.D. took off his helmet and spat out his mouth guard into his left palm. "I knew I could! I knew I could!" he shouted while nodding his head. The other bull riders came up to H.D. congratulating him and shook his hand. "Thanks, guys. You did a great job, too!" he replied earnestly.

The two walked around to the outside of the arena and watched the rest of the rodeo, sitting in their lawn chairs enjoying a cold Coca-Cola and cheeseburger. H.D. barely remembered what happened in the competition after his thrilling ride. After it was over, they gathered their belongings and headed to the truck. When they left the rodeo that day, H.D. was walking tall with his head in the clouds. It would be quite some time before he came back down to Earth.

The SIJRA award banquet was held the next month in New Albany. After a delicious buffet of country cooking, Terry Haller gave out the awards. When it came time to hand out the bull riding trophies, he called H.D. up on the stage. H.D. was decked out in his newest cowboy outfit, beaming from ear to ear. As he walked up to him, Terry said, "This young man has more gusto than a team of Budweiser Clydesdales. I have watched him work harder than anything to be the best he can be. Tonight, I am proud to announce H.D. Hogan is our year-end series leader in bull riding!"

Terry handed him a silver buckle with the words 1999 SIJRA Bull Riding Champion inscribed on it and a picture of a bull. H.D. took the buckle and stared at it intently as if to photographically memorize every detail of it in his mind and cherish the moment forever. "Smile, H.D., for pictures," said Terry. Cocking his cowboy hat upward, H.D. grinned as he displayed his belt buckle for his dad and the SIJRA members. It was one of the proudest moments in his life.

Later in the fall, Steve and H.D. were at the Professional Bull Riders (PBR) event at Freedom Hall in Louisville, Kentucky as spectators. One of the highlights of the rodeo for both of them was when Adam Carrillo (co-founder of the PBR) rode the bull, Jit. When Adam got ready to ride the bull, the announcer said, "We have Adam Carrillo riding Jit, the bull. This might well be the rankest bull here. No one's ridden him. He's got a real bad first two jumps then spins to the right- if you make it that far!"

The gate was opened and as if on cue, Jit did exactly what the announcer said: he made two powerful jumps and began spinning to the right. Adam held on, snapping back and forth like a twig in a hurricane. Jit made six turns to the right and just as he straightened back to the left, Adam came off the bull and crawled away.

"Jit has just been rode!" boomed the announcer in the microphone. The audience thundered in applause as Adam fell down to his knees and raised his arms up to the heavens. He stood back up, grabbed his bull rope, and walked to the gate. The announcer continued, "Adam just took the lead! You just gotta cowboy up if you draw Jit. You know he's a good bull, but he's pretty scary; and he will hook your britches off if you git in the way. Adam scored ninety-four and a half points!"

H.D. and his dad laughed at the announcer's comments and were thrilled they were able to see a piece of rodeo history unfold before their eyes. After the bull riding, Steve took H.D. by the chutes to get a better look at the bulls and pro cowboys. A stocky middle-aged cowboy came up to them and said, "Looks like a brand-new buckle you got there, boy." He looked at Steve, winking and grinning, as he continued, "You win that barrel racing or pole bending?"

H.D. looked straight at him and said, "I'm H.D. Hogan, the

Indiana State Champion! I rode against kids two years older than me." He grabbed his buckle, shaking his hips and showing it off.

"Really? What's it for?"

H.D. said without faltering, "I won it bull riding!"

"You did, hunh? Do you know who I am?" the man asked, raising his bushy, brown eyebrows.

H.D. said, "I know who you are. You're Don Gay, eight-time world champion bull rider. I know exactly who you are, sir!"

Don stepped back, nodded his head in approvement, grinned, and said, "Boy, you come on with me. You too, dad." He took H.D. and Steve back to the chutes and hoisted H.D. up onto the platform with the other pro bull riders. One asked, "Don, who do we have here?"

"Well, gentlemen, we have here with us the Southern Indiana Junior Rodeo bull riding champ, H.D. Hogan!" H.D. smirked and shook hands with every single one of them. He turned around to see who asked Don about him and saw none other than Tuff Hedeman. He swooned at the sight of Tuff and almost fell off the platform. Steve caught him and steadied him back up. Tuff reached out his hand and shook H.D.'s heartily.

"Nice to meet you, H.D.," said Tuff.

"Wow! I can't believe I finally get to meet you, Tuff!" stammered H.D.

Tuff smiled at H.D. and offered Steve his hand saying, "You must be one proud papa!"

"I sure am," said Steve, shaking Tuff's hand.

They spent the rest of the rodeo hanging out, drinking, and laughing with Don Gay, Tuff Hedeman, and Cody Lambert. The famous cowboys shared stories about their friend, Lane Frost, the rodeo, and traveling. H.D.'s head grew bigger than a watermelon! He could barely get it through the truck door when they left the rodeo.

As they rode back home, the song "July in Cheyenne" by Aaron Watson came on. Steve and H.D. sang along with the lyrics, "*In the rain in the mud in July in Cheyenne. They had to carry away that brave young*

38

man..." It was as if the spirit of Lane Frost was riding in the truck with them. Steve reached over and squeezed H.D. around the shoulder as he fell asleep, leaning against his dad.

6 DON'T BITE OFF MORE THAN YOU CAN CHEW

During August of 2000, H.D. changed schools and began fourth grade at Brownstown Elementary School. When he walked into his classroom the first day of school, he was surprised to see a boy he recognized. H.D. strolled up to him and said, "Hey, aren't you that kid I talked to at Muscatatuck Wildlife Refuge last year when we had a field trip?" The black-haired, brown-eyed boy looked at H.D. skeptically at first, but then smiled at him in recognition.

"Yes, I am. I'm Chase Plumer. What's your name?"

"I'm H.D. Hogan."

The two boys instantly became best friends and were inseparable all through school. They were two peas in a pod, cooking up some mischievous schemes together. While in fourth grade, the two decided they were going to be cool like cowboys and chew tobacco. One day, they formulated a plan and both snuck a pinch of tobacco from their dad's stash and hid it in a baggie in their boots- just a small amount at a time, so their dads wouldn't miss it or get caught by their teachers.

When it was recess time at school the next day, they met at the hallway door and sprinted to the far end of the playground by the pine trees and cornfield. They sat down on the green grass looking at each other.

"Chase, did you bring your chew?" H.D. inquired.

"Yeah, did you?" replied Chase.

"Yeah, you ready?"

"Yeah, you watch out for the teachers to see if they're lookin'," suggested Chase. H.D. looked into the distance to see where all the teachers were and said, "Okay, coast is clear. Now!"

Both boys reached into their cowboy boot, pulled out a baggie, and stuffed the chew in their mouth. They sat and stared at each other as the strong tobacco flavor filled their jaw.

"Mmmm," mumbled H.D. with a grimace on his face.

"Mmmm," mumbled Chase, scowling.

After a couple of minutes of chewing, the dark brown juice began pooling in their mouth and drooling out of the corner of their lips. H.D. glanced forward and saw a teacher look in their direction and point.

"Spit it out! A teacher's coming!" panicked H.D. Both boys went to the edge of the cornfield and spat out the tobacco. The teacher was headed right toward them. "What are you two doing way over here?" she yelled when she got closer.

"Nothin', just playing with our tractors," fibbed H.D. He showed her the two small John Deere tractors he held in his hand. She bought their lie and said, "Okay, listen for the whistle. We're going inside in five minutes."

"Okay," said the two boys, grinning.

When she left, H.D. asked Chase, "Wasn't that great chew?"

"Oh yeah. Great!" nodded Chase.

"We'll havta do it again next week," suggested H.D.

"Yeah," agreed Chase.

The boys snuck tobacco a few more times at school but became paranoid thinking the teachers were onto them and decided they'd better not bring it to school anymore. Later, H.D. invited Chase to his house after school to hang out. Chase got permission from his mom and rode the bus with H.D.

When they got to H.D.'s house, his dad wasn't home yet; so, they played outside roping and swinging on a tire hanging from a tall oak tree for a while. Shortly, they became bored and H.D asked, "You wanna try some more chew?"

"Yeah!" said Chase nodding his head. The pair went inside to the kitchen. "Okay, you keep an eye out for my dad. He's going to be home soon from work," ordered H.D. as he headed up the stairs to his dad's bedroom.

"I will," promised Chase.

H.D. went to where his dad kept the tobacco on his bureau, opened the can, took a small amount out, closed it, and replaced the can back in the same spot he snatched it from. As a final touch, he turned the can to face exactly as it was when he picked it up, knowing his dad had a knack for noticing when something was moved or missing.

He went back to Chase standing in the kitchen and gave him half of the chew. Both stuck it in their mouth at the same time. They were chewing for a few minutes when Chase saw Steve's truck pull in and yelled, "Hunter, your dad's pullin' in!"

H.D. immediately swallowed his tobacco. Instantly, his face turned guacamole green. His eyes bugged out at Chase, and he ran into the bathroom. Chase darted to the kitchen sink, spat out the chew, turned on the faucet to wash it down the drain, and rinsed out his mouth just as Steve was turning the doorknob. He wiped his wet mouth on his sleeve in the nick of time.

When he came into the house, Steve saw Chase standing in the kitchen and heard H.D. vomiting in the bathroom. "What's wrong with him?" he asked Chase.

"I think he ate something at school that made him sick. The school lunches are *awful!*"

"Yeah, H.D. complains about the lunch all the time," said Steve as he walked into the bathroom to check on H.D.

"You okay, Son?"

H.D. had flushed the toilet, watched the last remnants of the tobacco swirl down the hole when he heard his dad talking to Chase, and rinsed out his mouth in the sink. After wiping his mouth on the hand towel, he looked at his dad who was now standing in the doorway of the bathroom and responded, "Yeah, I'm okay."

Chase was standing behind Steve, peeked around him at H.D., and said, "I told your dad how bad the lunch at school was today and that I thought it made you sick." H.D. glanced at Chase, looked back at his dad, and replied, "Yeah, that's probably what it was. I'm starting to feel a little better now that my stomach is clear."

"Good! You two hang around the house. I'm going to check on the horses," instructed Steve.

"Okay," replied H.D.

Chase watched as Steve went outside and waited until he was well out of earshot before he said, "Whew! That was close!"

"Yeah, too close!" responded H.D.

"You okay?" asked Chase, concerned about his friend.

"Yeah, but I may be burping up wintergreen for a week!"

Chase laughed and H.D. had to laugh, too. Before Chase left for home, H.D. suggested, "You ought to come join the rodeo with me when it starts again in the spring. I think you'd like it."

"That sounds great. I'll ask my parents when I get home."

"Good. I hope they say yes."

"I do too."

Chase saw his mom pulling in the driveway and said goodbye to H.D. "See ya at school!"

"See ya," replied H.D.

Chase did start the rodeo with H.D. He tried the bull riding, but it wasn't for him. He decided he liked the calf tying and chute dogging. The rodeo changed locations from Terry Haller's farm to the fairgrounds in New Albany.

During one competition, Chase noticed H.D. wasn't watching the rodeo with the other kids. Instead, he was by the corral getting his bull rope ready. H.D. had looped his rope around the top rail of the corral and was using a wire brush to clean it well.

When he decided it was ready, he began wiping Rosin on the rope to make it sticky. Chase came up to him and watched him for several minutes. H.D. reached for more Rosin and warmed it on the rope, rubbing it hard with his gloved hand. "How long are you going to put that on the rope?" asked Chase.

"As long as it takes, may be a while," said H.D., sweat forming on his forehead.

"Okay, I'll catch you later," said Chase as he walked off to watch the rodeo until he competed. H.D. spent hours getting his bull rope ready. He used over half a bag on the rope. Later, Steve walked up to him, noticed a lot of the Rosin was gone, and said, "You don't need to put that much on, H.D."

"I'm gonna stay on!" insisted H.D.

"Okay, don't say I didn't warn you," replied Steve, walking off and shaking his head.

H.D. finished putting on the rest of the Rosin and waited his turn to compete in the bull riding. After a couple of riders, it was his turn to go. He climbed up to the platform and nodded at the cowboys assisting the riders. The cowboy helping H.D. get on the bull asked him what kind of wrap he wanted to use. H.D. handed him his bull rope and said, "I want to use the suicide wrap."

"You're sure, son?"

"I'm sure," nodded H.D. vehemently.

H.D. put in his mouth guard and pulled the helmet over his head. The cowboy helped him get in position on the bull after he wrapped the rope around the bull with the help of a second cowboy on the other side. On the last wind of the rope across his palm, the cowboy ran the rope between his pinky and ring finger. H.D.'s glove was good and sticky on the bull rope. He was proud of himself for adding extra Rosin. He nodded to the cowboys in the arena, signaling he was ready. They swung the gate open to release the bull.

"Git all over him!" yelled a young rider waiting his turn.

The bull stormed out of the gate snorting, snapping its head back and forth, and slinging snot three feet in each direction. It began trying to buck him off, but H.D. matched the bull's movements perfectly with each kick and turn. The bull did its best

44

to dislodge its rider, but H.D. stuck on for eight seconds. When he heard the eight second buzzer go off, he retorted, "Take that bull!"

H.D. tried to hop off as the bull turned, but his hand was caught in the rope. He was held captive, dangling on the side of it as the bull drug him all around the arena. H.D. kept trying to pull his hand free and tried to keep his cool. The rodeo clowns jumped into the arena and attempted to catch the bull, but it was too fast. It took off to the other side of the arena then came back around by the bucking chutes with H.D. dragging beside it.

All you could hear was *Ding! Ding! Ding! Ding!* as H.D.'s helmet hit every single steel panel along the way. The audience stood to their feet, gasping, feeling helpless and fearful for the young boy. The rodeo clowns finally caught up with the bull and pulled H.D.'s hand free. "You okay, H.D.?" asked one of the clowns.

"What?" mumbled H.D., taking off his helmet and spitting out the mouth guard.

"I SAID ARE YOU OKAY?" shouted the clown.

"YES!" shouted H.D. above the ringing in his ears.

He shook his head a few times trying to get the ringing to stop, reached down, grabbed his bull rope off the ground, and walked through the gate. He saw his dad standing there with his arms crossed, glanced at him, and yelled, "I DON'T WANT TO HEAR IT!"

Steve didn't say a thing and just shook his head. H.D. walked right past his dad to gather his rodeo gear, cursing beneath his breath. Chase came up to him and said, "That was some ride!"

"One I won't *ever* forget!" asserted H.D., and he didn't. He learned his lesson to use the Rosin sparingly.

7 BEATEN, BUT NOT BROKEN

H.D. began working with Chase on the Plumer farm, helping
bale hay. One weekend, they had some free time and decided to
ride Chase's four-wheeler around the farmland. Chase climbed on
the four-wheeler first and handed H.D. a helmet. After securing his
helmet, H.D. hopped on behind Chase and grabbed the rear carrier
bar with both of his hands. Chase put on his helmet and started the
engine. The four-wheeler whined loudly as he squeezed the
accelerator to begin the ride.

Chase steered the four-wheeler toward the cornfield along the
path by the woods. A small gray rodent darted out in front of
them. "Squirrel!" they both shouted at the same time. Chase
swerved the four-wheeler chasing after it for several feet until the
frightened squirrel made a quick left turn and disappeared into the
underbrush of the woods. The boys laughed in delight and H.D.
hung on tightly as Chase squeezed the accelerated a little more.
They were having a ball riding through the woods and cornfields all
afternoon whooping and hollering with each bump and turn.

The dirt on the field was slightly wet, making the ride even more
thrilling as they slid when Chase turned too sharply or stopped
abruptly. They rode past the tall stalks of corn, feeling the slender,
green leaves slap them on the arm and face. Dirt was flying
everywhere behind them and on top of them when they spun out.

H.D. slid one arm between the bar of the rear carrier to give himself more stability as Chase went faster.

Chase followed the tractor trails between the rows of corn, looped around the outside edges, and turned back down another trail. Unaware of the P.T.O ditches his dad had made in the field earlier in the week for irrigating the crops, he squeezed the accelerator tighter on the four-wheeler. One ditch snuck up on them suddenly. *Smack*! They hit it just right!

"*Yeowww*!" screamed H.D.

"What in the hell is wrong!" yelled Chase trying to regain control of the four-wheeler.

"I broke my arm! I broke my arm!" shouted H.D. with tears rolling down his cheeks.

"You didn't break your arm!" Chase yelled back at him. He stopped the four-wheeler in the field. H.D. slid off and stood there, solemnly. Turning to look at his friend, Chase saw H.D. crying with his arm dangling a weird angle at the elbow. Chase started to freak out and yelled at him, "Get back on! Let's ride up to the house and take you to the hospital!"

H.D. climbed back on. They rode about twenty feet, but he couldn't withstand the vibration of every bump on his broken arm and had a hard time hanging on. Chase's neighbor was working in his field nearby, saw what happened, and ran up to the boys. He gently inspected H.D.'s arm and said, "You'd better walk back to the house. Your arm's broke."

Chase parked the four-wheeler and they walked back to the house where Chase's parents were standing outside after they heard the yelling. They took one look at H.D.'s arm and knew it was broken. Deciding it was useless to call H.D.'s parents since his dad was on his way to pick him up, they just waited for Steve to arrive. When he arrived at the farm, Steve was surprised to see his son standing there with his arm in a sling.

"What happened?" he asked, staring at everyone.

"I broke my arm on the four-wheeler, Dad," stated H.D., "We were just riding along and hit a ditch. The bar broke my arm."

e saw the tear stains on his son's face and Chase's sorrowful 'Well, we'd better get you to the hospital, so they can fix it," he ~tated matter-of-factly. Steve helped H.D. climb into the truck. H.D. waved goodbye to Chase with his other arm as they drove down the dirt driveway.

After registering H.D. to the emergency room in Seymour, they sat in the waiting room for several minutes until x-rays could be taken. Once those were completed, they waited for the technician to read it and report to the doctor. The x-rays confirmed H.D.'s arm was broken and dislocated at the elbow.

The doctor came out to the waiting room and asked them both to come with him to an examination room. He showed Steve the x-ray and said, "I'll need to set the bone back in place before we can put a cast on it," he paused and continued, "I'll give H.D. a sedative to relax him and ease the pain."

"No, I don't want any shot 'til I know you set it right," interjected H.D.

"No shot? You don't understand how painful this will be, H.D.," urged the doctor.

"I understand. No shot," said H.D. adamantly, shaking his head.

"Okay, if that's how you want it," conceded the doctor, "Dad, you will need to step out into the hall for this," he said, looking at Steve. Steve walked out into the hallway and the doctor closed the door. He turned to the young boy sitting on the edge of the exam table and said, "Okay, H.D., I want you to pull your elbow back while I grab your lower arm and pull it forward. We'll do it on the count of three," he counted, "One, two, three!"

On the count of three, H.D. pulled his elbow back as the doctor pulled his arm forward. *Snap!* The bone straightened and H.D. felt the pain radiate throughout his entire body as if he were struck by lightning, but he fought the urge to yell. His eyes teared up and he calmly said, "Okay, I'll take the shot now."

After the doctor gave H.D. the sedative, he opened the door and stepped out into the hallway to talk to Steve. "Your kid's crazy. I've never seen a grown up, let alone a kid, not take the shot, *ever!*"

"He's a little stubborn, like his dad," chuckled Steve.

"You can come back in now. The bone has been corrected and we can put a cast on it."

The doctor and Steve walked back into the room where H.D. was sitting on the exam table with a silly grin on his face. It was obvious the painkiller was doing its job.

"What color do you want your cast to be?" asked the doctor.

"Pink! I dare the kids at school to say anything about it." smirked H.D.

The doctor and Steve laughed so hard it echoed down the hallway. After checking on available colors, H.D. was told they were out of pink, so he donned a plain white cast instead. When he went to school on Monday, all the kids asked him about his arm. He told them the story, "The doctor said he was going to have to pull to get it lined back up. I was pulling my elbow one way and the doctor was pulling my hand the other way. It hurt like hell, but I didn't yell!"

His classmates were amazed by the story and asked him to repeat it several more times. He let them sign his cast and a few teachers, too. H.D. was proud of his cast but secretly wished it could have been pink. Unfortunately, the broken arm kept him out of the last rodeo competitions of the year.

By the time he got his cast removed, it was the middle of November. H.D. was anxious to get back to the rodeo. Steve decided he needed a new horse to ride and began searching for a good rodeo horse at a fair price. They found an older team roping horse named Wrangler. Wrangler was a tall red roan American Quarter Horse perfect for H.D.'s growing, long frame. H.D. began using Wrangler in team roping events in the rodeo.

In June 2001, Steve saw an advertisement on TV for Equitana U.S.A. at the Kentucky Fair and Exposition Center in Louisville, Kentucky. The event featured hundreds of booths with equine products and services, educational seminars, hundreds of demonstrations- several focusing on improving communication and understanding horses. The keynote speaker was going to be Ty

Murray, co-founder of the PBR and seven-time winner of the World Champion All-Around Cowboy award. H.D. and Steve were especially excited to hear Ty's speech.

Father and son rode to the Kentucky Fairgrounds and parked in one of the sections of the enormous parking lot. When H.D. entered the center, he was amazed. He had never seen so many horses in his entire life! An assortment of every color, size, and breed was available to inspect and buy. Depending on the size of your wallet, hundreds of dollars or half a million could be spent on a single horse. A variety of animal breed exhibitions, demonstrations, lectures, and children's activities were also available at the show. The commercial shopping offered everything from toys to expensive horse trailers.

Thousands of people from all over the country attended the event, including famous professional rodeo cowboys and cowgirls and country music artists. Steve and H.D. were in hog heaven. One day wasn't long enough for everything they wanted to see and do. They walked all around the center to see every exhibit they could.

Later in the afternoon, they went into the arena where Ty Murray was going to give his lecture on "Cross-Train Your Brain." They stood along the side as Ty was announced to the spectators. Ty entered the arena riding in a rustic wagon led by a team of magnificent Clydesdale horses.

They thundered into the arena making quite an impressive entrance. Their coal black mane and white feathering around their ankles flowed like newly spun silk when they strutted. The children and parents cheered and clapped as the team passed by and stopped in the middle of the arena.

Ty held a microphone and introduced himself, "Howdy, folks! My name is Ty Murray. Welcome to Equitana U.S.A. Are you enjoying yourselves?" The audience whooped and hollered in appreciation. "Before I start my talk, are there any questions you have for me?" he asked, looking at the kids. H.D. was standing right in front of him, raised his hand, and waved it eagerly. "Yes, son?" asked Ty, pointing to H.D.

"Sir, I was just wondering. How do you always land on your feet when you get off a bull? I always land on my head!" inquired H.D. with a straight face.

Ty and the entire audience exploded in laughter. Ty just smiled and replied, "When I began training for the rodeo, I realized that at 5'8" and 150 pounds, there was no way I could ever control a 2,000-pound bull. But, I could learn to control myself and how I reacted and responded to them." He went on to say he began taking martial arts and gymnastics classes and used a trampoline to master his balance and reflexes. He called it "Cross-Training". H.D. absorbed every single word the famous cowboy uttered. Steve was also impressed by his speech.

When Ty Murray's lecture was over and he exited the arena with the Clydesdales, Steve and H.D. left and went back out into the corridor of the center. As they passed the West Wing, H.D. saw the stalls where the horses were kept. "Dad, can we go in there?" he asked.

"Not right now, I need to go check on prices of feed at the country store first," replied Steve.

"Awww!" moaned H.D., hanging his head down.

"I'll take you there after, H.D."

H.D. shrugged his shoulders and followed his dad to the country store located at the North Wing of the center. The country store was immense with everything you could possibly want: cowboy hats, jeans, jewelry, shirts, belts, toys, horse tack, corrals, horse trailers, and much more.

Steve located the feed booth, examined the livestock feed, and asked the owner questions when he realized H.D. wasn't standing near him anymore. "Did you see where my son went?" he asked the woman selling the feed.

"I thought he was over there looking at those belt buckles," she replied, pointing to the booth across from them, "I don't think he came back this way."

Steve stood still a minute, pondering where his son could have gone until he realized the horse stalls were what enticed H.D. the most. *That little shit, just wait 'til I get a hold of him!* he thought. He headed to the stalls and began looking into every one of them for his son. When he finally found him, H.D. was standing there covered in horseshit and holding his cowboy hat wadded up.

"Dad, come here!" H.D. yelled at him, "I want you to meet some of my friends!"

Steve was tempted to choke the daylights out of his son when he realized H.D. was standing there with Ty Murray, Jewel, John Lyons, and Buck Brannaman. "This is Ty Murray and this is his girlfriend, Jewel. Isn't she purdy?" announced H.D., grinning proud as a peacock.

"Thanks, guys! Sorry if he's bothering you," apologized Steve.

Ty responded, chuckling, "Actually, he's been pretty entertaining! You want a beer?"

Steve sat down with Ty, Jewel, John, and Buck to drink a cold beer. They talked about the horse show, things they found interesting, and the fine horses. H.D. shared some of his rodeo adventures with them, loving every minute of it. When it came time to leave, Steve practically had to drag H.D. out of there. "Thanks again for watching my boy for me," he said as they left.

"No problem," said Jewel, "He's been absolutely delightful!"

H.D.'s heart pounded so hard he thought it would jump right out of his chest! He smiled and winked at Jewel. She laughed sweetly and blew him a kiss goodbye. That was another moment he would never forget as long as he lived!

After Equitana U.S.A., H.D. began working more with Wrangler and practicing the techniques Ty Murray taught him. Steve took him and Wrangler to Monte Molden's place near Georgetown to have Monte break the horse in during the summer. Monte invited Steve and H.D. to a team roping and barbecue he was having on Labor Day. Steve met Monte at the SIJRA. Monte had two children in the rodeo: a daughter a couple of years older than H.D. and son four years younger.

H.D. practiced team roping with Chase in the SIJRA. The two worked on capturing the steer as quickly as they could. Chase was the header who came out on his horse first to lasso the steer by either roping both horns, the neck, or one horn on the head. H.D. was the heeler who followed on his horse and would lasso the steer's hind legs. The two would work together bringing down the steer in a matter of seconds.

On Labor Day, Steve and H.D. took the truck and trailer with Wrangler to Monte's barbecue. They met Gary, Laura, and Chase Plumer there. An hour later, it came time for H.D. and Chase to team rope. A black steer was let loose into the arena and Chase shot out of the gate riding his horse, lasso in hand, to catch it. He swung his lasso and caught the steer by its horns. As he was pulling on the rope turning it, H.D. approached on Wrangler.

Just as the steer was beginning to turn, it locked up in front of the horse. Before H.D. could get around the steer and make his loop, Wrangler t-boned into the side of the animal. The steer cut under Wrangler, causing the horse to flip over with H.D. on him. He landed smack dab on top of H.D. The only thing you could see sticking out was one of H.D.'s arms and his head.

Wrangler shook his powerful legs, rolled over, and rose up on all fours. H.D. slowly crawled up onto his knees and stood up. Steve came running out to him to see if anything was broken. "I'm okay. I'm okay," assured H.D. Steve shook his head and yelled, "Scared the hell out of me, Son!"

"I really am okay," nodded H.D., swiping the dirt off of himself.

They walked over to examine Wrangler, who appeared to be uninjured, and stayed to finish watching the team roping and enjoy the rest of the barbecue. When it was over, they said goodbye to Monte and thanked him for inviting them to the barbecue, loaded up Wrangler, and went home.

H.D. worked the next week at the Plumer farm baling hay and had another junior rodeo competition, competing in a bull ride. Ten days after the barbecue, while eating dinner, H.D. complained, "Something's wrong inside of me!"

"What are you talking about?" questioned Steve, raising his eyebrows.

"Something's poking me when I breathe," replied H.D., pointing to his side.

Steve didn't wait to call the doctor; he immediately took H.D. to the E.R. When the doctor took them into the examination room, Steve said, "My son broke his ribs team roping." He told the doctor about the horse wreck as H.D. sat quietly on the exam table.

"How long ago was that?" inquired the doctor.

"Ten days ago."

"Have you ever had broken ribs?"

"Yeah."

"You know how bad they hurt. What all has he been doing?" asked the doctor incredulously.

"He's been baling hay every day and had another bull ride," answered Steve.

"We'll go ahead and take some x-rays, but I highly doubt that he's got anything broke," replied the doctor, shaking his head and added, "I'll give you a call when they're done."

"I guarantee you he has broken ribs," retorted Steve as he left the room with H.D.

After H.D.'s x-rays were completed, the two left the hospital. When they arrived back home, the voice mail was flashing on their answering machine. H.D. did indeed have broken ribs.

Two weeks later, H.D. had another bull ride. They were at the rodeo standing under the awning of their horse trailer when Steve began to question whether or not H.D. should compete. "I don't think you should do this ride, Son," said Steve looking directly at his son.

"I'm not going to be out of another competition! I'm in the running. You can't let me be out of this!" yelled the boy, determination displayed on his face.

"Okay, H.D.," stated Steve. He grabbed some medical tape and wrapped it around H.D.'s chest. H.D. did complete the bull ride and ended up winning the event. Nothing could stop that boy from his love of riding bulls.

8 THE DAY THE WORLD STOPPED TURNING

It was six-thirty on a bright, sunny Tuesday morning. H.D. arose from bed after his dad yelled at him for the second time to get up. He knew there wouldn't be a third time. He looked into his closet, grabbed his favorite jeans, pulled a t-shirt off the hanger, finished dressing, and went downstairs to eat before he had to leave for school.

"You don't have time to eat breakfast. The bus will be here in ten minutes," said Steve. "You can just eat breakfast at school. Do you want me to pack you a sandwich for lunch?"

"Naw, they're having pizza today. I'll eat that," replied H.D.

"Okay, suit yourself," his dad replied as he poured himself another cup of coffee.

"I hear the bus coming. I'd better go!" H.D. interjected.

He ran into the hallway, pulled on his boots, grabbed his backpack, and shot out the door to catch the school bus. Excited to see his classmates, he spent the entire time chatting with the neighboring kids who rode the hour-long bus ride to the Brownstown schools. Even though it was a long journey, the time flew by as he shared stories with his friends.

The yellow school bus pulled up to the front of Brownstown Elementary School and the bus driver opened the door to let the students off. H.D. grabbed his backpack, pushed his way between students in the aisle, and departed the bus. He ran up to the

55

entrance doors and walked down the hallway on the right to his fifth-grade classroom with other students.

"Good morning, H.D.! Get your books out and hang up your backpack in the coat closet," said Amy Hartley, his fifth-grade teacher, smiling.

"I need to eat breakfast. I didn't have time to this morning at home," reported H.D.

Mrs. Hartley picked up a small container, found a plastic meal ticket with H.D.'s name and picture on it, handed it to him, and said, "Here you go, go eat, and be back here by 8:25."

"I will," replied H.D. as he grabbed his meal ticket and left the room. Just as he was leaving, Chase Plumer walked in. "I'm going to breakfast. Do you need to eat too?" asked H.D.

"Yeah, I do. I'll get my ticket and meet you there," answered Chase.

H.D. walked to the cafeteria, stood in line behind the other students, and handed Mrs. Hall, the cafeteria aide, his meal ticket. She looked up his name, typed in the amount to deduct on the computer, and kept the ticket to return to Mrs. Hartley later. She smiled at H.D. and told him to go ahead in line.

After looking to see what was available, he grabbed a strawberry pop tart and a white milk; and he went to sit down. Chase went through the line and joined him at the cafeteria table. They sat for a few minutes talking until they noticed it was 8:22. "We'd better get to class," said Chase.

So, they grabbed what was left of their breakfast, got up, and walked to their class munching on the remainder of their pop tarts. They walked into the classroom and sat down at their designated chairs. H.D. pulled his writing tablet and pencil out of his desk, began copying the daily oral assignment written on the chalkboard, and correcting the grammar and punctuation errors in the sentences. Chase followed suit doing the same thing, as well as the other students in the class.

Mrs. Hartley started taking roll call to see who was absent. When she got to Lindsey's name, Lindsey briskly came walking into the

room with a worried look on her face. "I'm here, Mrs. Hartley!"
she announced, panting as if she had just run a marathon. "Sorry
I'm late. My mom was watching the news, and she had to hurry to
get me to school. My mom said there's something going on. A
plane hit a big building!"

"It did? Well, we'll just flip on the TV and see what's going on,"
Mrs. Hartley replied and added, "Go ahead and hang up your
things, Lindsey, and sit down. It's okay." Lindsey did what she was
instructed and sat down as Mrs. Hartley walked over to press the
on button of the TV. The televisions were just mounted on the
wall of each classroom last year in order for each teacher to watch
Channel One (a kids' news television program with stories and
current events) in their classroom and show videos without having
to sign up and borrow one of the few televisions available in the
library storeroom.

Mrs. Hartley stood to the side and stared at the television along
with every student in her classroom. They could not believe what
they saw. The news anchor of Channel 3 out of Louisville,
Kentucky was saying, "At 8:45 a.m., Flight 11, an American
Airlines Boeing 767 loaded with 20,000 gallons of fuel and ninety-
two passengers took off from Logan International Airport in
Boston, Massachusetts headed for Los Angeles, California has just
crashed into the north tower of the World Trade Center in New
York City. We are not sure what happened and will keep the
broadcast going until we get further details."

Coincidentally, a person standing several blocks from the World
Trade Center, captured the crash on their cell phone, and shared it
with a news station in New York City. Towering high above the
skyline of Manhattan, the shiny, silver Twin Towers stood majestic
in the morning sun when suddenly a jet came into view. The image
stunned H.D., as well as his teacher and classmates. It showed the
jet directly hitting the eightieth floor of the 110-story skyscraper.

A gaping hole with flames and smoke came roaring out of the
building. They continued watching as the news anchor explained
that thousands of people inside the building were being evacuated

and many were trapped inside as the N.Y.C. firefighters were running into the building to help search and rescue victims. "Wow, that is *so* awful. Those poor people!" said one girl near H.D. It appeared to be some kind of freak accident until eighteen minutes later, at 9:03 a.m., a second plane was approaching the twin towers.

Chase jumped up out of his seat and shouted, "Another plane is going to hit!" Other students stood up and gasped. H.D. sat and listened, staring in horror at the TV as he saw the second plane turn sharply and plummet into the south tower of the World Trade Center near the sixtieth floor. There was a huge explosion, as if a bomb went off, sending an immense mushroom cloud of fire and smoke upward into the sky.

The plane had left a massive hole and sliced into the inner section of the skyscraper. You could hear yells and gasps from behind the news anchor's desk and people scrambling on the phone trying to find out what was going on. *This isn't an accident. Someone did this on purpose. Who would do that?* thought H.D.

"Mrs. Hartley, what's going on? Why are there planes crashing into the buildings?" asked Chase.

"I don't know, Chase. No one does yet. The news people are trying to figure it out." She stood with a worried look on her face and continued, "We will keep watching this for a little while to find out what happened."

The news anchor came back on and reported, "A Boeing 767, United Airlines Flight 175, departing from Boston and heading for California with sixty-five passengers crashed into the south tower of the World Trade Center. We believe these two crashes are connected and intentional. The south tower is also being evacuated and citizens of New York City are being told to leave the area. At this time, we do not know if there will be any more hits on New York City."

Everyone in the class was stunned. They felt the same as H.D. It was not an accident and hearing the confirmation on the news station sent a ripple of unrest and anxiousness about what was going to happen next. Many had the same thoughts going through their heads. *How could someone kill all those people? Why would they do this? What does this all mean? Am I safe?*

For H.D., every student in his class, every person in Brownstown, Indiana, and every person in the United States of America who was watching the images, it was surreal. You saw what was happening, heard the reports, but could not believe this is happening in our country on American soil. No one realized the impact this would have on their lives and for generations to come.

Mrs. Hartley's class watched the footage of people running out of the Twin Towers, firefighters rushing in, people running away through the streets of New York City choking from the thick fog of smoke. Ash an inch thick covered the streets and cars. People walking away from the area looked like ghosts covered in it.

You could see debris falling like confetti several blocks away from the towers. Images of people looking desperately out of the windows came across the screen, and you knew they were too far up for any fire truck to rescue. Everyone felt afraid for them and helpless to do anything about it. All you could do was watch.

Then, at 9:38 a.m., the news anchor reported American Airlines Flight 77, a Boeing 757, traveling from Dulles, Virginia to Los Angeles had just crashed into the Pentagon in Washington, D.C. It flew low, alongside the building, banked at a ninety-degree angle, flipped on its right side, and slammed into the lower two floors of the southwest side. It exploded as horrified commuters and visitors watched. Panicked employees scrambled out of the building through any open exit they could find. Later, the upper floors collapsed trapping and burying employees inside.

As images of the Pentagon were being shown on the broadcast, the room went completely silent. You could have heard a pin drop at that moment. No one stirred a muscle in their seat; they just kept staring at the TV. The station switched to live footage of the Twin Towers, showing more firefighters entering the buildings.

"Children, I know this is horrible. Firefighters are trying to help rescue these people. Let's pray many of them make it out," said Mrs. Hartley as she turned away from the TV and was looking into the sad, pitiful faces of her students who were all sitting at their desks watching the live footage. Suddenly, Chase jumped up out of his chair again and shouted, "They're going down! They're going down, right now!"

At 9:59 a.m., H.D. and everyone gasped in horror as they watched the south tower suddenly and unexpectedly fall like a stack of dominoes, leaving an enormous pile of rubble and sending more smoke and ash into the air. Then, at 10:30 a.m., they saw the north tower likewise disintegrate into a heap in a matter of seconds.

Next, the news channel showed live footage of the chief of staff whispering into President George W. Bush's ear as he was reading a story with elementary students in Florida telling him about the second crash. You could see the shock on his face as he sat and finished the story. He stood up quietly and solemnly left the building, boarded Air Force One, and received a military jet escort to an undisclosed secure place.

The principal of the school, Mr. Raymer, came on the loudspeaker and said, "A few minutes ago, we have learned that two planes hit the twin towers of the World Trade Center and one hit the Pentagon. We do not know who is responsible or have all the details yet.... This is the day you will never forget as long as you live," he paused and continued, "Let's have a moment of silence for the people in New York City." Everyone bowed their heads, closed their eyes, and were silent for one minute.

The class sat quietly as the news anchor came back on and announced a fourth plane had been hijacked, "United Flight 93 was hijacked after leaving Newark International Airport in New Jersey. It had seven crewmembers and thirty-three passengers on board. From what we can gather by telephone calls made to loved ones before the flight went down, there were four terrorists. A group of men stormed the cockpit and the plane went down in a field near Shanksville, Pennsylvania at 10:02 a.m. All those aboard were killed. We do not know at this time what the destination was. Our hearts go out to the families of those brave men and women on board."

The past hour felt as if it lasted an eternity and there seemed to be no end to the tragedies. The sheer magnitude of this day was just beginning to take shape. A few minutes after the announcer reported the fourth plane crash, President Bush came onto the air to make a short speech saying, "Our freedom is being attacked by a faceless coward. The U.S. will hunt down and punish those responsible for these cowardly acts."

The mayor of New York City, Mayor Rudy Giuliani, also appeared on TV calling for calm in the city, telling people to evacuate peacefully as emergency personnel help rescue people and give them medical attention. New York City looked like a war zone. Footage of people jumping into action was also shown: people were helping victims get to medical personnel, gathering water bottles, food, bandages, and donating blood. Everyone was working as a cohesive unit, tirelessly searching and helping victims from the buildings, those injured on the streets, and those wandering around dazed and confused. A group of people began singing the National Anthem.

As it was approaching lunchtime, Mrs. Hartley turned off the TV and tried to assure her students they were safe and it was going to be okay. She escorted them to the cafeteria. H.D. followed in line, unusually quiet with a frown on his face. He didn't feel like talking to anyone or eating lunch.

He sat with his classmates picking at the pizza, took one little bite, and put it back down on his plate. Chase sat by him and only took a few bites of his pizza as well. Other fifth graders in the cafeteria were talking and carrying on as normal. Even though they heard what Mr. Raymer had said, they had not seen what was happening or realized the gravity of the events. Only a few teachers had their televisions on in the morning. As the day went on, teachers were going to the office to pick up mail or make copies in the supply room and learning the horrific details.

The kids were allowed to go outside for recess. Chase and H.D. went to sit down on a bench together. "Wow, H.D., I can't believe this is happening! I wonder what the president will do?" Chase said. H.D. shrugged his shoulders but didn't say anything.

"Are you okay?" asked Chase, looking at H.D.

"I'm not sure," replied H.D. as a single teardrop fell from his right eye.

"It will be okay, H.D. You'll see," Chase responded, patting him on the back gently.

They sat quietly, went back inside when the whistle was blown, and returned to their classroom. Mrs. Hartley tried to assure her students again they were going to be okay. She said, "What happened today is big. This is history- just like Pearl Harbor was for my parents and the shooting of J.F.K. was for my generation. You will never forget this day in your life. Our lives *will* be different. It's okay to be sad, but you will be alright. Go home and talk about it with your parents." She read them some stories to lighten up the rest of their day and at 3:00 p.m. dismissed her class to leave for home.

Some parents had picked up their children early, some were picked up at the end of the day, and some rode the bus home. Many parents were hugging and kissing their children, thankful they were safe and not letting them out of their sight. Chase's dad picked him up from school. He asked Chase, "Were you able to hear what happened?"

"Yes, we watched the whole thing on TV most of the day," replied Chase.

"You'll never forget this day as long as you live. You'll remember this day: where you were at, what you saw, and when you're eighty. You will be able to go to the exact spot where you were standing," Gary Plumer stated. Chase got in the truck and rode home with his dad.

H.D. rode the bus home. The long ride home was torture. Kids around him were talking about what happened in New York, retelling the events. H.D. didn't want to hear it. Putting his hands over his ears, he tried to drown out the stories. He didn't want to be on the bus anymore, he wanted to see his dad and be home, NOW!

When the bus dropped him off in front of his driveway, he sprinted to the front door, jerked it open, dropped his backpack on the floor, and ran into the living room yelling, "Dad! Dad! Where are you?"

"I'm right here, H.D.," Steve replied as he turned the corner from the kitchen. It was as if a dam burst inside him. H.D. began bawling with waves of tears flowing down his cheeks. "You can't leave!" he sobbed. "They can't make you go!" He grabbed his dad around the waist and wouldn't let go.

"What? What are you talking about?" asked his dad, holding onto him to comfort him.

"The president said we are going to hunt down who crashed the airplanes into the trade center...... They can't make you go back into the Marines......You can't leave me!" H.D. managed to spit out between sobs.

"Son, let's go into the den, sit down, and talk," responded Steve calmly.

He took H.D. into the den where they spent an hour talking about what happened in New York, D.C., and Pennsylvania. He told H.D., "I'm not in the Marines anymore. They can't make me be a Marine again and go overseas. The Marines and other men and women in our military now will be the ones who will go over there to fight."

"Really? For sure?" questioned H.D.

"For sure. Cross my heart!" swore his dad, crossing his heart with his index finger.

Steve could see the relief and weight of dread leave H.D.'s body. H.D. wiped the tears from his eyes and gave his dad a big bear hug. Steve held onto his son for a long time. After a few more minutes, H.D. sat straight up, and his face had changed. He was no longer afraid or sad, another feeling he had never felt before swept over him.

Steve turned on the TV to see what was happening and if there were any new developments. They watched as America hunkered down. People rushed to get gas in fear that oil prices would rise.

The nation's workforce stopped and returned home. Schools and businesses canceled all athletic and entertainment events. At other skyscrapers and landmarks, troops stood by to evacuate visitors and workers. The nation's airports were shut down with 200,000 passengers stranded. Airplanes in route in the sky were approached by F-16s (air force combat jets). The commercial airline pilots were to report who they were and what their destination was, then forced to land with the F-16 escort. It was reported that the attackers were Islamic extremists from Saudi Arabia and other Arab nations supported by fugitive Osama bin Laden's al-Qaeda terrorist organization.

At 9:00 p.m., President Bush returned to the White House and gave a second speech from the Oval Office. In it he stated, "Good evening! Today, our fellow citizens, our way of life, our very freedom came under attack in a series of deliberate and deadly terrorist attacks…. Thousands of lives were suddenly ended by evil… Terrorist attacks can shake the foundations of our biggest buildings, but they cannot touch the foundation of America. These acts shattered steel, but they cannot dent the steel of American resolve."

He declared, "The search is underway for those who are behind these evil acts…. We will make no distinction between the terrorists who committed these acts and those who harbor them." At the end of his speech, he asked for prayers for all those who are grieving and for the children whose world has been shattered. Lastly, he quoted Psalm 23 of the Bible, "Even though I walk through the valley of the shadow of death, I will fear no evil, for you are with me…. None of us will ever forget this day. Yet, we go forward to defend freedom and all that is good and just in our world. Thank you. Goodnight and God bless America!" After his speech, the room broke out in song singing, "God Bless America".

H.D. turned to his dad, his face beet red, and asked, "Who are terrorists?"

"Terrorists are cowards who try to make people afraid by attacking them in their normal daily lives. They hate Americans because of our way of life and involvement in the Middle East. That's why they attacked us today," explained Steve.

"That's not right! What did we ever do to them to deserve this?" shouted H.D.

"Easy, Son, you're right. It's not fair," he agreed, patting H.D. on the shoulder.

"Well, I hope President Bush finds those sons of bitches and kills them all!" yelled H.D.

Steve's eyebrows raised and he looked at H.D., surprised at the maturity of his son at that moment. He couldn't bring himself to correct his son for his language, because he felt exactly the same way. So, he said instead, "I hope President Bush does exactly that, too."

They sat together to watch the news for another hour. H.D. was feeling better and got a sandwich to eat and some Kool-Aid. They talked a little more about the military fighting in Beirut where the French and U.S. embassy was bombed in 1983, killing 241 American servicemen and terrorism. Finally, at ten o'clock, Steve said, "It's time for bed, H.D., you have to go to school tomorrow."

"Okay, Dad, I'm tired. See you in the morning," H.D. said and gave his dad one more hug before he walked up the stairs to bed. The day was September 11, 2001. A day that will live in infamy for the rest of his life. It was the catalyst that changed how we live our lives today. Security measures were put in place at all American airports: you could no longer go with your loved one to see them board their airplane and going through security took much longer.

Our daily way of communication changed. Not many people had cell phones at that time. Now, we are used to carrying cell phones in our pockets and seeing text messages scrolling across the bottom of the screen of our TV, providing instant news and information.

Americans old enough that day could never forget the moment the first airplane hit the World Trade Center, the feeling of having our carefree innocence taken away, sense of security shaken, and anger toward those who inflicted these acts of terrorism. Those feelings tugged at H.D.'s heart and mind for many years to come.

9 AN ARM AND A LEG

H.D. and Chase attended Brownstown Central Middle School beginning in 2002. The three years flew by in a blink of an eye. The two spent infinite hours working on the Plumer farm for extra money, going to the Southern Indiana Junior Rodeo Association rodeos, and practicing riding their horses and roping at the farm.

One day, during the summer after their eighth-grade year ended, they were sitting on a hay bale in the barn discussing how to improve their rodeo skills. "You know what we need?" asked H.D.

"What?" replied Chase.

"We need an arena to give us a place to let steer loose and practice with our horses," suggested H.D.

"You're right! We do. How much do you think it would cost to build one?" inquired Chase.

"I don't know...a lot," sighed H.D., shrugging his shoulders.

"I've been saving my money. How much do you have?" asked Chase.

"Not sure, maybe a couple of hundred bucks."

"I have over six thousand dollars saved up," said Chase, matter-of-factly.

"What! How the hell did you get that much money?" gawked H.D., dumbfounded.

"I just never spent any of the money I earned helping my dad.

Do you think that will be enough?"

"Only one way to find out. Let's ask your dad how much it would cost," suggested H.D.

"Okay, let's do it," decided Chase, nodding his head.

The two boys strolled back into the house to find Chase's dad. When they saw him, Chase said, "Dad, we need to talk to you. It's important."

Gary was reaching into the refrigerator to get a beer, turned around, and looked at the boys. He saw the serious looks on their faces. *Oh, no! What have those two done now?* he thought.

"Dad, H.D. and I've been talkin'. We wanna build an arena to help us get better in the rodeo."

"Build an arena?" Gary repeated to be sure he heard Chase right, not expecting that statement.

"Yes. We have the money, Dad. We don't expect you to pay for it. We will."

"Chase, are you sure you want to spend all your money on an arena?" he asked his son.

"Yes! I'm sure, Dad. We have to have a place to practice where we can let the animals loose and be able to rope them without having to chase them down. Besides, if we decide to stop, we can always sell the panels and get our money back."

Gary saw the determination on both boys' faces and caved in. He couldn't argue with their reasoning. "Okay, you two, I'll call R&R Metal and tell Ron we're coming in to talk to him. We need to figure out how big the arena will be, so let's go out and step it off."

He led the boys to the field where the arena would be located. The grass was cut making it easier for them to measure the distance. The two boys stepped off the size for the arena as Gary wrote down the measurements on a notepad and calculated about how many panels it would take to set up the arena the way they wanted.

Having the information they needed, Gary picked up the phone and told Ron they were coming to his shop in Cortland to ask him about a project the boys came up with. The three got into Gary's truck and rode to the shop a few miles down the road.

Gary's cell phone rang when he parked the truck. "You two go ahead. I'll be in when I get done with this call. Tell Ron what you want," he instructed them. He flipped open his cell phone and began talking as the two boys got out of the truck and slammed the door shut.

Chase walked into the shop first. He saw Ron Lucas sitting on a stool welding something in the corner and shouted to him, "Hey, Ron!" Ron didn't hear him the first time, so Chase shouted louder, "RON!" Ron turned around, saw the teenagers, and stopped welding to see what they wanted.

"What are you two boys up to?" he asked.

"We want to talk to you about helping us build an arena," replied Chase.

"How big of an arena are we talking about?"

"We want fifty panels sixteen-feet long and six-feet high," said H.D.

Ron stood up, scratched his head, looked at the two boys incredulously, and exclaimed, "You two don't have that kind of money to build that big of an arena. It will cost you an arm and a leg!"

"Yes, we do. We've been saving up our money," replied Chase.

"So, what kind of panels do you want? Aluminum or steel?" asked Ron.

"We want the arena to last a long time, so we want steel panels," answered Chase.

Ron's eyes doubled in size and he warned the boys, "You realize that is going to cost thousands of dollars, don't you?"

"Yes, we know that. We have the money, Ron," responded Chase.

"You do?" asked Ron, raising his eyebrows in disbelief.

"Yes, they do," interjected Gary as he walked into the shop and approached the three. Ron looked at Gary, who nodded in certainty, turned back to the boys, and said, "Okay, I will charge you 100 dollars apiece and give it to you in increments of ten panels. That will be one thousand dollars for ten." Ron looked back at Gary and asked, "Are you okay with that, Gary?"

"Yes. The boys told me about their plan and I agreed to help them," assured Gary.

"Okay, it's a deal," Chase affirmed.

"Sounds good. I can't wait to see this arena, boys!" stated Ron, smiling at them.

"Thanks, Ron," replied Chase, grinning back.

"Thank you, sir," added H.D., grinning just as big.

They turned and left Ron's shop. As they were driving back home, Gary said, "Okay boys, I'll call Herschel Lucas to see if he'll help us weld the panels for the arena."

"Okay, Dad, thanks," replied Chase.

"You do realize this is going to be quite a job. I will help you, but you two are going to dig the holes for the stakes and do the lifting for the panels," said Gary sternly.

"We know, Dad. We're ready to work hard on it," responded Chase.

"Yes, sir. I will be here every day to help Chase work on it," assured H.D.

"Okay. I'm holding you two to your promise," said Gary.

H.D. told his dad that night about their plan to build the arena and asked if he would take him to the Plumers the days they were working on it. Like Gary, Steve warned his son about how much work building the arena would be and that it would take much longer than he thinks. H.D. assured his dad he understood how much hard work it involved but wanted to help Chase as much as he could. Steve agreed to take his son to the farm and pick him up after work and on the weekends.

Gary called Herschel Lucas who owned Herschel's Welding on Highway 258 in Cortland to ask Herschel if he would help weld the panels. Herschel agreed. Several weeks later when Ron got the first ten panels done, he called Gary. The next day, they picked up the panels in Gary's trailer and began building the arena.

Herschel, Chase, H.D., and Gary set out stakes and cables to make sure every side was straight and square with the world. Then, they began putting the arena together slowly after each increment of ten panels was completed. They also built boxes to practice roping. By the time it was finished, it was the spring of 2006.

Gary was selling hay to a man in Madison who had a herd of longhorn cattle. He made a deal trading the hay for the cattle. H.D. and Chase used steers and calves in the arena to practice roping. The two became members of the Indiana High School Rodeo Association (IHSRA) in 2005.

About the time the longhorn cattle came rolling in, H.D. got out of the roping events and focused only on the rough stock events: saddle bronc riding, bareback bronc riding, and bull riding. Once he began the bronc riding, H.D. was in pure heaven. He found what he loved the most in the rodeo and spent his high school years perfecting the saddle bronc riding and bareback riding.

The rodeo events took place in five surrounding Midwestern states: Indiana, Illinois, Kentucky, Ohio, and Michigan. Gary Plumer and Steve Hogan spent many weekends traveling with their sons to the IHSRA rodeo competitions. Just their freshman year, they were gone eighteen weekends. It was a hauling match. If you could afford to attend the events, you would most likely make the state finals. If you made the state finals into the top four spots, you could go to the National High School Rodeo competitions. H.D. made nationals in the bronc events.

Even though H.D. loved the bronc riding, the horses weren't always kind to him. During the summer of 2005, H.D. and Chase attended the Harry Vold Bronc Riding Clinic in Abilene, Kansas to learn bronc riding techniques. Harry Vold was born in Canada and grew up during the Depression. He started auctioneering, like his father, at the young age of fifteen. He was a cowboy himself and helped break and sell horses, trailing them seventy-five miles to Stettler, Alberta. In 1967, he got into the rodeo business in the U.S. and formed the Harry Vold Rodeo Company in 1970. He was a legendary stock contractor and earned the nickname "Duke of the

Chutes".

During the morning of the clinic, the boys would practice riding on dummies. In the afternoon, Harry was selling broncs and bulls. He let riders get on the animals during the day and did a competition each night. The boys got to choose a bronc they wanted to ride.

H.D. was watching the other boys ride but wouldn't get on a single bronc. Finally, on the second day toward the end of the afternoon, he saw a strawberry Roan come running up the corral. He jumped up and shouted to everyone, "That one's mine! I'm getting on that one!"

The Roan was restrained in the chute and H.D.'s saddle was placed upon its back. A thick rein made of rope was attached to the halter. For the saddle bronc competition, cowboys use the rein instead of a saddle horn to hang on with one hand while balancing with their free arm.

H.D. lowered himself down onto the horse and grabbed the rein with his left hand. The Roan went crazy- kicking its hind hooves into the wooden panels of the chute with such force you thought the panels would break. The cowboys assisting H.D. grabbed the Roan's halter to get it to stop while H.D. held on. Once the Roan calmed down for a second, he nodded his head to give the okay, and the gate was opened.

Just as he learned in practice, H.D. instantly "marked out" the horse by having both of his spurs touch above its shoulders when it made its first jump. The feel of the spur on its shoulders set the Roan off. It leapt into the air off of all fours with such an explosive force H.D. had never experienced. The Roan was truly a fantastic horse.

It came down and kicked its hind legs straight up at a ninety-degree angle sending H.D. somersaulting right over its head. He landed square on top of his own head and fell over completely knocked out. Steve shot into the arena as the Roan was steered back into the corral.

"Don't move, H.D., stay there!" yelled Steve as he was running up to him, unaware he was out cold. The medics on hand for the clinic ran up to H.D. along with his dad. He had quit breathing. His lips were turning blue and his face was an ashen white.

The medics were about to begin mouth-to-mouth resuscitation when H.D. came to. "Get the bull off me!" he shouted deliriously, swinging his arms out wildly.

"H.D.! You were bucked off a bronc! Remember?" yelled Steve kneeling beside him.

"You've been unconscious for quite a while," added one of the medics, kneeling on the other side.

"I'm okay," said H.D. as he sluggishly sat up. The crowd watching silently began clapping, relieved the young cowboy was alright. H.D. looked around trying to regain his composure and recall where he was and what had happened. The medics assisted him onto his feet and Steve helped walk him out of the arena.

As they were walking out slowly, H.D. began shrugging his shoulders and said, "You need to pop my back, Dad."

"You need to get in the ambulance," ordered Steve, immediately concerned with H.D.'s statement. H.D. did what he was told and sat down on the back of the ambulance. Chase and Gary came up and stood beside Steve to make sure his son was okay. "What is today, H.D.?" asked the medic standing beside him.

"Tuesday," answered H.D. It was Sunday.

"What's your dad's middle name?" continued the medic.

H.D. glanced at his dad with a puzzled face. "I'm not helping you," answered Steve, shaking his head.

"When is your birthday?" the other medic finally asked. H.D.'s face changed from bewilderment to a frown and he said, "We'd better go to the hospital. My back is startin' to hurt a little bit."

His statement alarmed the medics, and they sprang into action. One held H.D.'s neck still as the other placed a neck brace on him. Then, they put him on a gurney. After that, they went through their normal protocol checking his vitals and pupil reaction. H.D. wasn't letting them touch him until then. One medic went to the driver's seat, called into the dispatcher's office on his radio, and switched the ambulance siren on. The other strapped H.D. into the gurney, making sure the strap over his forehead was tight enough to keep his head from moving.

Steve told Gary, "Let Harry know about H.D., and I will call you with details later."

"Sure, Steve. Anything else I can do?" asked Gary with worry clearly visible on his face.

"No, I'll call you if there is," he shrugged.

"We are going to the Memorial Hospital in Abilene, if you want to follow," instructed the medic just before he closed the door. Steve got into his truck and followed the ambulance to the hospital. They did a C.T. scan on him, and the female doctor came to get Steve in the waiting room.

"There's no bleeding or swelling in the brain," she told him.

"Okay, we'll head back down to the ranch," responded Steve, not planning on letting H.D. ride, but he wanted to get all their equipment.

"You're not going anywhere," she protested. "He has a broken neck! The break is at the C7 vertebra." The C7 is the main vertebra holding the neck up straight. Steve stared at the doctor, speechless. He was surprised but had suspected something was wrong.

"I'll take you to his room," she offered and turned around walking down the corridor. He followed her into H.D.'s room, who was lying in bed with straps going across his legs, arms, chest, and forehead. Steve looked at him and said, "Son, you have a broken neck." Two enormous tears ran down the side of H.D.'s face and he sobbed, "When…. can I…. ride…. again?"

"I don't know, Son. The doctor will have to clear you first. It could take a while," answered Steve, shaking his head and empathizing with his son. H.D. wept in disappointment.

"We will need to transfer him to the Salina Surgical Hospital. They deal more with spine injuries than we do. He will get excellent care there," she stated and walked up to the side of the bed. "It will be okay, H.D.," she added, consoling him and patting his left shoulder.

After the doctor left the room, Steve called Gary, told him about H.D.'s injury, and asked, "Can you bring H.D.'s equipment to me? They are transferring him to the Salina Surgical Hospital."

"Of course, Steve. I've already gathered it all for you. Chase and I will be there soon," offered Gary. He brought H.D.'s equipment to Steve and Chase went to visit H.D. to make him feel better. He saw him in bed, all strapped down with tear stains on the side of his cheeks.

"Sorry, H.D. I know how bad you must feel," Chase comforted his friend. "I'll come see you when we get back home."

"Thanks, Chase. Yeah, I'll see ya later on," H.D. said softly, only able to move his eyes to look at his friend.

Gary and Chase went back to the ranch, and H.D. was transferred by ambulance to Salina that day. A spine surgeon looked at his C.T. scan and decided surgery was not needed. They discussed the best way to get H.D. home, since they were 800 miles away.

The doctor and a male nurse came out to inspect the truck to see where to put H.D., how far to lay him back, and how to strap him down. He rode in the passenger seat lain all the way back and strapped down completely. Steve drove to his sister's house in York, Nebraska. Then, they started back to Indiana the next day.

A broken neck didn't stop H.D. from pursuing his interests. He went hunting one week later with the neck brace on and ended up killing a huge 11-point deer. Three months and two weeks later, he was on a pro bareback bucking horse.

During the next year, 2006, Steve took H.D. to the Kentucky Horse Park in Lexington for the high school rodeo. High school students from all over Kentucky, Indiana, and Ohio were there. The park had an enormous arena to host rodeo events, as well as other sporting events.

H.D. entered the bareback bronc riding event. When it was his turn, he lowered himself down on the black Gelding and wedged his right hand into the rigging attached to the horse's girth. The rigging is made of leather and rawhide, and it mimics the tree of the saddle. There is no saddle, so the rider sits on the bare back of the horse.

The horse turned around, stared at H.D. with his eagle-like dark eyes, and whinnied. There was something about the horse that sent a shiver down H.D.'s spine, but he shook it off as just nerves. *I can do this!* he told himself.

H.D. nodded to the men to open the gate. As soon as it opened, the Gelding began kicking its hind legs up. H.D. clung to the horse, squeezing his legs and holding onto the rigging with all his might. As the horse's feet came back down on the ground, H.D. moved his spurs back over the horse's shoulders, causing the horse to buck again. This time, the powerful action of the horse sent H.D. somersaulting off its back. Before he hit the ground, H.D. felt the horse's hooves smack hard against his back. He landed in the dirt on his stomach as the horse sped off.

The EMS personnel came running out to check on H.D. "I'm okay. No problem," he told the medics as he saw them coming up to him. He slowly rose to his feet and brushed off the dirt. One of the medics said, "Stay there son, let us check you out!"

"No. No. I'm fine!" H.D. insisted, shaking his head.

"Okay, but if something starts bothering you, you come see us immediately!" the other medic instructed.

"Alright!" replied H.D. as he walked out of the arena and went up to his dad.

"Are you sure you're okay?" Steve asked his son, not completely believing him.

"Yes, Dad, I'm fine!" he insisted.

The two went to the food stand to buy some lunch and climbed the steps near the top of the arena to sit and watch the rest of the competition. Just as H.D. turned to sit down on the bleacher, he fell over and passed out.

Steve grabbed his son and laid him flat on the floor. He lifted up the back of H.D.'s shirt and found a hematoma the size of a basketball. He told one of the men standing near him to go get the EMS. The man quickly descended the stairs and requested help.

The medics carried a gurney up the stairs, placed H.D. on it on his stomach as the boy was opening his eyes, strapped him in, and carefully carried him down the steps. They put him in an ambulance and took him to the nearest hospital. After treating H.D. for the hematoma, he was released to go back home.

After he was cleared by his family doctor to ride again, Chase and H.D. practiced in the arena they built. Gary and Laura talked to the IHSRA about adding a rodeo at their farm. The association agreed. Once sponsors and vendors were lined up and all the arrangements were made, the Jackson County Rodeo held its first competition in August 2008 at the Plumer Arena. High school students from Indiana, Kentucky, and Ohio came to compete in the two-day rodeo.

Chase and H.D. were a part of the competition and proud as peacocks knowing they were the ones that made it all possible. Besides the competitions, the rodeo had a clown to entertain the crowd, vendors selling merchandise including a t-shirt promoting the rodeo, and food. The audience sat in the bleachers or in their own lawn chairs in the grass.

Young children ran up to the fence and peeked through the steel panels at the broncs and bulls. When one of the wild animals came charging up toward them, their parents would grab the back of their shirts to pull them away. Despite the yells to stay away, curiosity drew the youngsters back to the fence. Everyone was thoroughly entertained. The rodeo was a huge success, so the Plumers continued hosting it annually.

Later that same year, Chase and H.D. went to a high school rodeo in Wapakoneta, Ohio. Getting to the rodeo turned out to be an adventure in itself. Rain or shine, the rodeo always goes on. However, on the morning of Saturday, September 13th, it was beginning to look like this may be the day the rodeo would be canceled.

Earlier that morning at 2:10 a.m., Hurricane Ike hit land at Galveston, Texas. Immense waves crashed into the coastline causing massive flooding and damage to Louisiana, Texas,

Mississippi, and the Florida Panhandle. Strong winds and rain spread up into North America.

While they traveled up Interstate 75 in Ohio, they saw trees bending from the force of the wind. Gary was driving his truck with a trailer carrying Chase's horse. Laura and Chase were riding with him. Steve followed behind them with H.D. in his truck. They both saw the wind push Gary's truck over the center line several times. Luckily, there were no vehicles passing at the time.

As the wind kept blowing and the rain poured, the travelers could see the destruction of the hurricane. Trees and power lines were down along the way. They passed a refrigerator truck turned over on its side in the median of the highway. A barn was toppled into a heap of timber on one farm. Two men were removing a piece of plywood off the hood of a car in the driveway of another home.

When they arrived at the arena in Wapakoneta, the rain stopped and the wind started to calm down. The arena was a muddy mess. People were clearing away debris and helping contestants arriving find a spot to park. Despite the wind, the rodeo went on.

While the grown-ups were going to check on the schedule and talk to the hosts of the rodeo, H.D. and Chase sat in Steve's truck listening to music. H.D. cranked up the song "Kryptonite" by 3 Doors Down. He told Chase bronc riding was his Kryptonite. The boys laughed and sang out loud. After listening to it one more time, they got out of the truck to join their parents.

Chase entered the steer wrestling event. He was assisted by a volunteer who was the hazer. The hazer rides on horseback, keeping the steer running in a straight line while the bulldogger tries to capture it. Chase rode his horse, Dallas, a Palomino Quarter Horse.

When the signal was given, the black steer was released from behind the barricade. The hazer stayed on the right side of the steer keeping it straight. Chase rode along the left side of the animal. When Dallas pulled even with the steer, Chase eased himself down on the right side of his horse and reached for the steer's horns. As soon as he grabbed both horns, he slid off his horse and dug his heels into the ground.

The thick, deep mud from the heavy rainfall made it trickier, but Chase managed to slow down the steer. He lifted up on its right horn and pushed down on the left bringing the animal down on its side. The buzzer went off signaling he completed his mission. The whole thing happened in less than six seconds. Chase was proud of his time and exited the arena completely covered in mud.

H.D. entered the saddle bronc riding event. He wore a white long-sleeved shirt with a black vest, blue jeans, and chaps. The brown Mustang he was given to ride was strong and agile. When the gate opened, H.D. held onto the rein with his right hand this time and used his left arm to balance himself.

The horse bucked in the mud. H.D. held on tight as the animal's front hooves leapt upward, and its back hooves dug into the mud. H.D. rose up off the saddle, lowered his head, and kept his left arm up in the air. Laura captured the magnificent ride on her camera as well as Chase's ride.

The Mustang bucked a couple more times, finally dislodging H.D. from its back. He landed with a *splat!* and was also covered with mud from head to toe. His crisp, white shirt was no longer crisp or white. Chase and H.D. pointed and laughed at each other when they saw how much mud the other had on him. Both boys finished extremely well in their events. Not even a hurricane could stop those two from competing in the rodeo.

10 THE ROAD NOT TAKEN

Two roads diverged in a yellow wood,
And sorry I could not travel both
And be one traveler, long I stood
And looked down one as far as I could
To where it bent in the undergrowth;

Then took the other, as just as fair,
And having perhaps the better claim,
Because it was grassy and wanted wear;
Though as for that the passing there
Had worn them really about the same,

And both that morning equally lay
In leaves no step had trodden black.
Oh, I kept the first for another day!
Yet knowing how way leads on to way,
I doubted if I should ever come back.

I shall be telling this with a sigh
Somewhere ages and ages hence:
Two roads diverged in a wood, and I —
I took the one less traveled by,
And that has made all the difference.

By Robert Frost

H.D. and Chase began their senior year in 2008. Chase transferred schools and attended Seymour High School while H.D. remained at Brownstown Central High School. H.D. continued to work on the Plumer farm his senior year but began to pursue other interests besides the rodeo. He joined the football team; therefore, team practice meant less time on the farm for him.

Friday night football was a big deal in the small town of Brownstown. The stands were always packed full. Some spectators would set up campers or trucks with lawn chairs and grills along the road behind the visitor section of the stadium to tailgate and watch the game. Other spectators would bring their lawn chairs or blankets to sit along the left side of the fence while their young children played their own game of football in the grass. Rain or shine, there were always loyal fans of the Braves to watch the game.

H.D. loved those Friday night games. He would play hard and catch the adoring eye of a few young girls. He went out with a couple of them, but the relationships never lasted very long. After the game, there was often a bonfire at his house or a friend's out in the country. Music and laughter would echo out into the dark till the wee hours of the morning. Like many of his senior friends, he began to enjoy the taste of beer when they got together for a party.

After H.D. acquired a driver's license, his dad helped chip in on a good, used truck for him to drive, making it easier for him to get to work and school. He loved his blue Dodge Ram 3500 with a Cummins engine. With his new-found freedom, he spent more time with some of his school buddies after school and on the weekends.

One Saturday morning, H.D. was eager to get up and join his friends to swim on a sandbar along the White River. It was one of the last hot days of the summer and he didn't want to waste it. His dad told him he couldn't leave until his room was clean.

Some of the things growing under his bed would have been considered science experiments. H.D. knew they should be thrown away, but he was in a hurry. So, he quickly made his bed and shoved more items under it to get them out of sight. *Good enough!*

he decided and walked downstairs into the kitchen. "Dad, my room's clean," he announced.

Steve was at the kitchen table eating breakfast and looked up at him. "Oh, it's clean?" he said, raising his eyebrows in disbelief. "Let's go up and look at it!" He stood up and led H.D. back up the stairs into his bedroom. He paused at the doorway for a moment, peering into his son's room. "See, it's clean!" H.D. boasted, pointing at his bed.

"Unh hunh!" Steve replied, nodding his head. Then, he slowly walked over, bent down on one knee, and peeked under the bed. *Oh, Shit!* H.D. realized it was about to hit the fan.

"What the hell is all this doing under here!" Steve shouted as he began yanking everything out from under the bed. There were stinky socks, underwear, and half-eaten food with mold growing on it. He pulled out a baggie with something brown and unrecognizable in it, knowing he'd better not open that! Steve tossed the baggie on top of the pile. H.D. stood as still as a statue, waiting until his dad was done.

Then, Steve stood up and went to examine H.D.'s drawers. He opened every one of them, finding items jammed into the drawers that didn't belong there either and proceeded to toss those out onto the floor, as well. He began yelling, "Attention to detail, H.D.!"

Here we go again! H.D. moaned inside. He had heard those words a million times when he was growing up. "Everything you do, you want to do it better than the man asking you. That's how you get promotions! That's how you make more money!" Steve yelled, looking his son in the eyes. H.D. didn't say a word. "I don't care what you're doing- whether you're serving fucking ice cream or in the military! Always do more than what your boss asks you!"

Steve stepped closer to his son, poked his index finger into his chest, and shouted into his face, "I asked you to clean your room. Your room is a goddamn mess! Clean that shit up! Attention to detail!" He turned around, stormed out of the room, stomped down the stairs, and went back to finish his now cold breakfast.

H.D. groaned as he grabbed his trash can and bent down to pick up the garbage that needed to be thrown away. It looked like a tornado had hit his room. He had to reorganize all of his drawers. An hour later, he walked back downstairs and said, "My room is clean now, Dad. Can I go?"

"Yes, but you'd better be back by eleven o'clock!" his dad warned him.

"I will," he promised. He joined his buddies to swim and drink some beer on the riverbank but was wise enough not to push his limits and returned home on time.

H.D. began seeking scholarships to go to college and applied for several rodeo scholarships. He was hopeful he would get one to help pay for college. During the last week of September, Seymour High School hosted a College and Career Fair for Jackson and Jennings County students. Juniors and seniors had the opportunity to talk to different representatives from various colleges. They could take home pamphlets on each college, pick up applications, and find out about scholarships.

Over fifty colleges from Midwestern Indiana were represented at the fair. Large colleges such as Purdue, Indiana University, Indiana State, and Ball State were there. Smaller colleges such as IUPUI, Butler, Hanover, and technical schools were available. Also, recruiters from the various branches of the military had booths for students to seek information on serving our country.

H.D. drove his truck to the college fair and met a couple of his friends at the entrance. The high school auxiliary gym was crowded with students, parents, teachers, and counselors. After H.D. spoke to his high school counselors and signed in, he walked around to explore the college booths with his friends. Then, he spotted the Marine Corps booth.

He thought about joining the Marines like his dad but had put it in the back of his mind until he saw the two Marines standing behind the table in their uniform. Something about them struck a chord inside him. They had an air of confidence and pride that was clearly visible to anyone who talked to them. He wished he had felt that way about himself.

"I'm going over there to talk to the Marines," H.D. informed his friends. He approached the table and stood back while another student was finishing speaking to the two recruiters. As soon as the boy left, H.D. stepped up toward the Marines. "What's your name?" one of them asked him, who appeared older than the other Marine.

"Hunter Hogan. My friends call me H.D."

"Hello, H.D., I'm Sgt. Jarrett," the sergeant said as he reached out his right hand to shake H.D.'s. "Are you a senior?"

"Yes, I am. I just turned eighteen last week," H.D. said, giving the recruiter a firm handshake. Both recruiters glanced at each other and nodded.

"Are you interested in being a Marine?" Sgt. Jarrett inquired.

"Yes, sir," H.D. replied.

Sgt. Jarrett was impressed with H.D.'s manners. He could see something was different about this young man from many of the other students he talked to. "H.D., I'm Sgt. Delph. What made you interested in the Marines?" the other recruiter asked him.

"My dad was a Marine. He told me a lot about it. I've thought of other military branches, but the Marine Corps is what I'm mostly interested in," H.D. replied earnestly.

"Anything in particular you would want to do?" continued Sgt. Delph.

"I'm interested in infantry. I like shooting guns and hunt often," stated H.D. The recruiter raised his eyebrows in curiosity and asked, "You do? What kind of game do you hunt?"

"I hunt deer, squirrel, and turkey mostly. I shot an eleven-pointer last fall- made my dad mad when I got a bigger deer than he did," H.D. replied, grinning. Both recruiters laughed.

"Well, H.D., let me tell you a little about our program. After thirteen weeks in boot camp, you will be able to choose an area to specialize in. You can get four years of college classes, tuition free," Sgt. Jarrett informed H.D. as he pointed to the inside of a brochure listing the specialty areas.

"Here, take some of these with you," stated Sgt. Delph, handing H.D. a couple of the brochures on the Marine Corps. Then, Sgt. Jarrett handed him a clipboard with an information sheet attached and a pen. "Fill this out and we will contact you later to see if you're still interested in joining the Marines if we don't hear from you first," he said.

"Okay," replied H.D. as he grabbed the clipboard and began filling in his name and contact information. Sgt. Jarrett handed him his business card and suggested, "Call me to set up a meeting to talk to you more about it."

"Yes, sir. I will," promised H.D. as he handed back the clipboard and pen. Both recruiters shook his hand, and he rejoined his friends as they looked at other colleges. He kept the brochures and business card stashed in his room and kept thinking about what the recruiters told him.

Three weeks later, H.D. called the recruiter and set up a meeting to find out more about joining the Marines. They met at the Scottsburg office where Sgt. Jarrett answered all of H.D.'s questions and they completed a quick screening to see if H.D. was Marine material. He had no mental or physical issues preventing him from joining, so another meeting was arranged to do a full assessment.

At school, H.D. began to hang out more with his friend, Kyle Mails, who he met during their junior year. He had a positive influence on Kyle. Kyle moved away from the city and friends who used drugs. Embracing the country ways of H.D, he started wearing Wrangler jeans and cowboy boots. He enjoyed listening to old country music with his new friend.

The two began eating lunch together every day in the school cafeteria. They would spend all their money on chewing tobacco and beer and never had enough money to eat. The cafeteria had crackers, ranch dressing, and jalapenos for free. H.D. would load down his backpack with crackers, and the two would eat them the next period.

They would come into shop class together with cottonmouth

from the crackers, so H.D. would sneak out a can of his Copenhagen snuff from his backpack and give some to Kyle. While they were chewing it, they'd pass an empty pop can back and forth in class and spit the tobacco into it. The teacher would always catch them chewing and tell them to spit their candy out. The boys did what their teacher asked but later would sneak some more chew into their mouth.

One day, Kyle brought in a can of Red Seal powder snuff. It looked like ground cinnamon. Using the tip of a knife blade and his thumb, he dug some out and snorted it. Then, he handed the can to H.D. H.D. dug some out with the knife and snorted it, too. The snuff was awful. It would definitely sober you up from a hangover. Their eyes began watering, and they began sneezing and coughing.

"What are you two doing?" the shop teacher asked them from the other side of the enormous room.

"Nothing," replied H.D., trying to look innocent.

"Well, whatever it is, you need to stop!" he yelled at them. Their classmates burst out laughing, annoying their teacher even more.

"Stop goofing off and get to work!" the teacher instructed the class.

H.D. loved being the class clown. He would put tape in the middle of his safety goggles to make himself look goofy and get the two girls in their shop class to laugh. H.D. and Kyle enjoyed hanging out together and spent time at each other's homes.

One Monday evening in January, Steve was gone on a business trip; so, H.D. invited Kyle to come spend the evening with two of their friends, Tyler and Dalton. They picked up a couple of cases of one of H.D.'s favorite beers, Old Milwaukee's Best. While they were drinking and munching down on potato chips, H.D. noticed it starting to snow outside. As they watched the snow fall, it turned to ice. Ice kept falling until it covered the ground and tree limbs. The pine needles were completely covered in ice and drooped heavily on the tree limbs.

The boys turned on the TV and listened to the weatherman predict more ice and snow for the night and week ahead. School closings began to be displayed on the bottom of the screen. It looked like their school would be closed, so the boys kept drinking. They were listening to their favorite local country station and having a great time until about six o'clock in the morning. They heard the announcer on the radio say Brownstown Central had a two-hour delay.

"Oh, shit!" H.D. yelled at the boys. "We have to go to school! My dad will kill me if I don't show up!" He went to the medicine cabinet to get some Ibuprofen to help him and his friends get over their hangover. Kyle took a couple of them and began throwing up. He busted blood vessels on his face and had red spots all over. H.D. quickly cleaned up the mess from their party, putting the empty beer cans in a trash bag to throw away in a dumpster in town, and they left the house.

They all looked and felt horrible but went to school anyway. H.D. drove his truck along the icy back roads in the country to town. He blared the song "Riders on the Storm" by The Doors. The boys sang at the top of their lungs, pounding on the dashboard the whole way to school listening to classic rock music.

When they arrived at school, the parking lot was still icy. H.D. spun a doughnut with his truck in the middle of the lot. His friends thought that was hilarious. After he parked his truck, the four got out and walked into the school. They made it just on time. Teachers looked at them suspiciously, but none the wiser of their nighttime activities.

As the day went on, the boys struggled to keep awake. In Math class after lunch, H.D. sat at his desk holding his chin up with his hands and elbows. His eyelids kept closing, but he fought to stay awake. He saw Kyle asleep on his desk. Before he could warn his friend, the teacher saw Kyle sleeping, walked up to him, and smacked a yardstick hard on it. *Wham!*

Kyle was startled awake, jumped to his feet, and yelled, "WHAT THE FUCK!" All of his classmates, including H.D., burst out laughing. The teacher was extremely angry at the disruption and had Kyle suspended for three days.

A couple of days later, school was canceled due to the snow. In the afternoon, one of H.D.'s friends called him at home. "Hunter, I'm stuck in the Medora bottoms. Can you come and get me?" asked Clinton. H.D. and Clinton Luttrell knew each other ever since elementary school.

"I'm making snow ice cream with Tyler. I'll be there when we get done," H.D. told him. An hour went by and still no H.D. Clinton and his friend, A.J., were shivering in his truck. They kept running the engine off and on for a little while, but the heater didn't work very well. After another thirty minutes, H.D. finally came. When he got out of the truck, he handed Clinton a bowl of the snow ice cream and said, "Here you go, we saved some for you!"

"Thanks, asshole. It took you long enough. We were freezing!" Clinton complained but took the bowl anyway. Despite feeling like a frozen popsicle, he did like eating the delicious snow ice cream and shared some with A.J. H.D. helped pull Clinton's truck out of the ditch with a chain attached to his truck. "Thanks, Hunter!" Clinton told him when he got his truck back on the road. "Anytime!" replied H.D. as he took off back home.

By late winter, four colleges out West accepted H.D.'s application and offered him full scholarships if he attended their college. While H.D. was excited that he was accepted to not just one college but four, his mind was full of all the events that had happened to him in the past year. His parent's divorce was finalized. That hit him hard. The one thing he did learn was that life was uncertain.

His life was no longer the same as when he was growing up. He was changing and his view on the world was maturing. He wasn't sure what was in store for him but knew he was meant to take a different path than most of his friends. Many of them would stay around Jackson County and get a job in a factory. Some would go to college and have a career in a city. The city life never appealed to him, and he knew he wouldn't be happy stuck inside a factory all day.

Many nights, H.D. lay awake staring at the ceiling and weighing his options: stay with the rodeo in college or join the Marines? H.D. thought about college, but his interest in becoming a Marine had a stronger hold on him with each passing day. After three agonizing months of back and forth, he made up his mind and decided to tell his dad what he wanted to do after he graduated.

One evening in February, after the two were done eating dinner, H.D. stood up from the kitchen table and said, "Dad, I need to talk to you." His dad was putting the dirty dishes into the sink and was about to start the water. "Okay," replied Steve, stopping what he was doing and turning around to look at H.D. He saw the serious expression on his son's face and knew something was up.

H.D. wasn't sure how to tell his dad, so he just simply said the words, "I've decided I'm going to join the Marines." Steve's expression changed immediately. "No, you have a scholarship for rodeo. You need to go to college," he protested, his face turning red.

"I don't want to go to college. I want to be a Marine!" insisted H.D., looking intently at his dad.

"H.D., you are not joining the Marines. You need to go to college!" Steve repeated, raising his voice.

"Why not? Dad, you were a Marine and did your part. You had a scholarship and could've went to college, but you didn't!" H.D. questioned, holding his ground.

"Yes, I did. But, that was me," asserted Steve.

"Well, I want to do my part, too, just like you," H.D. told him, not backing down from his dad. He was prepared for a fight. "I've thought about this a long time, Dad. It's my decision. I've already filled out the paperwork for the recruiter."

Steve's mouth dropped, surprised his son had already taken the next step. He stood a minute in silence and finally gave in. He knew by now that once his son had something in his head, there was no changing it. H.D. was too much like himself. It was like looking in a mirror twenty some years ago. He hated the idea of H.D. putting off college to be a Marine, but he had to respect him at the same time.

"Okay, H.D. It's your future," Steve said and turned away from him to start the water in the sink. He felt a lump well up in his throat and swallowed hard. He knew what the decision meant and the challenges H.D. was about to face. He needed time to absorb the fact that his son was going to be a Marine.

H.D. was relieved he finally had that settled with his dad and went up to his bedroom to finish his homework. The weight of indecision was finally lifted. He knew what he was going to do and didn't have to think about college anymore. By the end of high school, the arrangements were made for H.D. to enlist in the Marines. He was scheduled to report to the Military Entrance Processing Station (MEPS) in Indianapolis, Indiana in October.

H.D. graduated from high school in May. A few weeks later, H.D., Kyle, and two of their buddies, Jeff and Skyler, went to get tattoos. This was going to be H.D.'s second tattoo- he already had a cross on his arm. It was going to be Kyle's first tattoo. H.D. took them in his truck, doing burnouts along Highway 446. They drove north along the scenic, windy road, across the dam of Lake Monroe, and headed toward downtown Bloomington.

When they got to the tattoo shop, Kyle was a little scared. He really didn't like needles. H.D. lightened the mood by daring Jeff to get the word 'bitch' tattooed on the inside of his lower lip. "If you get it, we'll pay for it!" he told Jeff.

"I'll do it. I don't care!" Jeff said, grinning.

H.D. and Skyler put up fifty dollars each for the tattoo. Jeff had it done. The others cringed watching their friend have a needle injected into his lip. H.D. went next and got a tribal tattoo added to the arm with his cross. Then, Kyle got a tribal tattoo, also. After everyone got a new tattoo, they went back to H.D.'s house to celebrate.

Once H.D. told Sgt. Jarrett he was planning on enlisting in the Marines, he began going to physical training at the recruiter's office in Scottsburg every Wednesday during the summer. Usually, they would run a mile and a half, stop at a gravel parking lot and do some butterfly kicks, hello dollies, and other exercises. Then, they would run a half mile back to the office. When they got back, they would hang out and talk for a bit with Sgt. Jarrett.

One Tuesday night, H.D. and his friend, Ronnie, stayed up late drinking. They woke up Wednesday morning hungover and miserable. H.D. called Clinton to come get them and go to PT. Clinton had also planned to join the Marines with H.D. and was taking the PT class with him and Ronnie. Clinton drove to H.D.'s house to get the two.

It was raining that day, so they couldn't do any exercises outside. Sgt. Jarrett told them to meet him at the YMCA in Scottsburg. Ronnie and H.D. were wearing yellow construction hard hats when they walked into the gym, laughing loudly. Sgt. Jarrett was furious when he saw the two. "You guys think it's cute to show up in those hard hats?" he yelled. "What did you two do? Stay up late and get drunk last night?"

H.D. and Ronnie giggled. Clinton just stood quietly. He wasn't about to be a part of the wrath he knew was coming. H.D. saw the other recruits playing basketball on the court and thought, *Sweet! We get to play basketball!* He and Ronnie started to walk out to the others playing ball when Sgt. Jarrett stopped them in their tracks. "Unh unh! You think it's funny to show up drunk!" he yelled. "I guarantee you won't ever show up drunk again. I'll make sure of it! You two are going to run laps around the court the whole time!"

The two boys groaned and began running laps while Clinton joined the others playing basketball. After fifteen minutes, both began throwing up all over the gym floor. Sgt. Jarrett handed them some paper towels to clean it up and made them keep running again. Neither one showed up to PT drunk again.

As time went on in the summer, H.D. was staying up later and later with his friends and sometimes would be too hungover to drive to work. Clinton would come pick him up and take him to the Plumer's farm, so H.D. could feed the animals. When he drove himself, H.D. would often show up late. Each day he arrived later and later.

One day, H.D. arrived at the farm extremely late. As soon as he parked his truck and got out, Chase walked up to him and yelled, "H.D. you're two hours late!" H.D. shrugged his shoulders like it was no big deal.

"You can't keep doing that. We have work that needs to be done. If you're not going to be here on time, there's no reason to come at all!" Chase declared, disappointed with H.D.

"Then I won't come at all!" H.D. yelled back at him, turning around heading for his truck. "I'm going to be leaving for the Marines soon anyway!" he added as he stepped into his truck, slammed the door shut, and drove away leaving a cloud of dust in his wake. Chase stood and watched him leave, shaking his head in disbelief. That was the last time H.D. was at the Plumer's farm. He didn't know why he acted so badly toward Chase and later wished he could have said a proper goodbye before he left to the Marine Corps. *Two roads diverged in a yellow wood....*

11 FOLLOWING IN HIS DAD'S FOOTSTEPS

On October 26, 2009, Steve drove H.D. to the Military Entrance Processing Station (MEPS) in Indianapolis, Indiana early in the morning. When they arrived, a Marine recruiter greeted and escorted them to a small room where H.D. completed one more physical exam to clear him for duty. Next, the recruiter took him to an office to finish the paperwork needed to officially join the Marines, which included signing a four-year contract. After that, H.D. and nine other recruits were gathered together in a spacious room where they were sworn into the Marine Corps.

The men lined up with their hands at their sides as the recruiter stood before them at a podium with the American flag and various military flags displayed on staffs behind him. He asked the men, "Does everyone understand their contract?"

"Yes, sir!" the recruits replied in unison.

He read off rules and regulations for the military, making sure the recruits knew the consequences of AWOL (leaving the military base without orders or permission to leave). Then, he asked, "Are you here of your own free will?"

"Yes, sir!" the recruits responded.

"Are there any questions?"

"No, sir!"

The recruiter instructed the young men to raise their right hand and repeat the allegiance after him. H.D. raised his right hand in the air and recited these words after the recruiter: "I, (H.D. Hogan), do solemnly swear I will support and defend the constitution of the United States against all enemies, foreign and domestic. I will bear true faith and allegiance to the same. I will obey the orders of the president of the United States and the orders of the officers appointed over me according to regulation and the Uniform Code of Military Justice, so help me God!"

Pride swept over Steve as he watched his son take the same oath he had taken twenty-eight years ago. After H.D. was sworn in, he went to say goodbye to his dad. Steve gave him a big bear hug and said, "I'm proud of you, Son. Stay strong!"

"I love you, Dad!" whispered H.D., giving his dad an extra tight squeeze back.

"Love you, too!"

The recruiter came over and told H.D. it was time to go. "Goodbye, Pap," he said with a smile on his face. "Goodbye, Son. Call me when you can," replied Steve, blinking back a tear forming in the corner of his right eye. H.D. and the other nine recruits followed the recruiter and boarded a shuttle bus for the airport.

On the airplane, H.D. introduced himself to the recruit sitting beside him. "Hello, I'm Hunter Hogan. I go by H.D.," he stated holding out his hand.

"I'm James Barnes, H.D., nice to meet you. You can call me Jim," replied Barnes with a huge smile. He grabbed H.D.'s hand and shook it vigorously. *Damn, what a grip!* thought H.D. Barnes was a tall, stocky young man the color of molasses with a voice as thick and rich that resonated whenever he spoke. He was definitely someone you wanted on your side and not your enemy. The two hit it off from the beginning and became friends throughout boot camp.

H.D. also met another recruit by the name of Mark Reynolds. Reynolds was a tall, tan, lean young man with thick, curly, sandy-brown hair and blue eyes. He was much quieter than H.D., but had a quick wit and keen sense of sarcasm that matched H.D.'s. The three recruits spent the next four hours joking and telling stories about themselves, helping make the flight go quicker. They had a one-hour layover in Phoenix, Arizona and flew for another hour and a half to their final destination: San Diego, California.

When they landed, they boarded a bus that took the ten recruits from Indiana as well as forty more recruits from other states to the Marine Corps Recruiting Depot (MCRD) in San Diego. The Marine on the bus escorting them was friendly and welcomed them to the Marines. The men laughed and told jokes on their bus ride, excited to start their training in the 1st Recruit Training Battalion.

As soon as the bus stopped at MCRD and the deafening hiss of the air brakes quieted, a sergeant entered the bus and looked intently at them. He was six-foot, three inches tall with jet black hair cut in the traditional military flat-top and wore a campaign cover. He had gray eyes and was very distinguished looking, commanding the presence of every room he entered.

It was as if the needle on a record player was suddenly jerked to a stop. The recruits immediately sat straight up, stopped talking, and stared at the sergeant. There would be no more music or laughter for a long time. The drill instructor began yelling, "Recruits, my name is Sgt. Shepard. Today, you have taken the first step to be a Marine. From now on, you will eat and sleep as a team. The words *I* or *my* will no longer be a part of your vocabulary. I will tell you when to eat, sleep, talk, and take a piss. You will follow every command and answer Yes, sir! or Aye, aye, sir! Do you understand?"

The recruits replied, "Yes, sir!" That wasn't good enough for the sergeant. "I'm sorry, ladies, I didn't hear you! Try that again!" he screamed.

"YES, SIR!" yelled the recruits at the top of their lungs.

At that moment, reality sank in for all of them. *What the hell did I do?* wondered H.D. as well as many others. The sergeant continued with his rant, "Today, you are no longer a weak and pathetic kid; you are a Marine. I expect you to act like one. Now get the fuck off my bus and line up on the sidewalk!" The recruits jumped up and departed the bus as fast as they could. "Go! Go! Go!" shouted Sgt.

Shepard outside the door of the bus.

The recruits gathered on the sidewalk unsure of what they were supposed to do next. Their eyes were as large as a deer in headlights. Sgt. Shepard stood in front of them and gave his next order, "You see those yellow footprints on the sidewalk? From the count of three, you will stand on those footprints and wait for my next command...3, 2, 1, Go! Go! Go!"

"AYE, AYE, SIR!" the recruits shouted and ran to get on one of the pairs of yellow footprints. H.D. hustled to get himself in place, trying not to be last. As he stood there, an image of his dad as a young recruit flashed in front of him. His dad turned around and winked at him. From that moment, H.D. told himself, *If Dad could do this, I can do this!* His dad's departing words, "Stay strong!" echoed in his mind. When the sergeant began yelling commands, his dad's apparition disappeared and H.D. was staring at the back of the head of another recruit.

The next moments were a series of orders issued by Sgt. Shepard. If a recruit wasn't quick enough, he would stand in their face or by their ear screaming at them. "Sir, yes, sir!" the unfortunate recruit would yell back trying to be quicker the next time. H.D. just stood still, staring straight ahead avoiding eye contact with the sergeant.

The footprints taught the young recruits how to stand in formation: how close you are supposed to be to the guy next to you and where you are going to line up for the guy in front of you and behind you. In the beginning, the recruits lined up with their elbow out like a chicken wing. When the guy next to you bumps into your elbow, then you are ready to put your arms down. They practiced this over and over until it wasn't necessary to have their arms out to get into position.

After the sergeant decided he had enough of the drills on the yellow footsteps, he ordered the recruits to go inside the building into a room with tables and bins to place their belongings in. They were told to drop everything in their hands into the bins as well as empty out their pockets. Everything they had on them went into the bin. H.D. followed his dad's advice and didn't have anything on him except his orders, a wallet with his ID, and twenty dollars in cash. Other recruits had pictures, jewelry, wadded up papers, condoms, gum, plastic water bottles, and whatnot. Another drill instructor joined Sgt. Shepard as he barked out orders for recruits to put approved items in a small green bag.

H.D. watched as other recruits became flustered and made unapproved movements. The two drill instructors would swarm upon the unsuspecting recruit and scream at him until he did exactly as he was told. H.D. was thankful it wasn't him.

After their approved possessions were placed in the small green bag, they were told to pick up their camouflage duffle bag with military issued items. As they were standing there, Sgt. Shepard read off part of the Uniform Code of Military Justice, which was projected on an electronic display on the wall.

"According to the Uniform Code of Military Justice, Congress shall have the power to make rules for the government and regulations of the land and naval forces. United States Constitution Article 1, Section 8. Article 15 states commanding officers can enforce non-judicial punishment. Article 86 states you are not allowed absence without leave. If you leave the premises of the base, you will be hunted down and punished. Do you understand?"

"SIR, YES, SIR!" the recruits yelled back.

The sergeant continued, "Article 92: Failure to obey orders or regulations. If you do not obey officer commands, you will be punished. Do you understand?"

"SIR, YES, SIR!" recruits shouted again.

"Marine Corps policy on drugs: Drugs will not be tolerated! Is that clear?"

"AYE, AYE, SIR!"

After Sgt. Shepard was finished reciting the rules, the recruits were divided into groups to complete other tasks. H.D. was placed into the group to make a phone call home. The recruits were instructed to dial 9 plus 1 and the rest of the phone number they were calling. If they could not reach the person they called, they were instructed to call another family member. A piece of paper was attached on the partition of each cubicle for the recruit to read a specified script.

H.D. dialed his dad's cell phone number. Before his dad could finish saying hello, he shouted into the phone over the noise around him, "Hello, this is recruit Hogan! I have arrived safely at MCRD San Diego! The next time I contact you will be by postal mail, so expect a letter in two to three weeks!" *Click!* H.D. hung up the phone before his dad could utter a word. Steve grinned knowing all too well what his son was doing next. At least he knew he arrived there safely.

H.D. was hurried to join the line following other recruits down the hallway to another room where barbers were shaving heads. As one recruit got up, another sat in the barber chair. It wasn't long before it was H.D.'s turn. He sat down and the barber asked, "Do you have any cuts or moles on your head?"

"No, sir!" reported H.D.

The barber promptly took the electric razor and began shaving off H.D.'s hair starting at the forehead, going back, then up the sides from behind the ears. He sat there with a blank stare, the same look the others had on their face, as his head was shaved. In a matter of seconds, all of his hair was scattered on the floor along with the recruits before him. He was officially a jarhead. The clean shaved head made him feel different. He somehow lost a part of his identity but began to embrace a new identity along with his fellow Marines.

When he got up from the barber chair, he followed other recruits in line to the squad bay. They entered through double doors into a large room about the size of a school cafeteria where there were rows of bunk beds on each side and two footlockers stationed side by side in front of each bunk.

H.D. followed the line and came to his spot. He ended up sharing a bunk with Private Reynolds. After putting his duffle bag down, he stood facing forward waiting for the next order. Pvt. Reynolds did the same.

After all the recruits joined them in the squad bay, Sgt. Shepard reintroduced himself and so did the other drill instructor, Sgt. Wyler. Wyler was six-foot-tall with cinnamon brown skin, brown hair, and amber eyes. He was less noticeable than Shepard, except when he yelled. His campaign cover kept him from blending in with the other recruits. A moment later, the double doors burst open and slammed loudly against the wall. In came the master sergeant.

The moment H.D. laid eyes on him, he knew it wasn't going to be good. The man was not very tall: probably only standing at 5'7" and weighing 140 pounds. He had blonde crew cut hair under his campaign cover and dark blue eyes that were cold as ice. He was a force to be reckoned with. There was no doubt that no matter how much bigger any of them were, he could take them down in a heartbeat. He had a scowl on his face with a look that said, "I'd rather be anywhere else than dealing with your dumbasses!"

"Hello, recruits, my name is Master Sergeant Neville. This is *my* platoon. You are under *my* command. Do you understand?"

"SIR, YES, SIR!" yelled all recruits.

"You are now in the Marines and will use Marine Corps terms: the door is called the hatch, the window is called the portal, and the floor is referred to as the deck. When I tell you to get on deck, you will stand at attention in front of your footlocker. Do you understand?"

"AYE, AYE, SIR!"

"When I give an order, you will do exactly as I say when I say to. You will also follow my two drill instructor's commands without question. Clear?"

"SIR, YES, SIR!"

"We will be with you at all times. If you need something, you will say, "Sir, Private Sorry Ass requests permission to whatever the hell you think you need. I will either grant or decline your request. Do you understand?"

"SIR, YES, SIR!"

"Since this is my barrack, I expect you to keep it neat and

orderly. You will keep your items in your footlocker and clean up after yourselves. I will not tolerate uncleanliness. Do you understand!"

"AYE, AYE, SIR!"

"Because you maggots are ignorant and need to learn how Marines perform certain tasks, I will teach you everything you need to know and you *will* do what I say!" MSgt. Neville yelled as he began pacing around the room examining each and every jarhead.

"First of all, when I give the command EYEBALLS, you don't move your head, just your eyes and will yell CLICK! When I shout EARS, you will yell OPEN! to let me know you are listening. Do you understand?"

"SIR, YES, SIR!" echoed the room.

"Recruits, the water fountain is called the scuttlebutt and the restroom or toilet is the head. Is that clear?"

"AYE, AYE, SIR!"

"Head calls! Head calls! Head calls on three! When you enter, you will do exactly as I say!" he commanded. "3, 2, 1! Go! Go! Go!"

H.D. hastened with the other recruits into a rectangular restroom with a water fountain, four urinals attached to the wall, and six toilets along one side. There were five open showers behind a four-foot tall cement block wall and six sinks along the other side. Neville stepped into the restroom behind the recruits and shouted, "EARS!"

"OPEN!" they all yelled out, standing still. He began walking along the line heading toward the front, staring at the faces of each recruit.

"Recruits, go to the head right now and begin urinating when I start counting down from ten. When I reach zero, you will be done, zip up, leave the head, and go back to your position in front of your rack (bunk bed).

The recruits looked at each other. *Is he serious? I have to share a urinal with other people?* H.D. felt very awkward but did what he was told. He stood at a urinal with five other recruits. When MSgt. Neville began counting down, he unzipped, pulled out his penis, and began peeing. He tried not to look at the other recruits as they were going, but it was hard not to and keep his stream of urine flowing into the hole.

Some of the recruits had a difficult time going on command and shutting off when Neville got to zero. One unlucky recruit kept peeing when Neville yelled, "ZERO!" *Big mistake!* Neville ran up to the recruit and began yelling in his ear, "What the fuck are you doing? I said zero. FREEZE, RECRUIT FREEZE! You need to shut that motherfucker off!"

The poor lad regretted his decision to drink a bottle of water on the bus, grabbed his penis as it was still dripping, and shoved it back into his pants leaving a small wet spot. "SIR, YES, SIR!" he shouted back at the sergeant. The sergeant grabbed the recruit's arm and shoved him out of the head as he continued the countdown with the remaining recruits waiting to go.

After all fifty recruits were lined back up again in front of their rack, MSgt. Neville continued with the next series of commands. "Now that you have relieved yourself, it's time you learn how to dress like a Marine. Take off your civilian shirt and pants. 3, 2, 1, Go!"

"AYE, AYE, SIR!" the recruits yelled, stripped off their clothes, then stood back up waiting in their underwear.

"Take out the trousers from your duffle bag and put them on by the count of ten: 10, 9, 8...!" The recruits scrambled to open their duffle bag, pull out their desert MARPAT pants, pull them on, and zip them up before the sergeant got to zero. They were relieved when everyone made it. "Now, pull out your t-shirt, put it on by the count of ten: 10, 9, 8, 7...!"

"SIR, YES, SIR!" Every recruit found their olive-green undershirt and put it on in time.

"Get out your blouse, put it on, and button it up from the count of twenty: 20, 19, 18...!" yelled Neville, pacing the room with the other two drill sergeants.

The recruits did what they were told, pulled out their desert MARPAT shirt from the duffle bag and put it on. This time, one nervous recruit missed a button hole and had to redo his shirt. Neville was on him like a bee on a honeycomb. "What's the matter, didn't your momma teach you how to button a blouse? Do it NOW!" he screamed in the recruit's face with a Georgia drawl. The recruit's hands were shaking as he tried to button his shirt, and he squawked, "Aye, aye, sir!"

The sergeant turned and told the recruits to tuck their blouse into their trousers. Then, they were told to get their belt out of their duffle bag and put it on. The recruits found their belt, wove it into their belt loops, and tightened it in the front. Next, they were told to get out their combat boots and shoelaces.

As MSgt. Neville was giving the step-by-step instructions on how to lace a boot, H.D. imagined him as Barney the Purple Dinosaur dressed as the sergeant and singing, "You love me. I love you. This is how we tie a boot!" He couldn't help but let out a little snort. *Crap!* Neville was in his face in an instant yelling, "You think this is funny, private?"

"SIR, NO, SIR!" yelled H.D., removing all expression from his face.

"Get down and give me fifty push-ups!" commanded Neville.

H.D. got down on his hands and toes and was able to complete the push-ups, thankful he was in good enough shape to finish them just as Neville counted down to zero. *Shit, now I'm on his radar!* worried H.D. He stood back up with his t-shirt and blouse soaked in sweat. Neville let him be and went back to his shoelace and boot tying instructions.

H.D. was careful not to make another slip that night. His dad made sure he knew how to lace and tie a boot, but some of the guys from the inner city or poor rural areas had no clue. He felt sorry for the ones who just didn't seem to catch on right away. Neville was like a dog with a bone: he wouldn't give them any slack, so the yelling and cursing continued over and over and over.

"Attention to detail, you idiot!" MSgt. Neville shouted many times. The words were like fingernails on a chalkboard every time he heard them. He hated it when his dad yelled those exact words at him whenever he screwed up.

Just when everyone was completely dressed and feeling pretty proud of themselves, Neville yelled out, "Now, let's try that again! Take off your boots and uniform. You have twenty seconds. 20, 19, 18…!"

Holy shit! H.D. and the recruits scrambled to disrobe, some of them falling on the floor trying to get everything off before Neville finished his count. They were a pretty pathetic sight. And so, the night went on.

Sgt. Wyler left the room and Sgt. Shepard assisted MSgt. Neville with the rest of the night's tasks. They were instructed how to mark all of their clothes, including underwear using their personal stamp supplied for them with their last name and first initial printed on it.

They were given step-by-step instructions on how to make their rack, making sure corners were tucked and blankets folded back correctly. Every rack had to look exactly the same. Every item had a place. If you left something out of place, there was hell to pay.

For thirty-six hours H.D. was awake, most of that time he was standing. He wasn't even sure what time or day it was. No one was allowed to wear a watch except the sergeants. Not until you stepped outside or were eating a meal would you know if it was night or day.

By the end of the barrage of orders, recruits were running on empty. When they were standing dressed for the final time, H.D.'s eyelids became very heavy, but he didn't dare fall asleep. Some of them would nod off, catch themselves, and stand up straight again. One recruit fell asleep while standing, fell over, and hit the ground with a *thud!* He woke up with a startled look and quickly stood back up, but it was too late. Neville was instantly on him, screaming at him. He decided they all needed to do 100 jumping jacks because "Private Sleepy" decided to take an extra nap. The recruits all glared at "Private Sleepy" as they performed their jumping jacks.

Neville was satisfied when everyone completed their exercise and barked out the next command, "I can smell some of you maggots from here. You need a shower. Every night you will take a shower and clean every hair and hole on your body. You will also clean underneath your fingernails. You will be thoroughly inspected daily. Once again, uncleanliness will not be tolerated! Do you understand?"

"SIR, YES, SIR!"

"Take off all your clothes, take out the soap, washcloth, and towel from your bag from the count of twenty: 20, 19, 18, 17, 16....!" The recruits rushed to get their clothes off and get the shower items. By this time, the men were so ready for a nice shower, they didn't care everyone was naked!

"Line up and you will enter the shower when I tell you to, clean yourself, and stop when I tell you to. Is that clear?"

"SIR, YES, SIR!"

"Now Go! Go! Go!" he screamed.

"AYE, AYE, SIR!" they screamed back and shuffled into the restroom.

The sergeants turned on all five showers. The first five recruits were ordered to enter the showers, wash, scrub their hands and fingernails at the sink, and use the urinal or toilet in a wagon wheel rotation. H.D. entered the shower when it was his turn. The water was freezing cold. MSgt. Neville shouted, "Soap on your body right now!"

"SIR, YES, SIR!" H.D. shouted and began washing with the soap. He was only about halfway done, when Neville commanded, "Rinse it off, NOW!"

What? I'm not done! He couldn't believe how short the shower was, even though he was freezing. The showers at boot camp were always either frickin' cold or scalding hot. It was pure torture!

When they left the restroom, they were allowed to dry off and put on their newly stamped skivvies and shower shoes. They stood in their underwear with their name stamped right across their dick. Neville ordered them to stick out their hands for them to inspect.

"When I ask you if you have any injuries to report, you will respond: Sir, Private Maggot has no medical issues and all valuables are secured, sir *or* you will report if there is an issue. Is that clear?"

"SIR, YES, SIR!" H.D. yelled out with the others.

The two sergeants went through the line, inspected each recruit from head to toe, and asked them the same question. MSgt. Neville came up to H.D., glanced at his underwear and asked, "Private Hogan, do you have any injuries to report?"

"Sir, Private Hogan has no medical issues and all valuables are secure, sir!"

"Hands out, Private Hogan!" H.D. held out his hands as the sergeant inspected them.

"Palms up, private!"

" AYE, AYE, SIR!" H.D. yelled as he flipped his hands over to have them inspected.

"Arms up and turn around, private!" ordered Neville.

"SIR, YES, SIR!" H.D. shouted as he raised his arms and turned around for the sergeant to inspect his arms and body.

"Arms back down, bend over forward!"

"AYE, AYE, SIR!" H.D. yelled as he bent forward for the sergeant to inspect his head. Neville looked at his scalp and ears carefully and said, "You are cleared, Private Hogan."

"AYE, AYE, SIR!" H.D. shouted and stood back up. Neville stared at him for a second, inches from his face. H.D. didn't dare look directly into his eyes. They were like tiny portals to the depths of hell. Neville turned and continued down the line. This inspection occurred every night for three months for every recruit.

Finally, the end of the night of day two came and the recruits were allowed to rest. Neville ordered them to get into their rack. They removed their shower shoes, put them in their footlocker and crawled into bed. Sgt. Wyler came back in to relieve MSgt. Neville and Sgt. Shepard to take over fire watch that first night. Neville flicked off the lights and said, "Sweet dreams, ladies. Don't let the bedbugs bite!"

H.D. was completely exhausted. *Thank God that's over. Surely, tomorrow will be better. It can't be this bad the whole time!* Little did he know Neville was just getting started.

12 THE DEVIL CAME UP FROM GEORGIA

It seemed that no sooner than he had closed his eyes to sleep, H.D. heard the sound of "Reveille" being played on a bugle on base. *Shit! It's six already!* He began rubbing his eyes when the doors burst open and in stormed MSgt. Neville. "The sky is blue, the grass is green, get off your ass and be a Marine!" he yelled. As if his voice wasn't loud enough to wake everyone up, he flipped on the lights, grabbed a trash can, and began banging on it. "On your feet and make your rack, recruits!" he ordered.

"AYE, AYE, SIR!" the recruits yelled out as they rolled out of their racks and began tucking in their sheets. H.D. hopped down from the top and was proceeding to make his rack when Private Reynolds stood up beside him and whispered, "Looks like Neville the Devil is in good form."

"You'd better be quiet. If he hears you, he'll burn your ass!" whispered H.D. back.

"So, you don't think I should ask for a drink of water?" Pvt. Reynolds said with a sly grin on his face.

"Not a chance in hell he'll let you get a drink of water," quipped H.D. with a crooked smile.

Pvt. Reynolds nodded his head and grinned back at H.D. As he was peeking over H.D.'s shoulder, he whispered, "Watch out! Here comes the devil now!"

MSgt. Neville strolled down the row of bunks inspecting each and every one of them. He looked at Pvt. Hogan and Pvt. Reynolds' racks as they stood at attention by their footlockers waiting for a response. He glanced at the two of them and moved on to the next rack. *Whew!* thought H.D., relieved that Neville didn't hear them and they passed the inspection. However, not everyone did. Neville would pull everything off the rack if it wasn't correct and yell, "Attention to detail, recruit! Make the fucking rack like you were told!"

After Neville was done screaming at the recruits who didn't make their rack properly and watching them redo it, he ordered the platoon to grab their shaving bag, line up, and proceed to the head. He stood in front of them in the hall. "Recruits, this is the drill instructor hut," he said, pointing to the office where Sgt. Shepard and Sgt. Wyler were sitting and chatting. "When you pass it, you will turn your head and shout *snap!* We don't want to see your fuckin' ugly faces when we are in there. Is that clear?"

"SIR, YES, SIR!"

"Now get the fuck into the head!"

The whole platoon passed by the drill instructor hut and each recruit yelled, "SNAP!" as he went by, being sure not to look in. "SNAP! SNAP! SNAP! SNAP...!" went the fifty recruits as they marched by into the head. After they were allowed to share a urinal to pee, the recruits were told to gather around a sink. "Shaving cream! Left hand! Right now!" ordered MSgt. Neville.

"AYE, AYE, SIR!" yelled H.D. and the other recruits as they squirted shaving cream into their left hand and waited. "Razors! Right hand! Right now!" shouted Neville.

"AYE, AYE, SIR!" replied the recruits as they grabbed their razors in their right hand.

"Put that shaving cream on the left side of your face! Right now!"

"SIR, YES, SIR!" The recruits followed the command and rubbed the shaving cream onto the left side of their face- only the left as they were told.

"Shave the right side of your face, right now!" screamed Neville. *What? There is no way this dude is expecting me to shave the right side of my face without shaving cream!* The recruits were stunned. H.D. began slowly shaving the right side of his face, glancing at the others to see if he heard correctly. Some of the recruits froze and didn't do anything at all; others began putting the shaving cream on the right side of their face. "I fuckin' said shave the right side of your face, you idiots." screamed MSgt. Neville right into the ear of a recruit who was just standing there.

"SIR, YES, SIR!" the recruits yelled, still in a state of confusion and not following the command quick enough to suit Neville.

"EVERYBODY CLEAN YOUR FACE AND GET THE FUCK OUT!" screamed Neville at the top of his lungs, disgusted at the recruits. They glanced at each other, quickly washed off the shaving cream, and hurried out the door back into the squad bay.

"SNAP! SNAP! SNAP! SNAP!" they went down the hall as they passed back by the drill instructor hut. Sgt. Wyler and Sgt. Shepard grinned as they watched the recruits sprint by. "Sounds like we had another epic fail at shaving," chuckled Sgt. Wyler.

"Boy is Neville mad! Let's go see what he makes the recruits do," suggested Sgt. Shepard. The two drill instructors got up and joined MSgt. Neville in the squad bay. Neville was on fire! His face and neck turned red and he began screaming out commands, "Get the fuck dressed. Put your trousers on, right now!"

"SIR, YES, SIR!" The recruits yelled, opened their footlockers, grabbed their camo pants, and pulled them on.

"Take off your trousers, right now!" he screamed.

Shit! This is going to be hell! "SIR, YES, SIR!" H.D. yelled as he took off his pants.

The next hour was a series of putting on this or putting on that. Then, they were taking things off. At one point, they were in their skivvies and told to put their boots on. The recruits put on their boots, laced them up, and tied them. Next, they were told to put their trousers on. *How the hell am I going to get my pants on over my boots?* questioned H.D. but attempted to do what he was told.

Finally, Neville had enough of the punishment and ordered the recruits to line up to go to the chow hall for breakfast. *Finally, food!* H.D.'s belly began to rumble at the idea. He wasn't sure of the last time he ate.

At the chow hall, the recruits were given a tray with biscuits and gravy, scrambled eggs, and sausage. Everyone got the same amount unless you were deemed a "fat body." Then, you were placed at the end of the line and half-rationed. Private Barnes was not very happy when he was placed on half rations, but there was nothing he could do about it.

After breakfast, the recruits lined up and went outside to practice line formations again and physical training exercises. When they finished the exercises, the recruits were instructed to rest a minute. MSgt. Neville informed the platoon they would be completing their Initial Strength Test today. Recruits must pass the minimum requirements to continue in training.

First, the recruits were required to complete a minimum of two pull-ups on a bar. H.D. had no problem completing twenty pull-ups. Then, he had to execute a flexed-arm hang on the bar for twelve seconds which he was able to pass easily. After that, he was required to perform forty-four crunches in two minutes. H.D. had prepared himself for this by practicing for two months before he entered the Marines, so he was able to knock off the crunches well under time.

Lastly, the recruits had to finish a mile and half run in under thirteen minutes and thirty seconds. Even though H.D. was tired from the previous exercises of the day, he was able to complete the run with a couple of minutes to spare. All fifty recruits made it, though some were vomiting by the end of the run and falling down exhausted. Everyone was completely drenched in sweat!

The day ended with a quick dinner, more PT, showers, and inspections. The recruits were beginning to get adjusted to those tasks; they just wished the showers weren't so terrible. You never knew if you were going to freeze or be scalded when you stepped in, but you always knew it was going to be one or the other.

The next morning, the first sound H.D. heard was MSgt. Neville slamming open the squad bay hatch and yelling, "It's time to get up! Get out of the racks! Drop your cocks and grab your socks! It's a beautiful Marine Corps day!"

What? It's not six o'clock. I didn't hear "Reveille", questioned H.D. As the lights came on, he got up as did the rest of the platoon. They didn't hear "Reveille" played for another hour and a half. The recruits quickly learned that they will be woken up at any time during the night or morning to do any number of tasks the sergeant so desires.

Every step was strictly controlled and monitored. They told the recruits when and how to do every little thing. Once you think you've figured something out, they would change it and find every little way to stress you out. Each day was another day of hell. The men were becoming more and more stressed and it showed on their faces.

MCRD is located right by the airport. You are constantly seeing or hearing planes taking off or landing. When you see one, you are thinking, *Shit! I wish I could be on one and leave this hellhole!*

Every day for the first three weeks, the recruits attended class and received instruction on the history of Marines, first-aid, uniforms, customs, leadership, and core values. Today was a repeat of the day before: more incessant commands, lessons, and exercises. More games where the rules were vague and there were no winners. Games to play with your mind and see if you will follow any order no matter how ridiculous it seems. You'd be in the middle of performing a task and the drill instructor will yell, "FREEZE!" You could be halfway performing heart surgery on another recruit, but you DO NOT MOVE!

This morning, they were in the head shaving as instructed. The recruits actually made it through a complete shave and felt pretty good about it. MSgt. Neville and Sgt. Wyler came through the line with a bottle of Mennen Skin Bracer aftershave and a bottle of Listerine. "Open your mouths!" yelled Sgt. Wyler. The recruits all opened their mouths. The two came down the line and sprayed the men. H.D. felt the sting of the Listerine on his face and tasted the aftershave in his mouth. They all began gagging and spitting it out in the sink, trash can, or floor- whatever was closest. That set off another series of punishment for over an hour.

After getting dressed, they were taken to the chow hall to get breakfast, but only given a few minutes to eat. They were ordered to get out and return to the squad bay. Another day of exercises, lessons, and a three-mile jog. At the end of the day came the inspections.

MSgt. Neville went down the line asking the recruits the same question: "Private, do you have any injuries to report?" This time, when he came to Private Barnes, who was standing directly across from H.D., Barnes replied in his deep voice, "Sir, Private Barnes has one medical issue and all valuables are secured, sir!"

Neville stopped dead in his tracks, put his face within an inch of Barnes' face, and yelled, "What's your fucking medical issue Barnes!"

"Sir, Private Barnes has hemorrhoids, sir!" yelled Barnes with a straight face. The whole platoon burst out laughing. Neville spun around facing the recruits. H.D. could see the blood creeping up from the sergeant's neck, past his cheeks, and popping the veins out on his forehead. He knew there was hell to pay for laughing.

"Ahhh, you ladies think it's funny that our Private Barnes has hemorrhoids?" Neville asked and quickly turned back to Barnes, "You got shit hanging out of your ass, boy?"

"SIR, YES, SIR!" yelled Barnes, feeling the blood drain from his face.

"You will report to the medic office in the morning to get you some medicine, Private Barnes," Neville replied. He turned back to the platoon and the torture began: jumping jacks, push-ups, burpees, squats, whatever type of exercise MSgt. Neville could think of they were doing. If they didn't do it fast enough to suit him, they did it again. Just when they thought it was about to end, Neville went up to each footlocker and dumped it out.

"You have thirty seconds to pick your shit up!" he screamed at them. H.D. and Private Reynolds scrambled to sort their items and place them back into their footlocker in thirty seconds, which of course was an impossible task. No recruit finished in thirty seconds.

Then, they were ordered to remove their linens from their rack, but "DO NOT let it touch the floor!" The recruits grabbed their sheets and blanket, held it in their arms, and waited for the next command. Neville gave them sixty seconds to fix their rack. Most of them made it, but a few didn't. So, the punishment continued.

H.D. was never so glad to finally hear Neville tell them to get into their rack. They all crawled into their sheets completely exhausted. MSgt. Neville ordered Pvt. Barnes to take fire watch that night. He was to report if anyone entered or left the room to Neville in the morning.

From then on, the recruits were taking turns with fire watch and cleaning out the head and squad bay. Neville flipped off the lights and slammed the hatch closed without saying another word. Not a peep was made that night as the recruits closed their eyes and fell asleep in a matter of seconds.

Every day for the next week, the recruits were running sprints and completing obstacle courses. Each man in the platoon was issued his M16A4. H.D. finally began to feel like a Marine when he held the rifle in his hands. They were instructed how to hold the weapon. Drills were performed holding the M16A4 vertically out in front of them with both hands and horizontally.

They were issued a mouth guard and had to complete the Bayonet Assault Course. Recruits would run the obstacle course, jab their rifle into tires hanging on posts, jump into ditches, run over piles of rocks, crawl through tunnels, walk over a swinging rope bridge, and crawl under barbed wire on their back holding their rifle with both hands the entire time.

Week three began more grueling physical challenges for the recruits. They were introduced to the Confidence Course: an elaborate obstacle course full of wooden platforms and walls, rope obstacles, monkey bars, and three high obstacle courses they would tackle later in training after successfully completing the low obstacles.

On the thirteenth day of boot camp, the recruits were given a few extra minutes to eat breakfast, completed their PT exercises, had lessons on military ethic, went on a quarter mile run, and taken to a large open field where they were introduced to the Log Drill. MSgt. Neville placed the recruits into groups of eight according to height. He had one group give a demonstration to the rest on how to perform various exercises with the log.

"Recruits, this is a team task. You are expected to give one hundred percent. Should any of you let go of the log, you will perform the exercise again. If you drop the log, you will be punished. Is that clear!" shouted Neville.

"SIR, YES, SIR!" the recruits responded.

MSgt. Neville, Sgt. Shepard, and Sgt. Wyler divided themselves amongst the teams. Sgt. Wyler was in charge of H.D.'s team. The eight recruits stood beside a twelve-foot-long and twelve-inch-diameter wooden log.

"Pick up the log and rest it on your right shoulder!" yelled Sgt. Wyler.

"SIR, YES, SIR!" H.D. yelled, reached down with both hands, and raised the log with his teammates to his right shoulder.

"Raise the log up and move it to your left shoulder and back on my counts as you march!" Wyler yelled out as he began pacing between the two teams he was in charge of.

"AYE, AYE, SIR!" the recruits yelled back, grunting as they raised the 200-pound log over their heads and began marching together as a unit.

"Up 1! Up 2! Up 3! Up 4!" Wyler counted until he got to twenty and yelled, "STOP!" The recruits halted where they were and stood with the log rested on their left shoulder. The sound of sighs and panting could be heard from all of the teams.

"Recruits begin bicep curls, counting to twenty-five!" commanded Sgt. Wyler.

"SIR, YES, SIR!" H.D. yelled out as he turned to his right and lowered the log from his left shoulder to rest it in his arms- as did the rest of his team. They began curling the log up and down, raising their biceps, and counting together, "Up 1! Up 2! Up 3! Up 4! …." By the time they reached twenty-five, the men began to feel the strain of holding the heavy log.

"Log up, overhead, and march, recruits!" screamed Sgt. Wyler.

"AYE, AYE, SIR!" H.D. and his team yelled out, raised the log over their heads, and began marching again. The recruit in front of H.D., Private Williams, began to weaken and was about to let go. "I can't hold onto this anymore," he said softly.

"Yes, you can! You've got to keep going or we'll have to do this again. You've got this!" encouraged H.D. from behind him. Sgt. Wyler heard what Pvt. Williams said, came up beside him keeping in step as they marched, and yelled, "Marines do *not* let themselves be defeated. They do *not* give up so easily. The word can't is not in our vocabulary! You hold that motherfucker up and will NOT let go. Is that clear, Private Williams?"

"SIR, YES, SIR!" yelled Pvt. Williams as he straightened up and continued holding the log above his head. Sweat was pouring from his forehead and dripping down his neck. The team proceeded on their quarter mile march performing log dips, log squats, and log side bends.

All, wearing their helmet and full camouflage utilities, were drenched in sweat by the end of the course. Exhaustion and dehydration were taking over the men. Arguing could be heard at one team. One recruit let go and fell down. MSgt. Neville began screaming at the recruit and ordered the team to perform the twenty-five squats again. The rest of the platoon watched them complete the squats and listened to them shout choice words for their teammate who fell down.

After the log drills were completed, the recruits lined back up into formation and marched back to the barracks. The sun was setting in the horizon and the light posts began flickering on as the sound of "Taps" played on a bugle could be heard echoing throughout the base. The music had a quieting effect on the men.

H.D. thought of the countless Marines who have heard that sound on that very base and how many times it would be played in the next year at funerals. The idea gave him a chill and haunted him for several minutes. When he walked into the chow hall, his empty stomach turned his attention toward the food displayed at the counter. He grabbed his tray and silverware. Then, he waited patiently in line to be served.

When the men returned to the squad bay, MSgt. Neville began his nightly torture. The recruits were commanded to perform Monkey Fuckers. H.D. held his ankles, squatted, raised his butt up, lowered his butt, and stood back up. They repeated these fifty times. Next, Neville ordered them to do Sun Gods.

They stood with their arms outstretched, began moving their arms in circles, and yelled, "One, two, three, one! One, two, three, two! One, two, three, three! This is what you asked for!" They repeated it until they reached fifty.

"Opposite direction, recruits, to the count of fifty!" Neville shouted as he paced up and down the deck.

"SIR, YES, SIR!" the recruits yelled, flipped their hands over, rotated their arms the opposite direction, and performed another fifty Sun Gods.

"Hands out front! Palms up, recruits! Count out fifty!"

"SIR, YES, SIR!"

The recruits put their hands out and counted out fifty more Sun Gods. By the end of this round, H.D. could feel his rotator cuffs burning. *Son of a bitch! When is he going to stop?* As if reading H.D.'s mind, MSgt. Neville ordered the men to raise their arms above their heads and perform fifty more circles. *Asshole!*

When they finished those, MSgt. Neville stated, "We are going to play a little game called Two Sheets and a Blanket. From the count of ten, you will grab your two sheets and hold them up in your left hand. You will also grab your blanket and hold it up in your right hand."

The men were standing at attention in front of their footlockers anxiously waiting for the command. "Two sheets and a blanket, on line, right now!" screeched MSgt. Neville. H.D. sprinted to get his sheets and blanket as MSgt. Neville was counting down, "10, 9, 8, 7, 6, ...!"

H.D. made it back online (standing at the end of his footlocker, facing it) in time. He glanced and saw one recruit did not make it on time. "Oh good! Private Slone doesn't want to have his shit online! Everybody put your crap back on your racks, right now!"

"SIR, YES, SIR!" the recruits hollered and scrambled to put their sheets and blanket back on their bunk. MSgt. Neville began counting down from sixty seconds. Everyone was hurrying, but their arms were exhausted from the log drills and Sun Gods. The count they give you is an impossible time, but not so impossible to keep you from trying to get it done. You try to hurry, but it just is never enough time!

MSgt. Neville reached zero and, of course, not one of them made their rack completely. "Oh, good! You don't want to do that?" Neville grinned and let out an evil chuckle, "Heh, Heh! Well, ladies, let's play Three Sheets and a Blanket! You will hold three sheets in your left hand and your blanket in your right hand online when I give the order."

Oh, Come on! Now I have to fight someone for their sheet! This is fucking bullshit! H.D. was fuming inside. If looks could kill, Neville would be a goner!

MSgt. Neville was pacing back and forth, letting the recruits stew on the task they were about to perform for a few more seconds. "Three sheets and a blanket, online, right now!" he finally yelled out.

H.D. hurried to grab his sheets before Pvt. Reynolds could steal one of his. He looked at Reynolds who was holding his own sheets. Reynolds grinned, shook his head no, and pointed to the rack next to them. H.D. saw Pvt. Slone working on getting his bottom sheet off, sprinted over and grabbed one from him, ran back to his bunk, grabbed his blanket, and dashed back to get online holding three sheets in one hand and his blanket in the other.

Pvt. Slone, with the look of utter fear, wrestled a sheet from his bunkmate who in turn scrambled to find a sheet from someone else, plus an extra one. It was total chaos! With not enough sheets to go around, there were several recruits standing back online with two sheets or only one sheet.

"So, nobody wants to have three sheets and a blanket online, right now? FINE! So be it! Everyone unlock your footlocker, right now!" ordered MSgt. Neville. He made all fifty recruits put their shower shoes in one pile, skivvies in another pile, books in a third pile, trousers in a fourth pile, blouses in a fifth pile, and sheets in a sixth pile.

After that, he made them lock their locks together and tear off the number that identified whose lock was whose. Lastly, the three sergeants poured laundry detergent over their clothes and sheets. They tore apart the whole place. *So, this is the infamous Hurricane Party!* H.D. heard stories about it from his dad but didn't expect it would actually happen to himself. Now, it's time to go to bed and get some sleep, but they are expected to have the whole place cleaned and fixed by morning. *Fuck! This sucks!* H.D. hated MSgt. Neville with a passion!

While a few of them cried a little, it made most of them fueled with anger despite their exhaustion. The night actually brought the platoon together for the first time to work as a team. The recruits worked all night, splitting the jobs into groups to have a remote chance of getting the squad bay back in order.

Some ended up with someone else's shower shoes or skivvy until they could swap or for the rest of boot camp. The men crawled into bed after the entire place was cleaned and items put away in the footlockers. They had the good fortune of sleeping for an hour before MSgt. Neville woke them up at five in the morning.

13 LEARNING TO TREAD LIGHTLY

The fourth week of boot camp brought a new challenge to the recruits: learning to navigate and survive in water. Marines are deeply connected to water and must be amphibious to be effective; they typically deploy from naval vessels. Being from the Midwest, H.D. was a decent swimmer but not as skilled as other Marines who spent more time in or around water as a youth.

The first day of Swim Week, after completing their morning routine and lessons, the recruits were ordered to line up in formation. Fully dressed in their camouflage utilities, they marched to the MCRD Fitness Center which contained an Olympic-size indoor pool. The pool was fifty meters long with a diving platform on the deep end, tapering off to a shallow part on the opposite end.

Once they arrived, Sergeant Neville introduced the recruits to Sgt. Rivera, the Marine Corps instructor on water survival. He was the senior swim instructor who specialized in combat water survival techniques and certified as a professional rescuer. Sgt. Rivera took over training at the pool while MSgt. Neville watched.

"Recruits, to be a Marine you must be able to swim and maneuver in the water with your combat gear. Remember, slow, easy movements! If you get into trouble, we are here to assist you. Is that clear?"

"YES, SIR!" the recruits shouted in answer, sitting on the

concrete bleachers.

"How many of you have been on a swim team?" asked Sgt. Rivera. Nine recruits raised their hand.

"How many of you do not know how to swim?" No one raised their hand.

"Good! First, you will swim twenty-five meters across the width of the pool with your uniforms on. I will put you in rows of ten. You will jump in when I blow the whistle and swim to the other side, exit the pool, and come back around to wait for the next instructions. Is that clear?" ordered Sgt. Rivera.

"YES, SIR!"

The recruits lined up extending their left arm to spread themselves out- one arm length from the recruit beside them. The first row sprang into the water when Sgt. Rivera blew his whistle. H.D. was in the second row of recruits to enter the water.

When he heard the whistle, he leaped into the pool. The weight of his clothes and boots pulled him farther under the water than he had expected. Once submerged, he immediately kicked his feet and used his arms to propel himself back to the surface. He raised his head just above the water, took a deep breath of air, and began swimming to the other side of the pool.

H.D. could hear the sounds of bodies hitting the water and splashing in the pool all around him. One recruit, Pvt. Cody Wilson, was struggling to keep his head above the surface and contorting his body in a way that kept him from going forward. H.D. approached Pvt. Wilson on his left side and swam beside him, barely keeping himself above water.

"Remember, slow and easy movements…..Stretch your arms out…..and kick, Cody!.... Relax…. you can….. do this…... I'll swim…..with you!" offered H.D., panting from talking while trying to keep afloat. Cody nodded his head, relaxed, and began swimming forward in sync with H.D. The two reached the other side of the pool and pulled themselves out. Dripping wet, they walked back to the other side and sat on the concrete bleachers for the next set of instructions. "Thanks, H.D.!" Cody whispered to him as they sat waiting for the rest of the recruits to join them. H.D. smiled and nodded his head.

After all fifty recruits made it across the pool and were sitting on the bleachers, Sgt. Rivera grouped them into two categories: the Blue Ducks and the Iron Ducks. Thirty-nine of the recruits were placed in the Blue Ducks- the ones who can swim well enough to advance to the next step. Eleven recruits were placed in the Iron Ducks- the ones that don't swim well enough to proceed and will get training on swim techniques.

H.D. was placed with the Blue Ducks. Pvt. Wilson was placed with the Iron Ducks. The Iron Ducks were taken to the other side of the pool with two other swim instructors to work on breathing and swim form. Sgt. Rivera escorted the Blue Ducks to the deep end of the pool. He demonstrated how to tread water and float on your back when you begin to tire and how to take deep breaths filling your chest with air to help keep you floating. He arranged the men into groups of six to practice treading water and floating for two minutes. The recruits were also taught three survival strokes: the backstroke, sidestroke, and breaststroke.

After the thirty-nine recruits finished, he took them to the ten-foot tower. He instructed the men on how to jump from the tower, "Recruits, you will use the abandon ship technique. You will jump off the tower when I blow my whistle, keeping your body straight and crossing your arms and ankles. Then, you will swim to the rope, exit the pool, and come back to the bleachers. Do you understand this?"

"YES, SIR!" the Blue Ducks responded.

When it was H.D.'s turn, he climbed the ladder to the tower platform and waited for Sgt. Rivera to blow his whistle. He wasn't nervous about the jump, but he could tell some of his peers were. When he heard the whistle, he leaped off the platform and used the abandon ship technique Sgt. Rivera showed them. He glided smoothly into the water and sank almost to the bottom of the pool.

H.D. held his breath, kicked his feet with all his might, and swam to the surface. He still had to swim twenty-five meters to the rope separating the two sections of the pool. He began to tire after fifteen meters and stopped to tread water on his back to rest a few seconds and regain his strength. After resting and breathing in deeply, he continued swimming until he made it to the rope. He was relieved when he could finally touch the bottom of the pool in his boots, walked to the side, and pulled himself out.

One by one, the recruits jumped off the platform and swam to the rope. One recruit made it about ten meters and began struggling to keep his head above the water. He bobbed up and down twice before Sgt. Rivera threw him a life preserve and pulled him to the side of the pool. Rivera ordered the recruit to join the Iron Ducks to practice treading water.

The last skill H.D. performed that day was treading water for four minutes. Four minutes didn't sound very long to H.D., but he realized after two minutes of treading in one place, four minutes felt like an eternity. Every stroke became a struggle. His clothes doubled in weight after absorbing so much water, and every muscle in his arms and legs throbbed from all the swimming that day. He reached down deep inside and pulled out just enough strength to finish the four minutes. When everyone completed the last swim exercise for the day, the recruits were told to get into formation by MSgt. Neville and marched back to the barracks, leaving a trail of water where they went.

The following day, the platoon returned to the fitness center. This time, they brought their combat gear: helmet, rifle, flak jacket (vest), and service pack. Sgt. Rivera took the recruits to the shallow end of the pool and ordered half of the men to stand in the water an arm length apart while the other half waited. He gave his next set of instructions, "Recruits, it's important to learn how to quickly shed off your equipment when you are in deep water so that you *don't drown*! We will practice this today in shallow water. When I blow my whistle, you will begin taking off your gear. You have ten seconds to do this. When you come up, place your hands on your head to signal you are done. Do you understand?"

"YES, SIR!" replied the men.

This sounded simple enough to H.D., but ten seconds was not very much time. When Sgt. Rivera blew his whistle, he slid his rifle off his right arm and feverishly removed the rest of his gear. He quickly unsnapped his helmet and let it sink slowly to the bottom of the pool. Then, he unlatched his pack and let it fall.

Taking off the vest proved to be the biggest challenge. He had to continue holding his breath while he unsnapped it, unzipped it, and shook it off his shoulders. As soon as he had removed the vest, H.D. stood back up and placed his hands on top of his head to signal he was done. He just finished in the nick of time when Sgt. Rivera blew his whistle. Some of the recruits struggled shedding their gear and didn't make it under ten seconds. The ones who didn't had to put their gear back on and try it again.

When the group was done, they retrieved their gear from the bottom of the pool and climbed out to let the second half of the platoon practice. After the last group completed the lesson, the whole platoon was instructed to go back to the deep end of the pool to learn one more skill. The men stood alongside the edge of the pool while Sgt. Rivera had one of his assistants demonstrate how to use their service pack and their cammies as a flotation device.

The platoon was split up into groups of eight to swim across the length of the pool, using their service pack to keep them afloat. Everyone was able to accomplish this skill. The rest of the time, the recruits were divided amongst the swim instructors to continue practicing skills they needed to work on.

The next two days, they repeated the same exercises and on the last day of Swim Week, each recruit was tested. Everyone had to obtain the Combat Water Survival certification at the basic level to graduate from boot camp. With extra practice, all of them did.

By the end of the week, H.D. began to feel more comfortable around water and confident in his skills to swim and float in full combat utilities. His small frame was an advantage for him when he was swimming, but he didn't have the strength he needed to float for several minutes when he was loaded down in his gear. H.D.

realized he needed to build more muscle to perform better as a Marine. He also understood the lesson Sgt. Rivera taught the platoon that day: "We are only as strong as our weakest link. You may discover that that Iron Duck may pull you out of the mud when you are at your weakest point. Every Marine has one no matter how strong they think they are!"

Once Swim Week was completed, the platoon packed up their belongings and boarded a bus for Camp Pendleton along with several other platoons belonging in the 1st Battalion. Camp Pendleton, named after Major General Joseph Henry Pendleton, is located thirty-five miles north of San Diego. It is the major West Coast base of the U.S. Marine Corps and spans over 125,000 acres. The California climate is ideal for year-long training. Camp Pendleton's topography consisting of wetlands, plains, woodlands, coastal dunes, and mountains makes it perfect for various land combat training. The seventeen miles of coastline also provide the Marines ample space for amphibious and sea-to-shore training.

The platoon moved to Camp Pendleton for the second phase of boot camp: Grass Week and Firing Week. During Grass Week, the recruits hike to the rifle range and learn about rifle safety, proper firing positions, and the fundamentals of Marine Corps marksmanship without using live ammunition. H.D. enjoyed the scenic view of San Diego on the hour-long bus ride to the Marine base.

The first day of Grass Week, the recruits were given a quick breakfast and completed their PT exercises: six rounds of 440-yard runs, thirty steps of walking lunges, twenty pull-ups, thirty crunches, and thirty burpees. When finished, they received class instruction going over their data book. The Primary Marksmanship Instructor, Sgt. Monroe, demonstrated on charts where to aim and how to adjust their sights. He also discussed eye relief.

"Improper eye relief or the lack of proper positioning of the eye will cause scope shadow. This will result in an improper shot placement," warned Sgt. Monroe.

Next, the platoon was taken to a classroom where they were able to practice with a computerized version of their rifle, shooting at a large screen display. Practicing with his PlayStation helped H.D. excel at the simulated target practice. Then, the recruits were taught how to dismantle their M16A4, clean it, and reassemble it.

After the lessons, they lined up in formation and hiked to the Edson Range. The range is set up in a large field with dunes serving as a barrier behind the targets. The field was dry and dusty from the lack of rain and the mountains could be easily seen beyond the range. The platoon spread out and practiced firing their M16A4 from a prone position at the 500-yard line.

H.D. lay down on the asphalt. He held his rifle out in front of him, using his elbows, and spread his legs out into a V-shape to anchor himself in position. He dry-fired his weapon about thirty times at a white barrel with three little black targets painted on its side. Sgt. Monroe walked around and observed each recruit. As he was standing by H.D., a seagull swooped down and unloaded itself right on top of H.D.'s utility cap. "Crap!" swore H.D. He glanced up, saw the sergeant looking at him, and said, "Sorry, sir!"

"It's okay, recruit. You have to watch out for the seagulls here. We get shit on all the time!" Sgt. Monroe grinned at H.D. and moved on to the next recruit. H.D. smiled and was relieved he didn't get reprimanded for his comment. He discovered that the marksmanship instructors were more lenient than the drill instructors. He took his water canteen, poured some on the bird dropping, wiped it clean with his fingers, and washed his fingers off with a few more drops of water and the inside of his t-shirt. He didn't want MSgt. Neville to get onto him for having a dirty utility cap.

The recruits spent hours that week preparing their bodies to remain steady while they shot in the four positions- sitting, prone, kneeling, and standing. They practiced breathing, zeroing in their rifles, and trigger control. H.D.'s body was extremely sore by the end of the week from lying on the sharp asphalt. He had dry-fired his weapon thousands of times before he even took his first actual shot and began to get more and more anxious to use live rounds with each passing day.

During Firing Week, H.D. finally found his niche. He grew up hunting with his dad and his dad's friend, Zach. Shooting moving targets was second nature for him. So, when Sgt. Monroe handed him his canister full of live ammunition for his rifle, H.D. wasn't nervous at all. He was waiting for this moment for weeks.

The platoon was divided in half. Half of the recruits set up the targets and the other half practiced shooting. H.D. was paired up with Pvt. Williams. He went to the pit first to move the target and record points on a scorecard for Pvt. Williams.

The pit is a deep trench dug underneath the ground to protect the recruits moving the targets. There were three different types of targets: a bulls-eye, a low-profile silhouette, and the large silhouette. The targets are loaded on heavy chain-driven carriages and manually pulled up and down by the recruits.

H.D. was ordered by a rifle instructor to raise the target. After he pulled the chain and raised the target supported by wooden beams, he could hear the command on the loudspeaker, "Stand by! Contact!" The next thing he heard was *Snap! Snap! Snap! Snap! Snap!* as the bullets passed through the target. "Cease fire!" the instructor yelled on the loudspeaker. H.D. was instructed to lower the target and mark points for Pvt. Williams.

This process was repeated many times. H.D. was in the pit for over an hour. The nice thing about it was he could unbutton his blouse and talk freely with other recruits around him. The pit also provided shade from the wind and sun. However, H.D. still had to be careful while he was down there. He was showered several times by dirt and had to occasionally dodge pieces of rock.

When it came time for H.D. to shoot, Pvt. Williams took his place and he went to the first shooting line. Pvt. Reynolds was next to him. They shot five rounds, slow firing (one shot at a time), sitting on the ground. Then, they shot five rounds standing and knelt, firing at a target 200 yards away. Sgt. Monroe was walking up and down the line observing and instructing recruits.

Sgt. Monroe approached Pvt. Reynolds, noticed his rifle was

jerking him back, and stated, "Put your tricep on your shin and lean into it. Keep your eye on the post. Breathe in and breathe out. Slow, steady, squeeze!" Pvt. Reynolds followed the sergeant's instructions and pulled the trigger. He was surprised that the rifle did not move at all this time. Monroe turned to watch H.D. He observed how comfortable H.D. was with the M16A4. He took out his binoculars, looked at H.D.'s target, and saw the bullet holes in the bullseye.

"What's your name, recruit?" he asked.

"H.D. Hogan, sir!" answered H.D., puzzled why the sergeant asked.

"Private Hogan, I want you to rapid fire ten rounds into that target," commanded Sgt. Monroe pointing to the target.

"Yes, sir!" H.D. replied and quickly fired off ten rounds into the target 200 yards away- each one hitting directly on or around the bullseye. Monroe looked through his binoculars and said, "Well done, Pvt. Hogan! You ready for a challenge?"

"Yes, sir. I am!" replied H.D. grinning.

"After the rest of the recruits finish practicing on the 200, we'll see what you got at the 300," Sgt. Monroe replied. When the platoon finished rapid firing, Sgt. Monroe raised up his hand. "Cease fire!" the instructor inside the booth called out on the loudspeaker. The men did as commanded and stopped firing their weapons. The recruits were ordered to move to the 300-yard line.

H.D. walked to his place on the asphalt and sat down. Pvt. Reynolds sat down in the spot next to him. They were ordered to slow fire five rounds into the target, which they did simultaneously. H.D. could hear the *click!* of the trigger, the *pop!* of the bullet firing, and the *ping!* of the brass casing hitting the asphalt. He could smell the gunpowder all around him.

The California sun was heating up and beginning to roast the recruits. The wind from the nearby mountain ranges was picking up and blowing the dirt in the field. H.D. had to adjust his rifle to allow for windage. When they completed the five rounds of slow fire, the recruits were ordered to get into the prone position and rapid fire ten rounds.

"Whenever you're ready, Private Hogan," stated Monroe, still standing by H.D. and gazing down the field.

H.D. positioned his rifle, looked into the scope, took a slow breath in, let it out, and squeezed the trigger rapidly firing ten rounds into the target. Sgt. Monroe took out his binoculars and studied the bullet holes. He was amazed to see six out of the ten shots hit the bullseye. He saw three holes just outside the center. He looked for the tenth hole but didn't see it at first. Then, he realized H.D. had hit the center of the bullseye *twice*!

Damn! *I can't believe this kid!* marveled Sgt. Monroe. "Nice job, Pvt. Hogan. You think you can hit the 500-yard target?"

"Yes, sir, I can!" answered H.D. without hesitation.

Sgt. Monroe signaled for the ceasefire and ordered the men to move to the last line of fire. The platoon got up and resumed the prone position on the 500-yard line.

"Take your time, Private Hogan!" ordered Sgt. Monroe. H.D. steadied his rifle with his elbows on the ground, took his time aiming, and listened to the sound of his own breath, completely shutting out any other sounds around him. Silence crept slowly down the row of men until not a single one was shooting. They noticed Sgt. Monroe was following H.D. and were curious to see why. No one moved. Frozen in their spot, they just stared to see what was going to happen.

H.D. slowly squeezed the trigger. Steadying his rifle again, he took another shot and repeated three more times. He was about to take one more shot when Sgt. Monroe yelled out, "Ceasefire!" H.D. quit shooting and looked up at Sgt. Monroe unsure why he was stopped. Sgt. Monroe raised up his binoculars and saw all five shots hit the bullseye. *No frickin' way!* He couldn't believe what he was seeing, rubbed his eyes, and looked through the binoculars again.

"Private Hogan, where the hell did you learn to shoot like that?" asked Sgt. Monroe, shaking his head.

"My pappy, sir. We just *love* to hunt squirrels!" yelled H.D.

proudly. Sgt. Monroe burst out laughing and patted H.D. on the back. The platoon shouted, "Oorah! H.D.!" giving him a standing ovation. H.D. stood up and looked around. He couldn't believe everyone was yelling and clapping for him.

"Private Hogan, I want you to advance to the expert training. How does that sound to you?" asked Sgt. Monroe.

"That sounds *just fine* to me, sir!" H.D. answered, nodding his head. After the rest of the recruits finished firing at the last target, MSgt. Neville ordered the platoon to line up and march back to the barracks. As H.D. walked by him, he nodded at him and said, "Private Hogan." That was all he said.

"Sir!" H.D. replied, glanced at him, and continued walking in formation. He knew he had to *tread lightly* with MSgt. Neville. Being cocky would get him nowhere and that wasn't in his character anyway. Shortly after dinner, H.D. requested to make a phone call home. His request was granted by MSgt. Neville.

When the phone rang, Steve picked it up and heard H.D. blubbering on the phone excitedly. "Slow down, Son. What happened?"

"Finally, I feel like I did something right, Dad!" hollered H.D. into the phone. Then, he told his father the entire story. "Can you believe it? He wants me to train to be an expert sharp-shooter!"

"Yes, I can believe it, Son. You were always a great shot when we were hunting!"

"Thanks! I gotta go. I'll call you later to let you know how it's going. Love you, Pap!"

"Love you, too!" *Click*! Steve hated that the phone call was so short but was glad his son called to share the news. His heart swelled with pride for his son's accomplishment.

H.D. practiced honing in his rifle skills the next three days. The last day of Firing Week was Qualification Day. This was the day that counted. The platoon woke up before dawn, prepared their rifles, ate breakfast, and performed PT exercises. Then, they marched back to the range.

All of the recruits were trying their hardest and striving to earn the coveted Rifle Expert badge or the "Crossed Rifles". H.D. was hoping he would earn enough points to get it. Every recruit had to at least reach 190 points to earn the Marksmanship badge. When it was H.D.'s turn to shoot, Sgt. Monroe walked up to him and said, "Care to have some competition, Private Hogan?"

"Yes, sir. I would like that," replied H.D. smiling. He was confident in his skills and always enjoyed a good challenge. It usually pushed him to do his very best. The two lay down on the ground in the prone position at the 500-yard line. Simultaneously, they inserted a magazine with thirty rounds into their rifles as did the rest of the platoon.

"Stand by...Fire!" yelled the voice on the loudspeaker. *Pop! Pop! Pop! Pop!* went the sound of the rifles as it echoed into the mountains. Gun smoke filled the air. It was raining brass as the casings fell to the ground all around the recruits. In less than a minute, the entire magazine was empty. H.D. stopped, inserted the magazine with twenty rounds and continued firing. When he finished firing all fifty rounds, he sat up and waited for Sgt. Monroe and the rest of the platoon to stop firing.

After everyone was done, Sgt. Monroe raised his hand. "Ceasefire!" ordered the loudspeaker. Their points were added up on their scorecard and the recruits in the pit came out to give the results to Sgt. Monroe. He looked at his points and looked at H.D.'s. H.D. glanced over Sgt. Monroe's shoulder and couldn't believe he outshot the guy. Sgt. Monroe hit the expert mark at 223 points. H.D. scored 235 points! He could hardly contain himself.

"Excellent shooting, H.D. You made a formidable opponent!" praised Sgt. Monroe, reaching out to shake H.D.'s hand. H.D. grabbed his hand, gave it a firm handshake, and humbly replied, "Thank you, sir!" He couldn't help but let a small crooked grin sneak out.

After every recruit was shown their score, MSgt. Neville ordered them to line up in formation. They returned to the barracks, cleaned their weapon, and proceeded the rest of their day under MSgt. Neville's command who jumped right back into barking out orders. Despite whatever MSgt. Neville made them do, he couldn't take away the feeling of pride and confidence that had replaced any sense of insecurity H.D. had before. In his mind, he was now a Marine!

14 WHEN IT RAINS, IT POURS

That night, after the platoon returned to the barracks from the rifle range, had their showers and inspections, H.D. was ordered to take over fire watch. While everyone else slept, he walked around the squad bay taking count of recruits and equipment which he recorded in a logbook. He also documented who came and went from the room. With little to do, he knew it was going to be a long and boring night.

Sgt. Shepard came on deck just after eleven o'clock. H.D. snapped to attention, saluted him, and reported that all recruits were present and accounted for. Sgt. Shepard nodded to him, strolled around the squad bay for a few minutes, inspected the recruits for himself, and left.

Thirty minutes later, MSgt. Neville came walking in. Every recruit was sound asleep except for H.D. When MSgt. Neville entered, H.D. saluted him and said, "Sir, all recruits are present and accounted for. There are fifty weapons on board."

"Good recruit," he replied, looked around, and added, "There is one thing you need to do for me tonight. I'm missing a fourth key for the weapon systems. It's your job to find that key for me."

"Yes, sir!" replied H.D.

MSgt. Neville turned around and left the squad bay. As soon as he exited the hatch, H.D. began to search for the missing key, feeling privileged that he was chosen to perform this task. He

usually had a knack for finding lost items. At least he had
something to do to pass away the time.

Each recruit had his own lock and key while the drill instructors
had locks and keys for the squad bay. They ran a cable between the
lower receiver and ejection port of each rifle and connected it to a
padlock that secured all of their firearms. H.D. quietly searched
under all the racks, lifted up corners of footlockers, and inspected
every nook and cranny in that room. No key was to be found.

After an hour, he began to get nervous that he would not be able
to fulfill his orders. At half past midnight, MSgt. Neville entered
through the hatch. H.D. again saluted him and reported the status
of the squad bay. "Hogan, where is my goddamn fucking key?"
barked out MSgt. Neville.

"Sir, this recruit doesn't know, sir!" stammered H.D. as a bead
of sweat trickled slowly down the side of his face.

"Then fucking find it, recruit!" yelled MSgt. Neville, loud
enough to stir some of the other recruits from their deep slumber.

"Aye, aye, sir!" responded H.D. and he began searching the
whole squad bay again for the key. At this point, Sgt. Wyler came
into the squad bay and asked MSgt. Neville what was going on.
After Neville explained that Private Hogan was looking for the
missing fourth key, he leaned sideways into MSgt. Neville and said,
"Neville, there is no fourth key. You know that, right?"

He was loud enough H.D. overheard his statement but acted like
he didn't hear what he said and continued to search for the key.
Neville looked at Wyler, shrugged his shoulders, and said, "Oh!
Oops!" Wyler chuckled, shook his head, and left the room.

MSgt. Neville didn't say anything and let H.D. keep searching
for the key that never existed. Finally, after ten more minutes, H.D.
had enough and went into the head to sit on the toilet and think
about his life. He wasn't going to waste anymore of his time
looking for a key that wasn't there. He pulled out a piece of paper
and started writing down things he would eat and do when he got
out of boot camp. MSgt. Neville came into the head and yelled,
"Hogan, what the fuck are you doing?"

"Waiting for an epiphany, sir!" replied H.D., looking up from his paper and keeping a straight face.

"An epiphany of what?" questioned Neville with a look of confusion.

"Where the fourth key would be at, sir!" explained H.D., maintaining his poker face.

"Get the fuck back into the squad bay, recruit. Forget the goddamn key and continue your duty!" he yelled. Boy was he pissed! He stormed out of the head, went down the hall, and slammed the hatch of his office. H.D. thought, *I bet that bastard doesn't even know what an epiphany is! Shit! Now what the hell is he going to do to me?* He roamed around the squad bay all night waiting for his repercussion, but it never came.

Sgt. Shepard entered into the squad bay at five in the morning to wake up the recruits. He informed them that, today, they were going to be completing the second phase of the Confidence Course. He warned, "Anyone who is afraid of heights, well that's too damn bad! You're going to get over it today!" *Great! No sleep and we have to do the most physically challenging course today!* H.D. secretly moaned inside.

The platoon dressed in their full camouflage utilities, ate a short breakfast, and marched out to the obstacle course. After Sgt. Shepard instructed the men through a series of PT exercises in the dirt for half an hour, they were led to the first obstacle course called the Stairway to Heaven. It looked exactly as its name. An impressive ladder made of huge logs, reaching thirty-six feet, stood straight up into the air. It began spaced close together but became farther apart as you climbed.

The recruits stood wide-eyed with their mouths agape in pure awe. Panic began to grab hold of several of the men. MSgt. Neville instructed the recruits on how to climb the ladder, and they were divided into three groups led by each drill instructor.

They were ordered to climb the ladder one at a time. H.D. was in the middle of the group. From behind him, he could hear Pvt. Barnes say, "I ain't ever climbed nothin' that high in my life!" The recruit behind Barnes said, "At least you're tall and strong. I ain't gotta chance!"

When it was H.D.'s turn, he grabbed the first log and pulled himself up. Then, he proceeded to climb one rung at a time by pulling himself up and standing on the log below. It took more strength and much longer than it looked, even for a monkey like him. He got to the top rung, swung his right leg over, and straddled the log for a second to catch his breath. He looked around and could see pretty far from the top of the obstacle.

He saw the other two drill instructors yelling at recruits screwing up. After his breathing slowed, he began the descent down the other side. He was relieved when his boots finally hit the dirt ground. He turned and watched the other recruits following him. Pvt. Barnes came shortly after. Barnes got to the top and completely froze. H.D. could see the fear on his face.

"Come on Barnes! You got this!" yelled H.D. up to him. Pvt. Barnes looked down at H.D., nodded his head, and began climbing down. His height did indeed help him with the climb. It was more of a mental game than a physical game for him to overcome his fear of heights. He did. He was sweating profusely when he got to the ground and said, "Thanks, H.D."

"Anytime," he replied, smiling at his friend.

The recruits were kept in constant motion. Between each obstacle, they were performing martial arts techniques they had learned the past several weeks while they were waiting for their turn. After one group completed the obstacle, a sergeant would lead them to the next one, give instructions and demonstrate how to conquer it, then watch them perform while the other sergeants finished with the rest of the recruits on the previous obstacle. Sgt. Wyler led H.D.'s group to the next high obstacle course- the "A" Frame. This was an elaborate course requiring upper-body strength.

H.D. had gained muscle over the last eleven weeks and his long wiry frame helped him to climb the rope. Grabbing the fifteen-foot rope, he climbed hand-over-hand right up, not even using his feet to help support him until he got to the middle section of the "A" Frame, where he had to walk over a horizontal log ladder. He slowly stepped over the gaps onto the logs with ease, climbed up the fifteen-foot ladder to the top, and descended hand-over-hand down a thirty-foot rope using his feet to support him and keep him from falling.

As soon as he finished, he was hustled to the final high obstacle course in the Confidence Course II- the Slide for Life. By this time, he was tiring out from lack of sleep and the muscle strain of the first two obstacles. But, he didn't want to fail and told himself, *This is the last one. You can do it!*

He climbed the twenty-five-foot tower to the top, crawled on his belly onto a ninety-foot cable which descended downward. The cable hung suspended over a pool of water. If any recruit slipped, he would land into the water and have to redo the obstacle. H.D. slowly slid on the cable, pulling himself with his hands and gripping the cable with his feet. He could feel the burn of the blisters forming on both of his hands. The recruit in front of him lost his grip on the cable and plummeted into the water below. H.D. stopped for a second to watch him splash in the water and continued pulling himself down the cable.

After he reached halfway, he swung his body down as instructed and continued the descent hanging below the cable. He mustered every ounce of strength he could to complete the obstacle. Even though the pool was enticing, he did not want to have to complete the obstacle again. When he reached the ground, he felt a huge weight leave his body- relieved he had accomplished one more step toward becoming a Marine. There were only a few more days left. He knew he could do it.

Once everyone completed the confidence course, the platoon was ordered to line up in formation and return to the barracks for dinner. They woofed down their food as fast as they sat down at the table. After showers, they had more physical exercises and the platoon was ordered to clean up the squad bay. Jobs were divided between the head, hallway, and deck. H.D. was assigned to mop the head with another recruit. He was in the middle of mopping the floor when Sgt. Wyler came in and said, "Private Hogan, I would like to talk to you in my office."

"Yes, sir!" H.D. replied, leaning his mop against the wall. He followed Sgt. Wyler into the office and stood in front of Wyler's desk. On the desk was a box of Domino's pizza and two cans of Coca-Cola. The TV was turned on and a football game was being televised. The Indianapolis Colts were playing against the New Orleans Saints. It was Super Bowl Sunday!

H.D. hadn't even realized the Super Bowl was that day. He suddenly missed being in Indiana and watching the game with his friends.

"Private Hogan, I want to commend you on how well you are performing at the tasks given to you so far," praised Wyler.

"Thank you, sir!" responded H.D., humbly.

"Go ahead, Hogan, sit down and watch some of the game," he ordered. Wyler pointed to his chair and offered, "You can have my chair." He opened the box of pizza and added, "Get you a slice. You earned it!"

The pizza was steaming hot and the smell was irresistible. The aroma drifted into the air and danced in his nostrils playing with his senses. He took a moment to just enjoy the smell. The pizza looked great! It was even pepperoni; H.D.'s favorite kind. He hadn't had some in so long, his mouth began to water. He grabbed a slice and began eating it.

"Take one of these Cokes. You'll need it to wash down the pizza," offered Sgt. Wyler. H.D. did what he was told and popped open the tab on the can of Coca-Cola. As he was taking a sip, Sgt. Wyler said, "Go ahead and enjoy some more of the pizza. I have to go check on something. I'll be back in a few minutes." Wyler walked out of the room.

H.D. watched the game, ate a couple more bites of pizza, and took another sip of the pop. Just as he took another bite, MSgt. Neville came into the room, looked at H.D., looked at the desk, and looked back at H.D. He calmly said, "This is Sgt. Wyler's desk.

That is Sgt. Wyler's chair." He paused a second and yelled at the top of his lungs, "BUT, YOU ARE NOT FUCKING SGT. WYLER!" H.D. froze: he didn't swallow; he didn't speak; he didn't move at all.

MSgt. Neville came around the desk and grabbed H.D. by his left arm and pushed him into the hallway. "GET THE FUCK BACK INTO THE SQUAD BAY, PRIVATE HOGAN!" H.D. gulped down the last piece of pizza in his mouth and sprinted back into the squad bay. When he entered with Neville just behind him, the platoon knew something was up. H.D. stood in front of them with pizza sauce all over his face in complete dismay and not sure what he was supposed to do next.

The platoon stopped cleaning and stood on line waiting for MSgt. Neville's orders. He explained loudly to the men, "While you boys have been paying the price, washing and hosing stuff off, Private Hogan has been watching the Super Bowl, sitting at Sgt. Wyler's desk, and eating fucking pizza!" Every recruit in the platoon had a look of shock on his face and stared at H.D. in disbelief.

"Inspection Footlocker, right now, recruits!" The platoon was used to this command by now. They unlocked their footlockers and pulled everything out. H.D. started to step forward to unlock his footlocker, but Neville stopped him. He screamed at him, "Freeze, recruit! You are not doing a fuckin' thing! You stand right there until I tell you otherwise!"

Neville went through the piles, inspecting everything. One recruit had a t-shirt with his name faded off. Neville grabbed the t-shirt and threw it into his face. "Stamp your fucking t-shirt, recruit!"

"SIR, YES, SIR!" the recruit screamed back.

MSgt. Neville continued to pick through items, throwing things here and there, until he had enough. "Right shoulder! Footlocker!" he yelled suddenly. The recruits looked at each other and began clumsily picking up their footlocker and placing it on their right shoulder. *Clang! Clang! Clang!* went the sound of the metal footlockers being lifted. The men moaned and grunted as they lifted it up and onto their shoulder.

Everyone stood there, balancing a footlocker on his shoulder and glaring at H.D. He could almost hear them saying, "You fucking dog! You dick!" Guys were standing, straining, trying to keep hold of the long, heavy footlocker. Their arms were shaking. Several began dropping their footlockers and getting screamed at.

H.D. felt awful. The thrashing continued for over an hour and he couldn't be a part of it. It was worse than any punishment MSgt. Neville could have given him. It went on and on and on. Everyone was pissed at him.

Finally, MSgt. Neville was satisfied and commanded, "Pick up your shit and hit the racks, recruits!" He turned to H.D. and said softly in his ear, "I hope that pizza was worth it, Hogan. You get the fuck in your rack, right now!" H.D. did what he was told.

Just after Neville left, one recruit shouted to H.D., "You motherfucker, because of you..." H.D. stopped him in his tracks and yelled back, "Boys, it's never been because of me!"

His stomach was in knots and his head pounded. He didn't look at anyone, took off his fatigues, wiped the pizza sauce off on the inside of his t-shirt, and crawled up into his rack. He thought about how hard he had pushed in boot camp to be the example. He tried helping dudes that were fucking up and helped them with their shit. He was so disillusioned. *Why did they do this to me?*

His dad had always told him that hard work paid off. Do what you are told and then some. You will be rewarded for it. He didn't know what to believe now. A hush fell over the platoon as they contemplated what H.D. said, and each recruit in turn went to bed. H.D. was completely physically and mentally exhausted. He slowly closed his eyes and fell asleep.

MSgt. Neville came bursting into the squad bay at four o'clock in the morning. He picked up right where he left off. The day was absolutely miserable. They did about every exercise he could think of, completed obstacle courses, and ran for six miles.

He had them do skull drags where they were crawling on the

ground with their face pressed into the dirt. He walked by and stepped on one recruit's ankle, crushing it into the dirt. Then, they had to do buddy drags. H.D. had to drag one of the largest recruits back and forth across the field.

As the day went on, the hotter it became. It was an unusually hot California day for winter time. The temperature climbed to 79 degrees. By the end of the day, the recruits were fuming. They were so over the shit they had to do at boot camp and furious with MSgt. Neville.

Neville didn't let up. At the hottest point of the day, he had the recruits go into the squad bay for another hazing. He made them shut all the portals and close the hatch. It was like a sauna in there. He began making the men do jumping jacks, burpees, lunges, running in place, and more. They did it over and over and over. The room was getting hotter and hotter and hotter. MSgt. Neville kept pushing them. The men thought they would pass out before he would stop.

Neville kept them at it until suddenly H.D. felt a drip on his head, then another and another. The men looked up and saw the condensation on the ceiling. There was so much water, it began to rain. The platoon couldn't believe it! MSgt. Neville was satisfied when it began to rain and ordered the men to stop. They stood quietly, letting the rain fall on them for a few minutes. Then, Neville ordered the platoon to go to the chow hall.

After dinner, the hazing resumed. More Sun Gods and Monkey Fuckers. On and on and on it went. The yelling continued relentlessly. Nothing they did was right. Everyone was fucking up. Finally, at ten o'clock, he ordered the men to take a shower and inspected them afterward. He walked up to Private Reynolds who was standing in his t-shirt and underwear beside H.D. and said, "What the fuck is this?" poking Reynolds on his chest.

"Chest hairs, sir!" yelled Pvt. Reynolds.

"What is the fucking regulation of chest hairs in the Marine Corps?"

"Chest hairs cannot come out of the collar of our uniform, sir!"

answered Reynolds. He knew they were allowed to come out of the top of their t-shirt, but not their uniform. He decided not to say anything else to Neville and kept quiet.

MSgt. Neville began pulling hair right out of his chest. Reynolds just stood still at attention, not flinching once, and let him continue plucking the hair until he was done. Neville looked a little disappointed, turned, and ordered the platoon, "Get the fuck into your racks, you maggots!"

When they climbed into their rack, they were so pissed off they couldn't fall asleep. H.D. was livid. He was lying in his rack, staring at the ceiling, and thought, *To hell with it all! If Neville wants to kick me out, he can kick me out!*

He began singing "Hey Jude" by the Beatles, "*Hey Jude, don't make it bad. Take a sad song and make it better!*"

"Shhh, H.D.," whispered Pvt. Reynolds from his rack below.

"*Remember to let her into your heart. Then you can start to make it better,*" sang H.D. ignoring his friend. From across the row, Pvt. Barnes joined in the singing. His deep baritone complementing H.D.'s tenor voice. "*Hey Jude, don't be afraid. You were made to go out and get her.*"

"Shut up guys. Neville is going to kill us!" yelled one of the recruits on fire watch.

Pvt. Reynolds joined H.D. and Barnes, his bass voice making it a perfect three-part harmony. "*The minute you let her under your skin. Then you begin to make it better.*"

Slowly, a wave of voices joined them as the rest of the men ignored the fire watch recruit and began singing. Pretty soon everyone was singing. They were all thinking, *Fucking come out here and thrash us! We don't give a fuck!*

They kept singing louder and louder waiting for MSgt. Neville to come in. "*And anytime you feel the pain, hey Jude, refrain. Don't carry the world upon your shoulders. For well you know that it's a fool who plays it cool. By making his world a little colder.*"

They ended singing at the top of their lungs, "*Nah nah nah nah nah nah nah nah nah! Hey, Jude! Nah nah nah nah nah nah nah nah nah!*

Hey, Jude!"

The words echoed throughout the barracks and flowed out into the night air of the Marine base. When they finished, they lay still in the dark waiting for someone to come. The fire watch recruits were scared to death. They would have paid the price for letting the singing continue. Sergeant Neville didn't even turn on his light. He didn't rip open the door or yell, "What the fuck is going on?"

The next day, nothing was said. The drill instructors began to treat them differently. It was still attention to detail and brutal, but it was different. It was as if they had turned a corner. Before, no one was on the same page, now they were in sync. They bonded over the common emotions of hatred and anger. No more blame was directed toward a single recruit. They were in it together until the very end. That evening, they cleaned their rifle and packed their rucksack to prepare for the Crucible the next day. The men couldn't wait to begin this last rite of passage to become a Marine.

15 *CLIMB EVERY MOUNTAIN*

At two o'clock in the morning, the platoon woke up to the sound of "Reveille". Today was the beginning of the most intense and physically challenging exercise for the recruits to pass in order to officially become a Marine- the Crucible. It is a fifty-four-hour test of fortitude and endurance. They will have to march for approximately forty miles during those fifty-four hours and will have twenty-nine problem-solving obstacles to complete, as well as a hike up a steep mountain at the end.

The platoon was ordered to dress in their full camouflage utilities and pick up their rucksack. Among the contents were skivvy rolls, extra socks, utility uniforms, ammunition packs, a poncho, night vision goggles, an IFAK (Individual First Aid Kit), and two MREs (Meals Ready to Eat). Each recruit was responsible for rationing his meals to last the entire fifty-four hours.

They attached two canteens and a sleeping bag to the back of their rucksack. Proper packing was important to prevent the load from shifting and causing discomfort for the recruit. Then, the recruits put on their Kevlar (body armor vest) and helmet, slung their rucksack over their shoulders, and picked up their M16A4 rifle. The gear weighed just over sixty pounds. For some of them, it was almost half their weight.

The platoon began marching toward the Edson Range at three

o'clock in the morning. They started out in two columns traveling down the gravel road toward the range and merged into one column as they veered down a dirt path, heading past the range toward the mountainous terrain of the Crucible site.

The anticipation of the men was clearly visible. Some were excited and ready for the challenge, and some were nervous and unsure of what to expect. They all heard tales from other Marines of how hard the Crucible was, but also heard how rewarding it was to finish it. Many of the recruits came from homes where everything was handed to them; they didn't have to work hard for anything. Other recruits came from poor homes where nothing was really expected from them. If they complete the Crucible, it will be the first real accomplishment many of them did on their own.

The platoon began jogging down the dirt path in the dark. The moon was the only thing lighting their way. The drill instructors were intermingled within the group, shouting at them to keep moving. Tripping over sticks and rocks and stumbling in the dark, the recruits kept jogging forward.

H.D. was near the head of the pack and keeping up the pace well. He could feel his canteens full of water thumping against his hips with each step he took. At least it was a cool, fifty-three-degree morning which kept H.D. from sweating so much under all his clothing and gear.

The platoon passed the fields and marshes and headed uphill where the conifer and oak trees grew thicker and provided more shade. The bright, full moon lit up the forest. H.D. could see eyeballs of opossums, raccoons, and deer reflecting in the light. He wished he could use his gun to shoot one of those deer. The thought of fresh venison made his mouth water. He missed that taste. *Quit thinkin' 'bout food! It'll be a long time before I can eat!* H.D. scolded himself.

It would have been a peaceful march if it weren't for the constant yelling from the drill instructors and recruits shouting back. H.D. focused back on the path in front of him, being careful not to bump into the recruit ahead of him. They hiked for six miles until they reached the Crucible site.

When the platoon reached the site, they were told how the events were set up. Each event had a specific name with "warrior stations". Many stations were named after a Marine medal recipient and had a plaque with their citation and picture posted for the recruits to read. The platoon was split into teams with one of the recruits chosen as the leader for the station. After each station, the drill instructors would choose a different leader, giving each one a chance to lead and a chance to follow.

The team would have to work closely together to overcome the obstacles or problems that needed to be solved. For the men who always wanted to take charge and make the calls, it was a good lesson on being a follower. For the men who were quiet and no one paid attention to, it was a chance to be heard. The quiet ones were usually the ones who had the most creative ideas.

The first event was named the Battle of Hue City. It was a one-hour event in which teams had to run through a course with trenches, wire fences, and walls. While crossing the course, they had to restock supplies of ammunition and water. Sgt. Wyler told the recruits about the battle, "During the Vietnam War in 1968, Viet Cong soldiers launched an attack on the city of Hue to bring power to communist insurgents. Three Marine Corps battalions were protecting the air base and faced rocket and mortar fire. Unaware of the enemy situation in Hue, General Foster C. LaHue dispatched the 1st Battalion, 1st Marine Regiment to relieve the 200 surrounded Marines. The 1/1 moved into Hue, resulting in one of the longest, bloodiest battles of the war with fierce house-to-house fighting."

After the speech, the platoon was given a mission with directions on how to complete the event and a leader was chosen for each team. One recruit led H.D.'s team as he followed. They ran through the field, jumped over a trench, and began crawling under razor-sharp wire fences. The leader instructed one recruit to go first, lie on his back, and hold up the wire fence with his rifle. The next recruit began crawling under and held the fence for the recruit following him.

The field was a muddy mess. The recruits had the added difficulty of maneuvering through the mud on their back as their boots kept slipping out from under them. While they were crawling under the fence, the recruits passed ammunition cans to each other. They continued this pattern until everyone reached the other side of the wire fences with the ammunition cans. During the entire event, they were on silent patrol and communicated only with hand signals to imitate conditions in real combat. The sound of gunfire was blaring from loudspeakers making the task more realistic.

After the resupply course came the first of four warrior stations in the Battle of Hue City- the Pfc. Jenkins Pinnacle. Sgt. Shepard had a recruit read from the citation of how the hero's actions exemplify the Marine Corps values. The recruit read loudly and clearly, "Robert H. Jenkins, Jr. received the Congressional Medal of Honor while serving in Vietnam in 1969. While under attack from the Vietnamese, a hand grenade was thrown into the Marine emplacement. Jenkins grabbed his comrade, threw him to the ground, and shielded him from the explosion. Jenkins died from his injuries, but his courage and valor saved a fellow Marine's life." There was a moment of silence as the men honored Pfc. Jenkins.

Next, the recruits were given a scenario and instructions on how to complete the Pfc. Jenkins Pinnacle, and a leader was chosen for the station. H.D. and his team had to cross two horizontal cable-supported logs. Sgt. Shepard told them one rule was they could not hold the bottom of the ladder or touch the cables supporting the logs, making the task more challenging than it looked. The distance between the two logs came up to most recruits' necks. While standing on the bottom log, one recruit would have to hoist another recruit up to the top log and pass the ammunition cans as the ladder was swinging. It took teamwork to complete the station in a timely manner.

The second station was Pfc. Garcia's Engagement. The recruits learned about Pfc. Garcia, were given a battle scenario, and told how to complete the station. In this station, the recruits performed hand-to-hand combat skills with a partner. Once everyone was done, they moved onto Lehew's Challenge. For this station, recruits climbed over an eight-foot high horizontal log. H.D.'s team helped hoist each other up onto the log and passed the ammunition cans to the recruit on top who in turn handed it down to a recruit on the other side. They took turns who was on top of the log passing the ammunition cans.

The last station was Corbin's Convoy. H.D. read the story of Lance Corporal Corbin to the platoon, "LCpl. Todd Corbin was a tactical vehicle replacement driver supporting Operation Iraqi Freedom in Haditha, Iraq. On May 7, 2005, his platoon was ambushed using a suicide vehicle. Three of the four Marine vehicles were damaged and eleven out of the sixteen Marines were injured. Corbin repositioned his truck directly between the enemy and the wounded and radioed for help. He ran to his injured leader, threw him onto his shoulder and carried him to safety. Then, he recovered the dead and wounded, one at a time, and drove to the battalion aid station five miles away. Due to his heroism, no Marine lost his life after the initial attack. He earned the Navy Cross, the second highest award a Marine could receive." The recruits were amazed at Corbin's actions and thought about what they would do if they were put in a similar situation.

During Corbin's challenge, H.D.'s team was crossing a small bridge when suddenly an improvised explosive device (IED) went off. There was a loud bang and smoke filled the air. The IED did not contain any explosive material, but the recruits had to react as if it did. Instantly, H.D. grabbed the recruit's arm standing next to him and shoved him out of the way. Pvt. Dillman did the same for another recruit. Sgt. Shepard told the team H.D. was injured and so was Dillman.

Pvt. Williams was the leader of the team. "Pvt. Anderson, you need to assess Pvt. Hogan's injuries and provide first aid. Pvt. Rodriguez, you need to assess Pvt. Dillman's injuries and provide first aid," Williams ordered the team. It was determined that H.D. had shrapnel in his right shoulder and leg, and the bleeding needed to be controlled. Dillman was told he had severe injuries to both legs requiring a tourniquet on both. H.D. could walk, but Pvt. Dillman had to be carried.

Using resources around them, they found a plank of wood and used rope to stabilize Pvt. Dillman on the makeshift gurney. H.D.'s right arm was placed in a sling and he used a stick to support him as they walked to the next station. When they were done, Sgt. Shepard went over the things they did well and what they needed to work on. He commended H.D. and Pvt. Dillman on their quick action when the IED went off.

The second event for the day was called the Battle of Belleau Wood. Sgt. Shepard told the team about the battle, "The Battle of Belleau Wood took place during World War I. During June of 1918, the Marines were assisting the French against the Germans in a wooded area. Using their bayonets, the Marines dug shallow trenches to protect themselves from the oncoming Germans. After days of battle, Gunnery Sergeant Ernest A. Janson fought against twelve German soldiers, killing two with his bayonet before the rest fled. Because of his action, he became the first Marine to receive the Medal of Honor in World War I. The Germans called the Marines "Teufel Hunden" which translated is "devil dogs", a nickname we proudly use today."

The Battle of Belleau Wood was a three-hour event where the teams had to perform six reaction course problems working as a team to solve each one. One problem was the team had to cross several tree stumps without touching the ground. They used wooden boards as planks to cross the stumps. They also used a wooden board to cross a water hole. Then, they had to cross over a wall using whatever they had available and transport a barrel over it. The barrel was heavy and large, making it difficult to carry. H.D.'s team used two long poles and a rope to help them move the barrel.

When they were done crossing the wall, the recruits fought in teams of two against each other using pugil sticks in a small arena. When one recruit was out, the team member left had to fight both opponents. The afternoon sun was warming things up for the recruits. Many were sweating heavily after the "battle" and had to stop to refill their canteens with water.

The third event was called the Core Event and Warrior Stations. During this one-hour event, six teams worked simultaneously through the stations. The first station was called Noonan's Casualty Evacuation. A recruit read the citation of Thomas P. Noonan, Jr., "Thomas P. Noonan, Jr. graduated from college and could have commissioned into any branch of the military. He chose to be a Marine as an infantryman. Noonan went to Vietnam in July 1968. While moving from their position on a slippery, muddy hill, the leaders came under heavy fire from the North Vietnamese Army. Four men were wounded and repeated attempts to save them failed. Noonan moved from his safe position, maneuvered down the treacherous hill shouting words of encouragement to the injured Marines. He dashed over to them and began dragging the most serious injured man away. He was hit and knocked to the ground by enemy fire but got up to continue dragging his fellow Marine to safety. He was mortally wounded and never made it to his destination. The other Marines were so inspired by him that they launched a spirited assault, forcing the enemy soldiers to withdraw. Noonan earned the Medal of Honor during Operation Dewey Canyon in 1969."

The Marine Corps suffered a loss of over 13,000 during the Vietnam War, making it their costliest war. On the Vietnam Memorial in Washington D.C., one out of every four names listed is a Marine. There are hundreds of medal recipient stories of these brave Marines who fought courageously for their comrades and country.

H.D.'s team had to recover a downed pilot and another recruit "shot" by a sniper and move them through the woods to a location one mile away where another helicopter was waiting to evacuate the wounded. They had thirty minutes to reach the helicopter. H.D. was appointed the leader for this event. He ordered Pvt. Anderson, who was the strongest recruit, to carry the pilot over his shoulder.

Then, they assessed the recruit "shot" injury and applied first aid to him. H.D. told Pvt. Rodriguez and Pvt. Dillman to use a two-man carry for the recruit "shot". They trekked through the woods down a narrow path. Pvt. Williams was ordered to lead the team, guard for enemy attack, and search for hidden IEDs. The team made it to the helicopter in time; but they had to go back, swap who was injured for who was going to carry them, and complete the station over again.

The second station was the Enhanced Obstacle Course. The team had to carry a ninety-pound dummy casualty from one end of the course to the other, going over all obstacles. They also had to carry ammunition cans through the course. The next station was the Marine Corps Martial Arts Program (MCMAP) Strikes Station. At this station, the team had to complete five-minute MCMAP strikes against an opponent.

The constant climbing, crawling, and carrying of the day in the heat brought leg and stomach cramping for many recruits. Drinking plenty of water was extremely important and helped fill their empty stomachs. The stories they heard of the brave Marines that came before them kept fueling them to push through till the end.

The last station for the evening was the Core Values Station. The recruits all gathered together inside a hut. Sgt. Shepard discussed the Marine Corps value of commitment, "Commitment is the spirit of determination and dedication within members of a force of arms that leads to professionalism and mastery of the art of war. It promotes the highest order of discipline for unit and self and is the ingredient that instills dedication to Corps and country twenty-four hours a day, pride, concern for others, and an unrelenting determination to achieve a standard of excellence in every endeavor. Commitment is the value that establishes the Marine as the warrior and citizen others strive to emulate."

After reading, Sgt. Shepard asked the platoon, "What lessons did you learn today about commitment?"

"Our team argued over how to get the barrel over the wall. We all had ideas but couldn't agree. We wasted more time than we needed to. As the leader, I finally had to choose an idea and stick with it until we accomplished our goal. We finally came together as a team, started acting more professional, and valuing each other's opinions," stated Pvt. Mills.

"I'm glad your team learned that. In combat, you will have to move quickly and listen to each other. If you don't, you won't make it out alive," stated Sgt. Shepard.

"During Noonan's Casualty Evacuation, our team learned that we must be committed to bringing everyone injured to safety. We came up with a plan and worked together to rescue all the Marines who needed rescuing. We had to work fast to keep anyone else from getting "shot"," added H.D.

"Good point, Pvt. Hogan. Always remember the story of LCpl. Corbin, recruits. He exemplified courage and commitment. Corbin risked getting hit over and over until he rescued every wounded and dead Marine from enemy hands. Marines leave no man behind," stated Shepard with pride shown on his face.

"SEMPER FIDELIS!" the whole platoon shouted in unison.

Sgt. Shepard smiled at the recruits. That was the first time H.D. saw him actually smile. It made him look at the drill instructor differently. He wasn't the enemy. He was a man and fellow Marine- a guy just doing his job trying to turn spoiled, snotty-nosed kids into Marines.

Semper Fidelis means always faithful. Marines are bonded together like no other branch in the military. It is truly a brotherhood. They will stick their neck out for another Marine whether they know them or not. H.D. was glad he chose to be a Marine.

When the lecture and discussion were finished, they stood outside the hut and watched the sun set over the mountains. H.D. marveled at the beautiful colors of red, pink, and purple in the sky reflecting off the puffy, white clouds. The view brought a sense of calm to H.D. He felt proud he had made it this far and of his team for working so hard together.

The last event of the day was the Night Event. During this event, the platoon had to complete a five-mile hike in the dark within the limit of three hours. He felt confident he would make it through this last event. Five miles wasn't too bad after all they had done that day.

One recruit was chosen as the leader of the march. He set a fast pace for the others. The rest had to try to keep up with him. The recruit took off jogging as the sun set beyond the horizon. For the first mile, many of the recruits kept up close behind him; but, as darkness and fatigue set in, they slowly began trailing behind.

H.D. was beginning to tire and fell back a few yards with several other recruits behind him. He was sore and hungry. His Kevlar vest began rubbing on his shoulders and his feet began to ache. He couldn't see very well and was tripping over branches.

The leader kept going, inching farther and farther ahead of him. H.D. came upon a ditch made from the downpour a few days ago and had to jump across it. It was difficult to see the other side of the ditch, so he just estimated the distance and sprang over.

When he jumped, he hit the ground wrong, felt his right knee blow out, and tumbled to the ground. It was the same knee he had injured in a rodeo this past year. He lay on the ground for a few minutes, rubbing his knee hoping it would feel better, but it didn't.

Pushing through the pain, he got up onto his feet and kept walking down the dirt path. He was falling farther and farther behind the rest of the platoon. Sgt. Shepard, who was marching in the middle of the pack, turned around and saw H.D. trailing behind. He jogged back to him and shouted, "Pvt. Hogan, are you injured?"

"Yes, sir. This recruit hurt his knee jumping over the ditch," he replied, truthfully.

"You need to go back to the medic tent and have them examine you," Shepard told him. He yelled at the platoon to stop and ordered Pvt. Williams to escort H.D. to the medic tent- a mile and a half the other direction. When he arrived at the medic tent, he told the medic who he was and what happened. The medic inspected his knee and said, "It looks pretty bad, H.D. You may have a torn ligament." Pvt. Williams heard what the medic said, thought H.D. was done for the day, and turned back to catch up with the platoon. He reported to the sergeants what the medic said.

Meanwhile, at the medic tent, H.D. asked, "Can you wrap it, so I can go back and join my platoon?"

"No, you can't go back with that injury. You're done!" asserted the medic, shaking his head.

"No! I can't be done. I worked too hard to get this far!" H.D. protested. "Put some ice on it. I'll rest for a little while and go back."

"I could do that, but I wouldn't recommend it, H.D.," stated the medic.

"I hear what you're saying, but I'm telling you I can handle it. Put some ice on it. I'll be okay!" insisted H.D.

The medic did what H.D. asked, made him sign a release form stating he refused medical attention, and gave him a pack of ice to put on his knee. H.D. rested it for fifteen minutes, got up, and left the tent. He put on his night vision goggles, walked back down the dirt path in the dark, hobbling the entire five miles.

The walk was lonely and quiet. He heard "Owooooah!" and recognized the howl of a coyote. The sound didn't bother him, because he was used to hearing it often when he hunted back home. The only other sound he could hear was his own panting.

He was sweating heavily in his uniform and stopped to take a drink of water from his canteen. As he did, he heard a rustle in the woods and saw a huge gray and red coyote that must have weighed close to forty pounds standing ten feet from him. The coyote saw H.D., stared at him with his blazing yellow eyes, and let out a deep and loud, "Grrrrr!"

H.D. froze. He knew he couldn't outrun the perturbed animal. Luckily, the coyote didn't perceive H.D. as a threat, turned, and walked deeper into the forest. Breathing a sigh of relief, H.D. continued hobbling down the dirt path. It was just after midnight when he approached the tents where the platoon was set up for the night. He took off his goggles and zipped them back up in his rucksack. The recruit on fire watch heard him coming and yelled, "Stop! Identify yourself!"

"I'm Private Hogan returning from the medic tent," explained H.D., stopping in his tracks.

"Come ahead, Pvt. Hogan," responded the recruit, waving him forward.

MSgt. Neville heard H.D.'s voice from inside his tent and came out to see what he was doing. He shouted, "Hogan, what the hell are you doing here?"

"I'm finishing the Crucible, sir!" H.D. yelled back. The rest of the platoon stopped what they were doing and peeked out of their tents out of curiosity. Neville started to say, "Pvt. Hogan, you...," but stopped when he saw the determination in H.D.'s eyes and added instead, "get into your tent and get some rest." He pointed to the second tent to the right for him.

"Thank you, sir," stated H.D., relieved he didn't have to put up any more of a fight to stay. He wasn't sure how much more energy he had left to give. He sat down, ate his first MRE of the day, took off his muddy outerwear, got into his sleeping bag, and dozed off. His tent mates told him they were glad he was back.

It felt like he had just closed his eyes when he heard "Reveille" being played on a bugle at four o'clock in the morning. He wasn't sure how, but he mustered his strength, put on a new uniform and pair of socks, and packed up for the next day of the Crucible. The pain in his knee was increasing by the minute. He tried to underplay how much it hurt and didn't ask for any pain reliever, because he knew they would make him go back to base for treatment if he did.

The day began with event four, the Battle of Fallujah. MSgt. Neville told the platoon the story of the battle, "On March 31, 2004, Iraqi insurgents ambushed a convoy of four American private military contractors in Fallujah, Iraq and hung them from a bridge. Leathernecks from the 1st Battalion, 5th Marine Regiment and 2nd Bn., 1st Marines blockaded the road to the city and hit the industrial center. They were met with harsh resistance from the insurgents. The battle lasted for months and would go down as one of the Marine's greatest urban battles since the 1968 Battle of Hue City."

The recruits tackled a bayonet assault course and headed to the first station of the day- Perez's Passage. One of the recruits read the citation of Perez to the platoon: "Joseph B. Perez received the Navy Cross for his extraordinary heroism as a rifleman. In Operation Iraqi Freedom on April 4th, 2003, while advancing into Baghdad, his platoon came under intense enemy fire. As the point man and most exposed member, he came under the majority of the fires. Without hesitation, he fired accurate shots for his squad, threw a grenade into a trench occupied by the enemy, and led a charge down the trench. He also fired an AT-4 rocket into an enemy machine gun bunker, completely destroying it. By his outstanding display of leadership and courage, Lance Corporal Perez upheld the highest traditions of the Marine Corps and the United States Naval Service."

After reading the citation, MSgt. Neville divided the platoon into different teams and a leader was chosen for H.D.'s team for the first station. H.D. managed through the assault course by putting most of his weight on his left leg. He hobbled along from spot to spot. When he got to Perez's Passage, the team had to swing on ropes from "safe spot" to "safe spot" over a "contaminated area". He grabbed the rope and swung hard over the area, landed on his good leg first, and wobbled a little as he put down his injured leg. He made it through that one!

The next station was called Kraft's Struggle. The team had to climb a ten-foot wall and climb down the other side using a knotted rope. The leader let one recruit go first and had another recruit help boost H.D. up as far as he could as the first recruit grabbed his arm and pulled him up to the top of the wall. Once H.D. was on top, the first recruit descended down the wall and he followed.

After that station was completed, the team moved on to the John Quick Trail (also known as IED lane). Another recruit read the citation for the Medal of Honor recipient. He told about Sgt. Major John H. Quick's gallantry as a sergeant during the Spanish-American war. He also earned the Distinguished Service Cross and Navy Cross during World War I.

Sgt. Wyler instructed the team on how to identify key components of an IED; such as the trip wire, pressure plate, and command detonation. The team split into pairs of two holding maps and began to patrol along the lane, keeping an eye out for IEDs. Throughout the half-mile course, IEDs were placed to test the recruits on proper procedures when they found one.

As H.D. and Pvt. Mills were patrolling halfway down the lane, one of the IEDs detonated, sending powder over the impact area. They were both shocked when they found themselves covered in white powder. Sgt. Wyler identified the two as casualties and the rest of the team had to evacuate them. When they were done, Sgt. Wyler went over the simulation and explained how the recruits should have reacted and repeated the procedures for encountering an IED.

The team went back to patrolling the lane and were evaluated on their basic map reading and grid coordinate plotting. H.D. continued hobbling along, standing on his left leg whenever he had the chance to rest. After they finished the John Quick Trail, the teams gathered in the drill instructor hut as Sgt. Wyler gave a lesson on the Marine Corps value of Honor.

He stated, "This is the bedrock of our character. It is the quality that empowers Marines to exemplify the ultimate in ethical and moral behavior: to never lie, cheat, or steal; to abide by an uncompromising code of integrity; to respect human dignity; and to have respect and concern for each other. It represents the maturity, dedication, trust, and dependability that commit Marines to act responsibly, be accountable for their actions, fulfill their obligations, and hold others accountable for their actions."

Sgt. Wyler asked the platoon, "What lessons on honor did you learn today?"

"When the IED went off, I was angry. Before, I would have blown a fuse and blamed the other recruit for setting it off. Today, I accepted my part of the mistake as a team and we went on," confessed Pvt. Mills.

The platoon all nodded their heads in agreement. As they were completing the Crucible, they noticed their behavior was changing. Despite being hungry and tired; for most of them, their thought processes were maturing. They were trying to be better team players and much like a caterpillar were completing their own metamorphosis into a refined version of themselves.

While H.D. knew he wasn't perfect, he believed he upheld the values of commitment and honor. He tried to do his best at all times and looked after his friends. He made a promise to himself then and there to exemplify Marine Corps values to the best of his ability from then on.

The next and fifth event of the Crucible was the Battle of Mariana Islands. MSgt. Neville led the instruction of this event. He told the men the story of the Battle of Mariana Islands. The battle took place on the Mariana and Palau Islands in the Pacific Ocean during World War II. The U.S. Marines, Army, and Navy fought the Japanese and set up an airfield for the United States to use B-29s for strategic attacks on the enemy.

The first station of the event was the Combat Endurance Course. The teams had two hours to complete five events of the modified Confidence Course. By this time, H.D.'s right knee was throbbing. He kept drinking water to help hydrate himself and keep the swelling down, but because he couldn't elevate his leg at any point during the day, the knee began to expand. His team helped him as much as they could through the course.

When everyone finished, they moved onto the Skyscraper. The team had to recover a "wounded" dummy from the top of an eighteen-foot tower. H.D. was told to stay on the bottom and help grab the dummy as it was lowered to the ground by three of his teammates. Then, they had to move onto the next station- the

Stairway to Heaven. After completing this obstacle before, H.D. knew what to expect. He volunteered as the leader which helped him rest his leg for a while as he instructed his team on how to move two ammunition cans over the top of the thirty-six-foot ladder.

The next warrior station they tackled was the Two-Line Bridge. The team had to carry ammunition cans and water resupply cans across two fifty-foot-long ropes with their hands and feet suspended on the ropes two feet and ten feet off the ground. H.D. prayed he didn't fall. He couldn't risk more injury to his leg or he would be out for good. He used his upper body strength and balanced on his good leg to help move the ammunition cans and water.

When he was done, he stopped to drink more water and checked his leg. He rolled up his trouser and inspected his knee. It looked deformed. The knee was red and swollen to almost twice its normal size. The pain was tremendous! He wished he could take something to help with the pain, but he couldn't. He rolled his trouser back down quickly before anyone could see it, and the team moved on to the next obstacle course. This one about killed H.D. because of its difficulty.

The Weaver is shaped like an upside-down V. The recruits were required to climb over and under the logs to go through the obstacle. There were twenty-four logs, forty-two feet in length ascending to fourteen feet. As if the weaving wasn't difficult enough, they had to carry the ammunition cans and water resupply cans with them.

H.D. climbed up on top of the first log and lay on his stomach, grabbed the next log with his right hand, turned sideways, and moved his left leg to wrap it under the second log, followed with his right leg, leaving him hanging from the bottom. Then, he had to reach up with his left arm to grab the next log, raise himself up, and wrap his right leg over the top of the log, following with the left leg. He repeated this eleven more times!

It took tremendous core strength for H.D. and his team to finish the Weaver. His team was very patient and helped H.D. as much as they could to pass the equipment, but he had to climb across on his own. The only time he could rest a moment was when he was passing the ammunition cans and water to the next recruit.

The strain of hanging on his injured leg was excruciatingly painful. He felt if he stopped moving, he wouldn't be able to keep going. He prayed, *Lord, just give me the strength to finish the Crucible. That's all I ask.* He thought of earning his eagle, globe, and anchor emblem and how proud he would be showing it to his dad. That was enough to push through his pain and keep going on.

Event six was called the Battle of Khe Sanh. Sgt. Shepard told the platoon the story of that battle: "On January 21, 1968, forces from the People's Army of North Vietnam (PAVN) fired massive artillery on the U.S. Marine garrison at Khe Sanh. The Marines with the help of South Vietnamese allies fought off the communist army. While attention was focused on Khe Sanh, the PAVN and Viet Cong forces launched the Tet Offensive- a series of coordinated attacks throughout South Vietnam."

Sgt. Shepard instructed the platoon how to complete the Battle of Khe Sanh station. In teams of four, they were to position themselves on simulated building structures and fire at unknown distance targets in a time limit of seventy seconds. They had two magazines of five rounds to use. The amount of unused ammunition and targets hit was recorded. Afterward, recruits ran into firing positions and engaged with pop-up targets using ten rounds in two magazines.

Because shooting was H.D.'s strength, he was able to complete the course successfully. He had a few minutes until the last event of the evening started, so he sat down on a tree stump and propped his right leg up on another stump to rest his knee. He pulled out another MRE to eat while the rest of the team was completing the firing range and stopped to eat as well.

The sun set over the mountains as he was finishing his beef ravioli meal. The freeze-dried food didn't have much taste, but it helped fill his empty belly. He got up to walk again and could barely put any weight at all on his leg. When he did, there was a squishy feeling on his kneecap followed by shooting pain. He forced himself to walk, ignoring the pain. His teammates had finished their meals and the group joined together to prepare for the last event of the day- the Night Event.

This three-hour event was a simulated combat obstacle course at night. The teams had to resupply ammunition, water cans, and MREs. The platoon was instructed how to complete the event, then the teams split up. H.D.'s team charged together with one man on point to watch for IEDs, grenades, and enemy fire.

They crawled under the barbed wire, using their rifles to hold it up like they practiced before. Pvt. Barnes and Pvt. Reynolds were on H.D.'s team today. They both crawled ahead of H.D., held up the wire for him on both sides, forming a tunnel for him to crawl through. H.D. was thankful they were there to help. Crawling through the slippery mud wasn't easy holding his rifle and using only one leg to push himself under the wire.

"Thanks Jim and Mark!" H.D. told them as he was crawling between them.

"Anytime," replied Reynolds.

"You helped me, H.D., when I needed it. Now, it's my turn to help you. Marines leave no man behind, remember," Pvt. Barnes told him.

"You have no idea how much that means to me, especially right now!" H.D. told them.

The three made it through the barbed wire together and got up. Pvt. Barnes took hold of one of H.D.'s arms under his armpit and Pvt. Reynolds grabbed the other side. They lifted him up and ran with him through the field, following the other three men on the team.

Boom! went the sound of IEDs exploding around them. *Rat-a-tat-tat!* went the machine gun fire blaring on the loudspeaker. *Pew-pew-pew-pew!* went the tracers being shot over their heads in the sky, resembling fireworks with their pink and red colors. The team shouted battle cries as they went charging. The cries could be heard in the darkness all across the field.

For the last part of the night event, the teams had to reach a designated point on the map four miles down the dirt path avoiding explosives and capture. The drill instructors gave them a ten-minute head start and began hunting them down. H.D.'s team got a jump start and headed down the trail. One recruit was put in the lead and one was put on the end to watch out for the drill instructors.

The moon peeked in and out of the clouds, lighting the way for them part of the time. When they got half a mile down the trail, they decided to split up in groups of two to avoid getting caught. Pvt. Reynolds and Pvt. Hogan were paired together. Pvt. Reynolds took hold of one of H.D.'s arms and helped him hop down the path on one leg. It was slow going for the two of them. When the moon hid behind the clouds, it was pitch dark. They decided to rest behind a tree a few feet into the forest until the moon came back out.

"You rest your eyes, H.D., for a few minutes. You need it. I'll keep watch," suggested Reynolds.

"Okay, that sounds good. I'm beat!" admitted H.D.

He sat down and leaned against the tree and dozed off. While he was sleeping, he had a dream. In his dream, MSgt. Neville was coming after him. But instead of looking like himself, his skin was bright red. He had sharp teeth and horns protruding from the top of his forehead. He was wearing his camouflage uniform and holding two chains in both hands.

On the end of one chain was a Rottweiler with a spiked collar on. The dog was black with brown patches on his face, chest, and legs. He had razor sharp teeth and was foaming at the mouth. H.D. saw his brown eyes. They didn't look like a dog's eyes, but more like a person's. H.D. swore he knew those eyes.

On the end of the other chain was a German Shepherd wearing a spiked collar. It was completely black with gray fur on its legs. The Shepherd also had razor sharp teeth and was foaming at the mouth. Its gray eyes stared at H.D. He recognized something about them, also. Then, it hit him like a lightning bolt! *Wyler and Shepard!* The devil with his two devil dogs were coming for him out of the darkness down the dirt path. They had a fiery glow about them illuminating the woods. As they were getting closer, H.D.'s heart was racing, and he was startled awake. He heard Pvt. Reynolds say, "H.D., H.D., are you okay?"

"What? Are they here?" asked H.D. rousing from his nightmare.

"You were mumbling in your sleep. Is who here?" asked Reynolds, patting H.D. on the shoulder.

"The devil and his dogs!" said H.D. The dream seemed so real, he couldn't quite shake it off.

"You must've been dreaming. No one is here," answered Reynolds. He looked down the dirt path, straining to see in the darkness. "I don't see any sign of the drill sergeants, but we need to go. They will be coming soon!" He reached under H.D.'s arm and helped him up. The two men continued hobbling down the trail. It was a long trek to where they needed to be.

They looked for their teammates but couldn't see them in the dark or hear them. When they got close to the point they were supposed to meet, a Humvee crossed the path in front of them. It looked like a road intersection was just ahead of them. But, when Reynolds blinked his eyes, the road and vehicle were gone. "Did you see that?" asked Reynolds.

"The Humvee crossing in front of us?" questioned H.D.

"Yeah, I saw that, too!" replied Reynolds.

The two stood shaking their heads. There was no way they both saw the same mirage at the same time.

"We must be hallucinating," said Reynolds. He looked at H.D. and said, "How are you feeling?"

"Not good!" moaned H.D., feeling like he was going to collapse at any minute. Food deprivation and dehydration were hitting them both like a sledgehammer. Reynolds felt H.D.'s forehead with the back of his hand. It was hot with no sweat. *That can't be good!* Reynolds thought to himself. "I think you may have a fever, H.D.," he told his friend. "Let's stop and get a drink of water. You need to hydrate," he suggested.

The two stopped and pulled out one of their canteens of water to drink. After taking a drink, Reynolds took a bandana and poured the rest of his water on it and said, "Let's put this around your forehead, maybe it'll help cool you down,"

"Okay," whispered H.D. weakly.

Reynolds wrapped the bandana around H.D.'s forehead. When he turned, the moon peeped from behind the clouds giving just enough light he could see shadows coming behind them on the dirt path.

"They're coming, H.D.," warned Pvt. Reynolds. He grabbed H.D. by the arm, lifted him up onto his shoulders, and started jogging down the path carrying him. They were getting close to their destination, and Pvt. Reynolds was determined they weren't going to get caught. He kept jogging forward. The shadows were coming closer and closer.

Just when he thought he couldn't carry H.D. any farther, the leaves beside them rustled and out of the bushes came Pvt. Barnes. The only thing you could see clearly was his pearly-white teeth smiling in the moonlight. Barnes grabbed H.D. from Reynolds and the two ran down the path at full speed. H.D. was amazed at Barnes' infinite strength. He didn't know how he could have that much left after two days of exhausting obstacle courses. The three made it to the end of the course just in time.

Most of the platoon was standing there waiting. A few of the men were missing. H.D. figured they probably got caught by Neville and his cohorts. Moments later, MSgt. Neville, Sgt. Wyler, and Sgt. Shepard emerged from the shadows with eight recruits who got captured. They were very surprised H.D. didn't end up being one of them. The three even made a bet on how long it would take to catch him. None of them won.

The platoon returned to their tents, cleaned their rifles, drank more water, and took off their muddy uniforms. Gently sliding off their boots, they inspected their feet. Blisters were visible on almost everyone's toes and soles. Some were oozing and pussy. H.D.

didn't even realize he had blisters. All he could feel was the intense pain in his knee. *Just one more day! Let me make it just one more day!* he pleaded as he crawled into his sleeping bag to get some rest.

16 DON'T FEAR THE REAPER

It was three o'clock in the morning when H.D. heard the sound of "Reveille". At first, the music was faint and seemed far off in the distance. He had heard it played so often, he felt as if he was dreaming it. As his mind slowly woke from the fog and the tune played louder, H.D. knew he wasn't dreaming. It was time to get up. Every muscle in his body ached. He wished he had more time to rest.

When his tent mate, Pvt. Reynolds, saw him lying still in the sleeping bag, he came over to check on him. "H.D., it's the last day of the Crucible. You've got to get up. You made it this far," he encouraged H.D. as he patted him gently on the shoulder. "Come on, buddy, we can do this!"

"I know. I just wasn't sure what I could move that wouldn't hurt," mumbled H.D. He unzipped his sleeping bag, slowly rolled over onto his left side, and got onto his left knee. Pvt. Reynolds reached out, grabbed his arm, and helped him stand up on both legs. H.D. winced in pain as he put his right foot down, but somehow managed to stand up. The two put on new skivvies, socks, and uniforms; and they grabbed their equipment to start the last part of the Crucible.

With the full moon helping to light the way, H.D.'s platoon joined with other companies until the entire 1st Battalion was formed together and began the nine-mile hike up the 700-foot-tall mountain known as the Grim Reaper to the Marines. From the sky, the marching men looked like a massive trail of ants following each other up the hill.

They started off in short strides. The entire battalion of recruits and drill instructors were hungry and drained from two full days of training and lack of sleep. They each carried two canteens of water. The DIs recommended they drink at least twelve canteens during the hike to prevent dehydration. Following the group, a supply vehicle carried more water and first aid equipment for the recruits.

The mountain trail headed up a small hill first, then gradually got steeper. All they could see was dirt, rock, and sagebrush along the sides. They hiked a third of the way and stopped to refill their canteens, adjust their gear, and change their socks. Several of the men had holes in their socks from the constant rubbing of their feet inside their boots. After two days with no showers, they were a stinking, slimy crew. It was a wonder they could stand being so close together with the rank smell of body odor in the air.

As H.D. was taking a drink from his canteen, he saw a Polaris all-terrain vehicle (ATV) come up the trail. Everyone stopped what they were doing and watched the driver and passenger approach the battalion. MSgt. Neville stepped out from the crowd, greeted the Marine guard, and saluted the Navy chaplain. The chaplain asked, "Where is H.D. Hogan?"

"He's over there with his platoon," answered Neville pointing his finger to the left with raised eyebrows.

"If it's alright with you, I'd like to join your platoon on the rest of the hike," stated the chaplain- not as a question, but as a statement.

"Yes, sir, you're welcome to join us," replied MSgt. Neville. The Marine guard made a U-turn in the ATV and headed back to the Marine base. The chaplain with his own rucksack on his back walked over to Neville's platoon. When he approached the group in the dim light, he asked, "Which one of you is H.D. Hogan?"

"This recruit is, sir!" stated H.D. trying to stand up. He

recognized the man as soon as he came close enough to see him. He could see the lieutenant's silver bar on his camouflage uniform and realized he was Father Griffin. The chaplain came to their barracks every Sunday to offer spiritual advice to the young men. Not many took him up on the offer, but H.D. did every time he came. His father raised him in the Catholic church; therefore, a strong faith was important to him.

Father Griffin and H.D. had some very deep and interesting conversations. The chaplain was often surprised at H.D.'s honesty and perceptiveness for his age. They spent part of their time telling jokes to each other. H.D. was astonished to see him standing in front of him at this moment. That never happens on the Crucible.

"No need to stand up. Sit and take a drink," stated Father Griffin, motioning for H.D. to stay down. "One of the medics assigned here came back to the base and was talking about you and your injury in the chow hall. I overheard him and asked him how you were doing. He said he didn't know, so I came to see for myself," he explained. "How are you, H.D.?"

"My knee is really sore, but I'm going to make it, Father Griffin," H.D. answered modestly.

"Here, maybe this will help you," replied the chaplain, knowing full well that the young man was in a great deal of pain. He reached inside his shirt pocket, pulled out two aspirin, and handed them to him. H.D. took the aspirin, popped them into his mouth, and swallowed them down with water from his canteen.

"Thank you, sir!"

"You're welcome. Now that I'm here, I plan to see that you get to the top of this darn mountain. That okay with you, H.D.?"

"Yes, sir, I'd like that," he grinned. He loved how down-to-earth the lieutenant was. Father Griffin made him feel valued and was very easy to talk to. He always felt better after their talks no matter how bad the day had been and was glad he was there to support him today.

After the ten-minute break, the battalion was ordered to line up and continue the hike. Father Griffin helped H.D. stand up and marched beside him the entire way. There was something about his presence that lifted H.D.'s spirits. He began to regain his strength and confidence. The whole platoon began feeling it, too. They knew it wouldn't be long before all their blood, sweat, and tears would pay off.

The hill increased to a sixty-degree incline. The platoon struggled slowly up it and was relieved when it leveled off. As they were marching along, they began to chant:

"Way back when at the dawn of time.
In the heart of Death Valley where the sun don't shine.
The roughest toughest fighter ever known was made.
From an M16 and a live grenade.
He was a lean mean green fighting machine.
He proudly bore the title of US Marine!"

The cadence gave them the fighting Marine spirit and they picked up their stride as they continued on the hike. The sun came up behind the clouds to the east, giving them light to see. When they reached the point just before the last steep hill, they stopped again for their final ten-minute break.

H.D. took off his boots with the help of Father Griffin, changed into his last pair of clean socks, and put his boots back on. Then, he drank some more water. Pvt. Reynolds sat on the other side of him and pulled out his last MRE. He gave half to H.D., hoping it would be enough to give his friend the strength he would need to finish the worst part of the hike. H.D. thanked him for it and ate it quickly. It did help to fill his empty stomach.

The battalion was ordered once again to resume formation after the ten minutes were up. H.D. and Father Griffin got up together and continued marching up the mountain. When they reached the last hill, there was no doubt how the mountain got its nickname. It was so steep, H.D. could reach out and touch the sand in front of his face. He took about twenty steps and started to stop. "Keep going! Come on, H.D., we've got this!" yelled Father Griffin, who was struggling himself with the climb.

H.D. knew he had to keep up his momentum or he wouldn't make it. He dug his boots into the sand, took one more step, and another and another- half standing, half crawling up the mountain. He stared at the sand in front of him, looking at the other countless imprints of boots that came before him. The sand was so deep from the impressions, it made it hard to get a foothold.

H.D. kept digging in, taking one step at a time until he finally reached the top. He didn't know how he did it, but he did. He was the last to make it to the peak. After he stood up straight, he hobbled over to join his fellow recruits and complete the platoon.

As they were resting and inhaling deep breaths of fresh air, the sun broke through a hole in the clouds with a stream of golden rays shining down on the mountain. H.D. gazed to his left and could see the Pacific Ocean. It was truly a magnificent sight. Straight ahead and to the right side far down below was a plush, green valley with more mountains behind.

The whole battalion stood quietly taking in the view. The sight sparked a passion inside them. Pride shone on their faces as they realized what was just accomplished. An intense emotion began welling up within their core- a new feeling deep inside that was undefinable. Only a Marine who climbed that mountain would understand it.

"Company, Atten-hut!" yelled out MSgt. Neville. The men stood at attention. Each platoon leader called out their presence, holding their red platoon flag with their number printed in gold. The American flag was placed in the ground and recruits passed up state flags to stand in the ground beside it. H.D. smiled when he saw the Indiana flag proudly dancing in the breeze. The battalion saluted the flags as the "Star-Spangled Banner" was played on a bugle. Tears were welling up in the men's eyes.

When the song was done, MSgt. Neville stepped forward to read the citation displayed on the peak of the mountain. It belonged to Col. Merritt A. Edson after whom the Edson Range was named. "During the battle of Guadalcanal, Edson's Raider Battalion, consisting of two companies from the 1st Parachute Battalion, was guarding an airfield when they were attacked by Japanese forces. Under Edson's leadership where he was encouraging, cajoling, and correcting as he continually exposed himself to enemy fire, his 800 Marines withstood the repeated assaults of more than 2,500 Japanese soldiers. Edson was later awarded the Medal of Honor for his honor, courage, and commitment."

MSgt. Neville continued speaking to the recruits, "During the past two days, many of you had to rely on your fellow recruits to get you through the Crucible. Today, you are now a member of the finest fighting force in the world. When you look down on your left breast pocket and see that emblem, you get to wear it with pride. You have earned this. You have done something here few could ever achieve. You are a Marine!"

Weeping could be heard from amongst the men; the feeling deep inside was now pouring out of them. After eleven grueling weeks in boot camp, they would no longer be called "recruit". They would be called by their name. Now, they can call their superiors by their rank and name instead of "sir".

The drill instructors went down the row of Marines, handing them their eagle, globe, and anchor emblem. Sgt. Shepard came up to H.D. and said, "Pvt. Hogan, I was hard on you, because I knew you had more to give than what we saw. You have proven in the last two days that I was right. You have exemplified each of our values of honor, courage, and commitment. I would want you fighting beside me in battle any day. I am honored to give you this emblem and to say you are a Marine."

He placed the emblem in H.D.'s left hand as he shook his right hand firmly. H.D. felt a tear trickle from his right eye. He couldn't be more proud and happier than at that moment. "Thank you, Sgt. Shepard," he replied, smiling.

The drill instructors finished passing out the emblems to everyone in their platoon. When they were done, the whole battalion began singing "The Marines' Hymn":

*"From the Halls of Montezuma
To the shores of Tripoli;
We fight our country's battles
In the air, on land, and sea;
First to fight for right and freedom
And to keep our honor clean;
We are proud to claim the title
Of United States Marine.*

*Our flag's unfurled to every breeze
From dawn to setting sun;
We have fought in every clime and place
Where we could take a gun
In the snow of far-off northern lands
And in sunny tropic scenes,
You will find us always on the job-
The United States Marines.*

*Here's health to you and to our Corps
Which we are proud to serve;
In many a strife we've fought for life
And never lost our nerve.
If the Army and the Navy
Ever look on Heaven's scenes,
They will find the streets are guarded
By UNITED STATES MARINES!"*

The words echoed into the valley and over the ocean waves. The men, overflowing with pure joy, hugged each other and yelled, "OORAH!" Father Griffin grabbed H.D. and gave him an enormous hug. He said, "I'm proud of you, son!" He sounded so much like his dad that H.D. was overcome with emotion and his legs began to give way.

Father Griffin grabbed him on one side and so did Pvt. Barnes who stood on his other side. The two held onto him until he could regain his composure and stand up again on his own. The battalion spent a few more minutes celebrating and enjoying the view before they were ordered to line up in formation to descend the mountain.

They had to hike the nine miles back to their tents, pack up, and return to the barracks. Father Griffin radioed for the Marine guard in the ATV to return for him at the same spot he dropped him off. The guard arrived just as the platoon was coming down the hill.

Father Griffin ordered H.D. to get in the back, so they could take him to the medical clinic on base and get his leg treated. H.D. didn't utter one word of protest. He was worn out and had accomplished what he set out to do that morning.

After arriving at the clinic, they took an x-ray and hooked him up to an IV to treat him for dehydration. The x-rays confirmed he had a torn anterior cruciate ligament (ACL) and a torn medial collateral ligament (MCL). The medical staff was amazed he walked on it for two and a half days. H.D. was told the injury was so severe, he would need surgery to correct it.

"Can I get a brace on it today, so I can join my platoon for a few hours. We just finished the Crucible," begged H.D. to the female doctor. With his big brown eyes and charming smile, he had a way of convincing anyone to do things they normally wouldn't do. Because of the circumstances, the doctor agreed to let him return for two hours on the condition he would come back to the clinic to get more IV fluids and rest. H.D. agreed to the terms.

The male nurse unhooked him from the IV and let him take a shower to remove the dirt and scum from his body. He put on his last fresh uniform from his rucksack; and the nurse placed a brace on his right knee and gave him a pair of crutches to use. An assistant transported him in a golf cart back to the barracks. H.D. knew the platoon would be at the chow hall and had the driver drop him off there.

When H.D. entered the chow hall using his crutches, his platoon, who had just sat down to eat, rose to greet him. The room thundered with clapping, whoops, and hollers. Even all three drill instructors stood up and cheered for him. Private Reynolds signaled for him to come sit by him for breakfast. The whole battalion was treated to the Warrior's Breakfast. It consisted of everything a starving Marine would want to eat: steak, eggs, waffles, pancakes, hash browns, bacon, sausage, biscuits and gravy, and even chocolate cake.

The ravenous pack devoured everything in sight. There was so much food and everything tasted fantastic! H.D. ate as much as he could, but his stomach told him he needed to stop. A couple of the men ate so much, they began puking in their trays. The battalion laughed and spoke freely for the first time in almost three months.

After breakfast, the recruits returned to the squad bay where they cleaned their rifles and washed their dirty clothes. Afterward, they had to clean the deck from all the sand that poured out of their boots and pockets. H.D. cleaned his rifle and went to the drill instructor's hut to turn it in. MSgt. Neville was sitting at his desk and reading the orders stating that H.D. would be at the medical clinic for an indefinite amount of time. Neville stood up and took the rifle from H.D., sat it down on the desk, and looked at him directly in the eyes.

"Pvt. Hogan, I hope your surgery goes well and you're able to return to duty," he said, looking like he actually meant it.

"Thank you, sir. I hope I can, too," H.D. replied as he left to return to the squad bay and gather up his things. It felt a little strange to once again be able to refer to himself in first person, instead of third person. Sgt. Wyler gave his personal belongings back to him that were taken away the first day of boot camp. He grabbed his duffle bag with clean clothes and shaving equipment to take back to the clinic with him. The assistant, who dropped him off in the golf cart, returned to pick him up when the two hours were up. After he returned to his room in the clinic, the nurse hooked him back up to the IV.

H.D. called his dad to tell him he injured his knee and was going to have surgery to repair it. He was extremely exhausted at that point and said, "Dad, I'm getting tired. I'll tell you all about it when you come see me."

"That's okay, Son. We'll have plenty of time to talk when I get there. Get some rest. I'll see you in a few days. Love you!"

"Love you, too!"

H.D. hung up the phone and was sound asleep in a matter of seconds. The Sandman didn't even have time to reach in his bag to sprinkle some sand on him. Steve had received the graduation packet H.D. mailed to him three weeks ago, so he had already planned on coming there to watch him graduate from boot camp.

The platoon packed up their equipment and rode in a bus back to MCRD for the last week of boot camp. After getting another day of fluids and rest, H.D. was taken back the following day to MCRD and assigned to a medical hold platoon (BMP). He wasn't sure if he could participate in the ceremony and requested permission the next day. Under restrictions from the doctor, he was allowed to participate in the practice for the ceremony and the graduation festivities but had to return to the BMP as soon as both were done. The surgery was scheduled the day after graduation.

Four days later, Thursday, was Family Day. Families of the graduates came to visit with their Marine at the Depot Theater the day before graduation. When they entered the theater, each Marine walked up to greet their family and escort them inside. H.D. saw his dad come through the door, leaned his crutches against the wall, limped up to him, and said, "Hi, Pap! I'm glad you came!"

"Wouldn't miss it for the world!" stated Steve, grinning.

H.D. took Steve's right arm with his left arm leaving his right hand free to salute a higher-ranking Marine. He escorted him into the theater where they took a seat together in the auditorium. Steve was surprised at how much his son had changed. He was no longer a kid; he was a well-mannered man who stood up straight and proud. It was amazing what three months in boot camp could do.

After the families were given information on rules and etiquette for the base and graduation services, they ate a buffet dinner together at the Bay View Restaurant. H.D. introduced his dad to his friends, Pvt. Reynolds and Pvt. Barnes, before they sat down to eat. He was so excited to spend time talking with his dad, he began spilling out all the details about the Crucible, including how he injured his knee. Steve listened and recollected his own experience of the Crucible with his son. It was a bond they now shared as Marines.

The next morning, Steve and the other family members went to the Shepherd Field Parade Deck for the graduation ceremony. The parade deck is a long asphalt pavement the size of a football field. It is a revered site because of its rich history of Marines who trained and graduated on it. Only uniformed personnel are allowed to walk on it. The families walked around the perimeter and sat in the bleachers by platoon number.

At precisely ten o'clock, the six platoons approached the deck with each leader carrying their platoon flag and stood at the far right. The Marines were dressed in their khaki dress blouse and tie, sky blue dress trousers, and white cap. They were an impressive sight. Steve watched the Marine band march up toward the bleachers and play a song.

Afterward, Father Griffin was introduced as he walked over to the microphone and said a prayer, "These fine Marines behind me have shown honor, courage, and commitment in their training here at MCRD. I have had the privilege of speaking to several of them personally and am proud of their accomplishments. They have earned the honor of being called a Marine. Lord, bless them in their future in the Marine Corps and life. We thank you for the drill instructors who have given up time from their families to train these young men. Lastly, Lord, bless each family member here today and provide them with a safe journey home. Amen!"

The audience clapped in appreciation for the chaplain, drill instructors, and Marines. A female announcer told about the history of the Marines and MCRD. Next, the band played as the platoons marched along the rear of the deck toward the center. When they stopped, the band played the National Anthem as everyone stood holding their right hand on their heart. Each Marine held his cap over his heart and placed his left hand behind his back.

When the song was done and the audience sat down, Father Griffin came back on the microphone and said, "Once a Marine, always a Marine. Anyone in the audience who is a Marine, please rise." Steve stood up with a handful of others in the bleachers. The audience clapped and whistled for them. After a few seconds, they sat back down.

For the final part, the band played "The Stars and Stripes Forever", the well-known marching tune composed by John Sousa, as the platoons marched along the rear of the parade deck in rows of two, down the left side, and passed in front of the audience as families clapped and called out the name of their beloved Marine. Once all the platoons were standing in front of the bleachers, they stopped and turned facing the audience simultaneously.

H.D., who was standing on the sidelines, joined his platoon on crutches. The audience clapped for him as he hobbled up and completed the platoon. Lastly, the colonel of the battalion introduced each drill instructor before the platoons marched off the deck to the beat of steel drums and thunder of applause.

The families met once again to eat lunch together at the Bay View Restaurant. H.D. proudly went up to his dad, shook his hand, and gave him his eagle, globe, and anchor pin. Then, H.D. handed him his Marine Corps ring. Steve nodded, pulled his own Marine Corps ring off his finger, and handed it to his son. They both grinned and hugged each other tight.

After they sat down to eat, Steve saw Father Griffin talking to a couple of the Marines, got back up, and walked up to him to introduce himself, "Hello, Father Griffin! I'm Steve Hogan, H.D.'s father. I heard what you did for my son. Thank you for being there for him when I couldn't."

"You're welcome, Steve. You have a remarkable boy. I really enjoyed getting to know him. You must be very proud," replied the chaplain, reaching out to shake Steve's hand.

"I am proud of him," replied Steve, clasping the chaplain's hand and giving it a firm shake.

"I'll go visit him after the surgery to keep an eye on him and make sure he didn't lose his sense of humor," chuckled Father Griffin.

"I'd appreciate that," said Steve, smiling.

He turned to rejoin his son for lunch. Afterward, most of the recruits left the base to fly back home with their families for their ten-day leave. H.D. returned to the BMP to prepare for his surgery the next day. Steve stayed two more days to be there for his son's surgery and recovery.

H.D. had his knee repaired and began physical therapy. The rest of his platoon received orders and went on with their Marine Corps training: the School of Infantry. Part of them would go to Camp Lejeune in Jacksonville, North Carolina and part moved to Camp Pendleton. H.D. spent the next year and a half with his medical hold platoon. It was a long and physically demanding recovery, but not without some benefits.

17 *FALLING HEAD OVER HEELS*

Steve flew back home and H.D. began his recovery. During this time, he was given plenty of protein to build muscle and increase his strength. He used the time to work on his upper body as well as his legs. Because he was working with weights every day, H.D. began to fill out and develop bulging biceps and pecs. After six months, he was looking pretty sharp. He had more privileges, including internet access, while he was there and posted a picture of himself on Facebook with the caption "Look, I'm a beast!"

His dad would come visit him when he could. H.D. made new friends and continued his recovery for a year and a half. He liked his gunnery sergeant, Joe Restivo, who was in charge of the platoon. Everyone called him "Gunny". Gunny would leave the base on the weekends and help his fiancé cater weddings.

Sometimes, he would ask the men in the platoon to go with him to boost their morale and get them off the base for a little while. One week, he asked two of the Marines at the BMP to help him with a wedding on October 16, 2010. Just before the wedding, one of the Marines was discharged from the Marine Corps for medical reasons, so he asked H.D. to take his place. "Gosh, I told Gunny I would go with him to help out with this wedding. Is there any way you can go take my place, H.D.?" he pleaded.

H.D. thought, *Oh, God! I really don't want to do that!* Instead, he replied, "Okay, fine. I'll do it for you." He let Gunny know he would be helping him instead of Colton. Gunny told him he'd get him at 9:00 a.m. on Saturday. H.D. and the other Marine, Savage, were picked up and drove to the wedding venue an hour and a half north of San Diego.

When they arrived, H.D. loved the sight of horses in the pastures. It had been so long since he had ridden one, he suddenly realized how much he missed riding and the rodeo. He felt a little homesick. The wedding was at the Brookside Equestrian Center in Walnut, California.

After parking, the three men helped the women unload the SUV. Gunny introduced the two young men to his fiancé who was about to grab a tray of food from the back of the vehicle. "Kristie, this is Hunter and Savage. Let them know what you need help with," said Gunny.

"Nice to meet you, ma'am," replied H.D. He thought, *Gunny is a lucky man!* She was a very pretty petite blonde wearing red lipstick.

"Nice to meet you, Hunter. I'm glad you came to help. Just start grabbing a tray of food and take it inside to the kitchen. My daughter is in there. She can tell you where to put it," instructed Kristie. H.D. grabbed a tray of vegetables and walked inside the center.

When he entered the kitchen, he stumbled a second and about dropped his tray. He quickly straightened up, balancing the tray with his hands and hoping no one saw him. *Wow!* he thought when he saw the attractive girl wearing a white long-sleeved blouse, black skirt, and black stilettos. She was petite, like her mom, standing five-foot-tall without heels. She had silky, black hair that fell just past her shoulders and striking honey-brown eyes with thick, black eyelashes. He hadn't seen anything that gorgeous, *ever*, except in movies. She introduced herself to him, "Hi, I'm Brittney." She reached out her hand. He grabbed it and shook it gently.

"Uhhh, I'm Hunter Hogan. My friends call me H.D.," he stammered, not sure why he felt so nervous. He wasn't normally this awkward around girls.

"I love your name, Hunter!" exclaimed Brittney as she smiled warmly at him.

H.D. laughed. He was blown away by her smile. He wasn't sure what to say and before he could think of something, he was interrupted by Savage.

"Quit lollygagging around, H.D., go get some more food!" barked Savage as he came in carrying a tray. H.D. walked back out to the SUV and thought about what he would say to Brittney. H.D. and Brittney were so busy carrying food into the kitchen and setting up, they didn't get a chance to talk for several minutes. Every time they passed by each other, they would steal glances and smile.

When Kristie and Gunny started to cook the food on the stove, there was no electricity. They had to stop what they were doing and get hold of the manager to get it turned on. While they were gone, Savage took a walk around the grounds. Finally, Brittney and H.D. were alone. They went outside and sat on the back of Gunny's tailgate to talk.

"So, what do you do for work besides helping out your mom?" asked H.D.

"I'm a wedding coordinator- just started a couple of months ago. I live in Los Angeles," replied Brittney and asked him, "Where are you from?"

"I'm from Indiana. I tore my ACL and MCL during the Crucible. That's how I ended up at the BMP with Gunny. He's a great guy," he told her.

"How awful! That had to hurt. Too bad you couldn't finish it," Brittney sympathized, frowning.

"Oh, no, I finished the Crucible," corrected H.D.

"You did? How on Earth did you do that!" she gasped, putting her right hand on her cheek.

"I just did," said H.D. nonchalantly, shrugging his shoulders.

Brittney didn't know very much about this Marine, but she was beginning to realize how exceptional he was. As he shared more of the story on how he injured his knee and the obstacles he had to still complete to finish the Crucible, she thought he was truly amazing. She wanted to learn more about him.

The owners got a generator going an hour before the wedding. Everyone scrambled to get the food cooked and carried outside to the serving table. Once the wedding guests were served, H.D. and Savage had more time to talk to Gunny, Kristie, and Brittney. Kristie noticed how polite he was and loved Hunter instantly. She confessed, "Oh, man! You are so sweet! I wish that I could give you to one of my girls. Brittney has a boyfriend, Chloe's too little, and my oldest is already married!"

"Thanks!" smiled H.D., blushing a little. He wasn't used to being gushed over like that. He looked at Brittney. Brittney smiled sweetly back at him. *He really is adorable!* she thought. She loved his southern accent. They talked for a little while and helped load the remainder of the food back into the SUV.

Shortly after they cleaned up, Gunny had to take him and Savage back to the base. Just before he went to get in the truck, Brittney said, "Hunter, I'd like to talk to you some more. Let me give you my phone number." They both pulled out their cell phones and exchanged numbers. "I'm on Facebook if you want to contact me that way, too" she suggested.

"I'm on Facebook, too. I'll call you when Gunny lets me have some free time," H.D. grinned mischievously.

"Yeah, yeah, I'm a slave driver. Get in the truck, H.D.!" commanded Gunny, laughing.

Kristie gave H.D. a big hug and thanked him for helping out. She squeezed his arms and exclaimed, "Boy, you really have some muscles there!" H.D. grinned at her and walked around the back of the truck to the passenger side. "Bye, Hunter," Brittney hollered to him.

"Bye, Brittney," he replied and smiled once more at her.

Brittney and H.D. connected on Facebook and called each other as often as they could. She told her mom how much she liked Hunter. Her mom understood why. Just before Halloween, Kristie and Gunny told Brittney, "You should invite Hunter and his friends to your sister's party." They were having a party to celebrate Tara's husband coming home from Afghanistan. Brittney texted H.D. and invited him and his friends.

Gunny picked up the Marines and took them to his house- just a few minutes from MCRD. H.D. and Brittney were so excited to get to see each other again. They immediately hit it off and were more relaxed around each other. They enjoyed sitting outside, eating the barbecued chicken and hamburgers, and talking.

Brittney liked meeting H.D.'s friends and H.D. had a chance to talk to Brittney's brother-in-law for a little while about what it was like in Afghanistan. He told him a little bit but didn't want to talk about it anymore. He was thankful to be back and wanted to enjoy the party. After the party, Gunny drove H.D. and his friends back to the base. H.D.'s friends told him they really liked Brittney and that she was "a keeper".

Brittney drove back to LA the next morning and went to her boyfriend's place. She told him she didn't want to see him anymore, knowing H.D. was the man she wanted to be with. Her boyfriend knew it was coming and wanted to see other girls himself, so they parted amicably. H.D. called her the very next evening. She told him she had broken it off with her boyfriend. So, he asked her, "Well, since you're single now, will you be *my* girlfriend?"

"Yes, I will!" she immediately replied. They talked for a few more minutes and he told her he would call her soon. The next week, he invited her to the Marine Corps Ball on November 10, 2010. The ball is an annual event honoring the birthday of the Marine Corps.

Since H.D. didn't have a car, Brittney drove to the base for the ball. When he saw her step out of the car in her little black dress, his mouth dropped. When she saw him, all decked out in his Marine dress blues, her heart skipped a beat. *Wow! Is he handsome!* she swooned.

He asked her if it would be okay to drive her to the ball and promised he was cleared to drive. She said it would be okay and he walked her around to the passenger side, opening the door for her. She got in. He closed the door and walked around to get in the driver's seat.

He drove her to the ball at the Manchester Grand Hyatt in downtown San Diego. After parking the car and opening the door for her, he escorted Brittney by holding her right arm into the resort. They walked through the lobby, down the hall, entered a large conference room, and sat at their designated platoon table with H.D.'s friends.

The first part of the evening was the formal celebration. Officers marched out in pairs down the middle of the aisle, parted, and stood at attention. The Marine Corps Band bugle players played "Taps" honoring Marines of the past who have passed on.

Afterward, the band began playing a more upbeat tune as Marines dressed in uniforms from past years to present came down the aisle. After that, "The Marines' Hymn" was played as six officers wheeled in a huge birthday cake honoring the 235th year of the Marine Corps. The colonel cut the first piece of the cake and it was rolled to the dessert area to be cut and served after the main course.

They ate dinner with their friends and enjoyed a piece of the birthday cake. Once speeches were done, awards were given out, everyone had finished eating, and the dishes were cleared away, the lights were lowered and a D.J. began playing dance music with disco balls illuminating the dance floor. H.D. and Brittney talked and danced all night long.

A variety of songs were played and some of the Marines showed off their dance moves. They line danced to the "Cha Cha Slide" by DJ Casper. H.D. surprised Brittney with how well he could dance. She assumed, being a country boy, he wouldn't know how to dance at all.

He taught her how to do the line dance for "Copperhead Road" by Steve Earle. Being from California, Brittney didn't know a lot of the country songs like H.D. did. She loved embracing the country music side of H.D. Their favorite songs for the night were "Mary Jane's Last Dance" by Tom Petty and "Can't You See" by The Marshall Tucker Band. They discovered they both liked classic rock music.

H.D. loved what a spitfire Brittney was. She was vivacious and would tell him exactly what she thought. She loved his sarcasm and sense of humor. He would make a comment out of nowhere that would make her laugh so hard she would have tears rolling from her eyes. Like magnet and steel, they were drawn together and could not deny the strong attraction they felt for each other by the end of the night.

Near the end of the evening, H.D. whispered in her ear, "Come on, let's go explore the hotel!"

"Okay!" she giggled and followed him out into the hallway. He grabbed her hand and they dashed down the empty corridor. H.D. spotted a door that led toward the back of the resort, glanced to see if anyone was watching, and they sneaked outside. Walking out onto the stone patio, they saw the sun setting over the ocean and the lights flicker on from the San Diego shoreline. A lighthouse cast a beam of light out onto the ocean waves as they gently rolled onto the sandy beach.

With a soft love song playing in the background from the ball, it was so beautiful and romantic. H.D. couldn't resist the moment and grabbed Brittney by the arms giving her a long, smoldering kiss. They stood kissing each other passionately for what seemed like an eternity, not wanting to let go. A waitress came out and said, "Excuse me, everyone is leaving and the doors will be closed in fifteen minutes." They both laughed out loud at being caught and walked back to the car, holding hands.

Once they left the resort, H.D. drove Brittney back to the base, walked around the car, and opened the door for her. She stepped out, and he escorted her to the driver's seat. He gave her one more kiss before she got into the car and drove away. She spent the night with her mom and Gunny, telling them all about her date. Neither were surprised the two hit it off so well.

For the next month, Brittney drove from LA to San Diego to spend time with H.D. every weekend. She didn't know anything about military life and thought he was going to be discharged because of his knee. H.D. was honest with her and told her he wasn't sure what was going to happen. Gunny encouraged H.D. to hang in there, get stronger, and he could possibly stay in. He knew that's what H.D. wanted to do.

"I'll follow you wherever you go, no matter what happens," Brittney told Hunter when they were talking about the future one day. Brittney decided to move to San Diego at the end of November, because she didn't want to have to drive back and forth every weekend and could spend more time with Hunter. She moved into her mom and Gunny's house for the time being.

Meanwhile, Steve had arrived to his house in Nebraska with Hank. The trip down memory lane helped fill up the long and boring twelve-hour drive. He was relieved to finally be home and exhausted from the long day. He went to bed and unpacked the horse trailer the next morning.

Later in the afternoon, H.D. called and told him he had met a girl he knew he loved. He explained that she was his gunnery sergeant's fiancé's daughter, how they met, and what happened at the Marine Corps Ball. Steve could tell by the way H.D. talked that this could be the one. He couldn't wait to meet the girl that captured his son's heart.

On December 12th, it was a beautiful eighty-degree day. There was a nice breeze, so H.D. and Brittney packed a picnic lunch and bought some cheese at the commissary. H.D. had a friend buy a bottle of wine for him, because he wasn't twenty-one yet and neither was she. They drove to the bay on base and found a picnic bench. While they were sitting across from each other eating their lunch, H.D. looked at Brittney and said, "I want to ask you something."

"Hunh?" mumbled Brittney, just putting a cracker with cheese in her mouth.

"Babe, you have to finish eating before I ask you," replied H.D., staring at her intently.

"Why?" asked Brittney between crunches.

"Because, it's really important! Just swallow your cheese!" persisted H.D.

"Okay," she replied, chewing some more and swallowing the rest of her food.

H.D. came around to her side of the picnic table and got down on one knee. "I don't have a ring, but today is so perfect and I love you so much. I want to know if you'll marry me?" he asked, peering deeply into her eyes. Brittney jumped up and yelled, "Yes, I'll marry you!" She squeezed him so tight around the neck, he started to choke. She laughed and let go. He stood up, hugged her, and kissed her tenderly. They were so excited and took a bunch of pictures to capture the moment forever.

After packing up their picnic lunch, they drove to Kristie and Gunny's house. Brittney ran inside, excited to share the good news. "Hunter asked me to marry him! We're engaged!" she burst out when she saw them in the living room. They stood up and gave them both a hug, excited for the two of them. They loved H.D. from the moment they met him. Kristie was impressed with his manners and how well he treated Brittney.

The next week, H.D. and his two friends, Scooter and Eto, went to the commissary with Brittney. They walked into the mall area to go shopping. H.D. told Brittney," Why don't you go look at some girl stuff with Eto while Scooter and I check out some guy stuff?"

"Okay," said Brittney, not sure why Eto would want to go with her to look at girl stuff. She was glad to have company, so she didn't question it. Scooter and H.D. took off in one direction while Brittney and Eto went to look at some clothes in another direction. H.D. and Scooter were gone a long time. Brittney tried calling him on the phone to see where he was, but he didn't answer. They walked around the mall searching in some of the shops for several minutes.

"What's taking him so long and why isn't he answering his phone?" complained Brittney to Eto.

"Oh, you know H.D. He gets caught up looking at stuff and loses track of time!" assured Eto, knowing full well what H.D. was up to.

"I just don't understand why we can't find him?" said Brittney, becoming extremely agitated at her fiancé.

"Hey, let's go look at some shoes. I need some new tennis shoes," suggested Eto, even though he was wearing a brand-new pair of Nikes.

"Okay," replied Brittney, still miffed, but she did love looking at shoes.

While she was distracted holding up some red stilettos, H.D. came up behind her and tapped her on the shoulder. She sat the shoes down, turned around, and saw him on one knee holding a beautiful diamond engagement ring in an opened box.

Brittney was so surprised, she squealed in delight. H.D. said, "Brittney, I love you so much. You deserve a beautiful ring to show how much I love you!" He slid the ring onto her engagement finger and stood up to kiss her. Everyone in the shoe store clapped and whistled for the happy couple. Eto and Scooter laughed out loud and hollered for the two.

They left the shoe store and went to the commissary to get some food for the barbecue they were planning to have that evening. It was going to be their engagement party. While they were in the store, H.D.'s dad called. Hunter stammered into the phone, "So, uhhh, Dad, I have something to tell you."

"What is it?" asked Steve thinking, *What the hell did you do now, H.D.?*

"Remember the girl I told you about that I'm dating?" asked H.D.

"Yeah," answered Steve, waiting for the other shoe to drop.

"Well, Brittney and I are getting married, Dad!" H.D. said, excitedly

"What? You are?" Steve was stunned. He wasn't expecting the news but wasn't really surprised either. Every time H.D. called the last month, he was gushing about how wonderful Brittney was and how much he loved her. He congratulated his son and said he hoped to see him soon and meet his fiancé.

They posted an engagement picture on Facebook announcing their love to the world. They held their engagement party that night at Brittney's mom's house. All of H.D.'s friends were there that could come. They drank and listened to music all night long. It was so much fun for the young couple and their friends.

On December 29, 2010, H.D. married Brittney at the courthouse in San Diego. They kept it a secret, because they didn't want to have a big wedding and weren't sure what was going to happen to him. If he was going to stay in the Marines, the only way they could stay together was if they were married. They knew they would get married eventually, so they just did it. Brittney told her family the next day and H.D. called his dad to tell him, also. Both parents were surprised at how fast it all happened but were happy for the two of them, knowing how much they loved each other.

The following month on January 22, 2011, Gunny and Kristie got married. They had planned their wedding before H.D. and Brittney were married. That night at the reception, H.D. told Brittney, "I passed the physical exam, and I'm approved to stay in the Marines." Brittney began crying and exclaimed, "Oh, Hunter!" She was so upset and afraid of him going to war.

"It's going to be okay. I know I'm going to come home, because I have you to come home to," soothed H.D., holding Brittney tightly and kissing the top of her head as she sobbed into his chest.

"Okay," she sighed as she finally accepted the news and dried her tears. They spent the rest of the evening enjoying the wedding reception and told Kristie and Gunny the news after they got back from their honeymoon. H.D. called his dad and told him even though he could have got a medical discharge, he wanted to stay in.

He let him know he passed his physical exam and was cleared for duty. Steve wasn't really surprised. He knew if anyone could come back from an injury like that, it was his son. H.D. was always a fighter and never gave up once he started something.

They rented an apartment right next to Brittney's mom and Gunny. H.D. was released from medical hold in February. He left to Camp Pendleton to continue his training in the School of Infantry (SOI). He was there for four months. Brittney would drive there every weekend and pick him up. It was only an hour drive from the apartment. The weekend was the only time they could talk and be together, because H.D. didn't have phone privileges while he was in the SOI.

H.D. graduated from the SOI on June 23, 2011. That day, he went to see Father Griffin. He and Brittney had been to see him several times for marriage counseling before they got married, which was recommended for any recruit thinking about marriage. H.D. walked into the chaplain's office and said, "I need to speak to you, Father Griffin."

The chaplain was on his computer and replied, "I'm busy, but I can see you in a few minutes, H.D." He didn't look at the young man and kept typing on his computer. H.D. replied, "I can wait. This is important." H.D. sat down in the chair in front of the desk, opened up a can of Copenhagen, put a piece in his mouth, and chewed in silence.

After a minute, the chaplain turned to look at H.D. and saw the serious look on his face. He immediately closed his laptop computer, deciding it could wait, and asked, "So, what are we going to talk about today?"

"I'm leaving for Afghanistan soon after I go to Lejeune tomorrow. I wanted to thank you for all you've done for me here and tell you goodbye," said H.D. with tears forming in his eyes.

"Don't look so down, H.D. This won't be the last time we talk. You can call me when you get back," encouraged the chaplain.

"I won't be back. I'm going to be killed just before the end of my tour," stated H.D., looking directly in Father Griffin's eyes.

"Oh, come on, H.D.! Don't talk like that. Look at me, I survived Vietnam and your dad came back from his duty, too. You'll be back," Father Griffin replied back, but suddenly had a cold chill run down his spine.

"No. I don't think I will," H.D. said, shaking his head and frowning, "but it's not me I'm worried about. I'm square with God, so I'm not afraid of dying. It's my dad that I'm worried about. He won't do too good when I'm gone. I want you to talk to him."

"I will, H.D., but don't you give up hope," assured the chaplain with tears in his eyes.

"I won't," replied H.D. as he stood up and went around the desk to give the chaplain a final hug. "Goodbye, Father Griffin."

"Goodbye, H.D."

H.D. picked up his can of Copenhagen and walked out of the office. The chaplain, who was usually used to having these final conversations with Marines leaving, was deeply moved by H.D.'s words. He closed the door to his office and wept a few minutes, praying for H.D.

The very next day, H.D. was sent on a duty plane to Camp Lejeune, North Carolina. Brittney had to stay in San Diego and figure out a way to move all their possessions clear across the United States. Gunny talked to people on base and helped her figure out how to do it.

18 SEE YOU WHEN I SEE YOU

When Brittney told her family she was moving to North Carolina, they all said, "We're coming with you. We don't want to be away from you and Hunter that long. We're all moving to North Carolina." Brittney was so happy to have her family's support and willingness to make this huge change for her. Tara and her husband divorced and she moved into Brittney's apartment with her. The two women packed all their things and planned the route to Camp Lejeune.

They loaded up the car, left on August 1st, and drove across the country. When they arrived, H.D. lived on base while they stayed in hotels as Brittney looked for a house. The military paid for the hotels until they could find a permanent residence. Camp Lejeune is located close to Jacksonville. After looking around the area for a house, Brittney didn't like the idea of living there. She told H.D., "I'm not living here. It's just a dump!"

She searched on the internet for homes for sale and found one she liked an hour away from base in a little town called New Bern. When H.D. called her later that day, she said, "Honey, I found a house for us!"

"You did! Where?"

"It's in New Bern."

"What? That's an hour away. I'm not going to drive there every day!" protested H.D.

"It's the cutest little place and it's beautiful there. Trust me. You'll love it!" Brittney pleaded.

H.D. wasn't convinced the drive was worth it. After a little bit more persuasion, he caved in and told Brittney to buy it, because he loved her and wanted her to be happy. He ended up loving the place and was grateful to get away from the military base and big city. It was a three-bedroom house with an acre of land and cost them $700 a month. H.D. bought himself a truck, so he could drive there every day from Camp Lejeune.

Brittney started decorating the house and making it their home. Brittney's mom, Gunny, and younger sister came later and moved thirty minutes down the road from them. H.D.'s grandparents on his dad's side lived there, too. They were also only thirty minutes away from their house.

H.D. would train from 7:00 a.m. to 4:00 p.m. and drive home every week day. He had the weekends off, except when he had to go into the field for training. The newlyweds went fishing and explored the area to see everything they could. They weren't far from the beach, so they would drive to see the ocean as often as they could. They loved swimming in the ocean together and watching the dolphins swim by. H.D. didn't get a chance to swim in the ocean much while he was at Camp Pendleton.

H.D.'s Meema and Papa invited them over often for dinner. H.D. loved spending time with them, since he didn't get to see them very often when he grew up. His Meema would bring out different wine for them to try. H.D. loved sampling the wine. Brittney was surprised at how sophisticated he was at tasting wine. Most young men don't like drinking wine. She thought it was really cute. Every holiday they would spend with Meema and Papa and Brittney's family.

While in North Carolina, Brittney and H.D. made new friends. H.D. was so likable; he had a ton of friends. They would invite them over for barbecues and campfires all the time. They bought a big barbecue grill and would grill out every night. H.D. loved to cook like his dad and grandparents. He had their family recipes and taught Brittney how to cook some of them, except she didn't put as much hot sauce on the food like he did. As her cooking improved, Brittney made him dinner every night during the week.

He would come home, drop all his gear on the floor in the middle of the kitchen, and ask, "Can you wash this stuff for me?" Then, he would jokingly say, "Where's my beer, woman?" They would laugh and he would swing her around the kitchen.

Just after they moved into their house, Hurricane Irene hit on the morning of August 27th. H.D., Brittney, and her sisters went to Meema and Papa's house, so they wouldn't be alone. They played cards and board games to entertain themselves and ride out the storm. Meema and Papa were glad to have the company. At times the wind was so loud, they could barely hear themselves talk and thought it was going to take the roof off!

The Hurricane ended up being the seventh costliest hurricane in the U.S. with fifty-six deaths. It hit the Bahamas, went out to the ocean and came back in full force. The eye of the hurricane made landfall at Cape Lookout, North Carolina, and spawned several tornadoes and floods. Its winds reached one hundred miles per hour, causing damage along the entire Atlantic coast and up into Canada. H.D. and Brittney helped his grandparents pick up fallen tree limbs, sticks, and debris scattered on their lawn. Luckily, no severe damage was done to either of their homes.

The following month on September 17th was H.D.'s twenty-first birthday. His Meema and Papa invited him, Brittney, and Tara over for dinner. Meema asked him, "Are you sure you want to celebrate your birthday with us? Don't you want to go out with your friends?"

"No, Meema, I want to spend my birthday with you!" he told her on the phone.

They drove to his grandparent's house and ate a delicious Hogan dinner with a birthday cake and drank wine. There were so many bottles to choose from. Then, they went to visit friends of Meema and Papa for a while and had more wine to drink. They passed the bottles around sampling them all, trying to decide which one they liked the best. It was getting late, so Papa left to go home in H.D.'s truck and left his car, so the youngsters didn't have to drive. Meema drove Papa's car back home with Tara in the passenger seat and Brittney and Hunter in the back seat.

Meema headed toward her house. They were stopped at a traffic light when H.D. said, "I'm going to throw up!" He grabbed his door to open it but couldn't get it to open, so he decided to lean over Brittney and puke out of her door. She barely got the door open when he began vomiting all over her and the back of the car. "Damn it, Hunter!" she yelled at him.

The door was open and he continued projectile vomiting out onto the asphalt. People in passing cars were pointing at him and laughing. Brittney quickly closed the door when the light turned green and rolled down the window. H.D. kept hurling out the window and laughing so hard. "Oh my God! What are you doing, Hunter!" Meema yelled, "You couldn't wait till we got home?" H.D. laughed even harder.

When they arrived at the house, he was so scared Papa was going to be mad at him. He wasn't. He just laughed and told H.D. to clean it up. He cleaned up the mess and rolled down the windows to get the smell out. Meema washed their clothes for them while they borrowed some t-shirts and shorts to wear for the night. They spent the night in the spare bedroom and H.D. drove home with Brittney and Tara the next morning.

For Thanksgiving, H.D. was in the field training. Brittney spent the holiday with her family. Early in December, Steve came to visit and brought Hank to live with H.D. and Brittney. When Steve pulled into the driveway and let the dog out of the car, Hank was so excited to finally see H.D. again. He ran up to him, jumped up on his lap, and licked him all over his face. H.D. laughed and rubbed him all over. Hank missed those rubs!

After hugs were exchanged with Brittney and H.D., Steve helped them rake their yard and hang up Christmas lights. Steve's girlfriend, Shelley, and three children (Ali, Karah, and Eli), who also lived near them, came over to help decorate. Shortly after, Meema and Papa arrived to visit and so did Brittney's family. Later that evening was when H.D. told everyone he got the orders that his unit (1/8) was going to Afghanistan sometime in January.

Shortly after September 11, 2001, Operation Enduring Freedom began to stop the Taliban from providing a safe haven to al Qaeda and their use of Afghanistan as its base of operations for terrorist activities. H.D.'s deployment, Operation Jaws 5, was launched to stop the Taliban supply chain and eliminate key enemy leaders in the Helmand Province, Afghanistan. Working with the Afghan National Security Forces, the leathernecks helped clear out many areas and trained the Afghan Forces to take over security and stabilize the area.

The family was saddened by the news, but knew it was inevitable, since other Marine units from Camp Lejeune had already deployed in the past year to Afghanistan. It was part of H.D.'s job. They just hoped for the best for H.D. and spent the remainder of the year with him enjoying the holidays and thankful for each moment they had with him.

For Christmas, Brittney made a turkey since H.D. didn't get any at Thanksgiving. They ate it on Christmas Eve. After eating part of the turkey, H.D. found the wishbone and said, "Let's make a wish!"

"Okay!" exclaimed Brittney.

Brittney grabbed one side and H.D. grabbed the other. They pulled at the same time. *Snap!* went the bone. When they held their pieces up together, they both had exactly the same amount!

"Okay, we have to do this then. Don't tell me your wish and just write it down on a piece of paper. I'll write mine down, too," suggested H.D.

"I love it!" replied Brittney. They wrote down their wish and folded it up. H.D. put them in a Ziploc bag and put it in the freezer.

"Don't open it until I get back from Afghanistan. Don't look at them," he told Brittney.

"Okay. Why?" she replied, puzzled.

"Just don't!"

"Okay. I won't," Brittney promised and she didn't.

On her Mom's birthday, Brittney found out she was pregnant. When she told H.D., he hugged her and kissed her. He was so happy. She took a pregnancy test and wrapped it in a box for her mom as a surprise. They knew they should wait three months to tell others about the pregnancy, but H.D. said, "I don't want to be stuck over there and gone when you tell everyone!"

"It's fine. We'll just tell everyone now," Brittney replied, knowing how much it meant to H.D. So, they did. When Kristie opened the box, she was so surprised. It was the best gift she could have ever received. They called Steve and told him the good news. He was also surprised and happy for them both.

H.D. was promoted to Lance Corporal and ordered to be deployed on January 13, 2012. It was Friday the 13th. They prepared for the call ordering him to base. H.D. drove Brittney's little black car with Brittney and Tara. Shelley drove behind them with her kids and Papa drove his car with Meema. They all drove to Jacksonville.

On the way, H.D. suddenly made U-turn where he wasn't supposed to. Shelley turned her wheel sharply, trying to keep up behind him, just missing a head-on collision with a car. They were on the phone with H.D. and he could hear them screaming. "Are you guys okay?" he asked.

"Yes, damn it, H.D. We almost got hit by a car!" yelled Shelley. H.D. laughed at them. They got to Jacksonville and waited. They had been up for twenty-four hours and it was getting late. So, they decided to eat at Red Robin.

After they were done eating, H.D. said his goodbyes to Meema, Papa, Shelley, Ali, Karah, and Eli. He picked up Karah and squeezed her so hard her back popped. It was their special hug. Karah kissed his cheek and he put her back down.

Then, he went over to say goodbye to Papa. Papa looked at him and thought, *My little grandson is a man. Now, he's leaving to war!* A feeling so overwhelming came on him and he made a little squealing noise under his breath. H.D. wiped the tears from his grandfather's eyes and said, "Goodbye." Everyone watched and waved goodbye as he got in the car and drove away with Brittney and Tara to the base.

The buses didn't come until 2:00 a.m. While they were waiting, H.D. told Brittney, "All the other Marine wives have been through this before, so they don't get too upset. If you don't cry, I'm going to be pissed!" Brittney thought, *Perfect! I'm trying to be strong and not fall apart, but he wants me to cry!* She brought her baby book and they recorded a message for the baby. Before H.D. had to get on the bus, he kissed Brittney and said, "I love you so much! I'm going to miss you, Babe!"

She began sobbing and was a blubbering mess. She tried to tell him how much she loved him and would miss him every day but couldn't talk. He hugged her, kissed her, and told her just before he stepped on the bus, "We can't say goodbye. I'll see you when I see you."

H.D. loved the Jason Aldean song where he heard those words. He gave her one more passionate kiss and got on the bus. H.D. sat down by a window and waved to Brittney. Brittney blew him a kiss and waved to him as the bus drove away. Tears were streaming down her face as she drove back home with her sister. They got there at four o'clock in the morning.

She was so distraught, she began bleeding and cramping that morning. Her sister took her to the emergency room where she had a miscarriage. Brittney was heart-broken. She didn't know how she was going to tell her husband she lost the baby. At least she had her sister there to help comfort her.

The bus took H.D. to the airport on Camp Lejeune where the Marines boarded a 757 civilian airplane to Frankfurt, Germany. It was the most uncomfortable way to travel, ever. They were crammed into the plane with their day pack full of all of their serialized equipment: optics, night vision, thermals, scope, bayonet,

PEQ15, PEQ16, binoculars, and compass. They placed their rifle between their feet with very little legroom for the long flight.

During the flight, questions ran through his mind: *Did we cover enough in our battle drills? What will it be like? I hope everyone comes out alive!* He dozed in and out, awakening only to bumps of the plane hitting turbulence or hearing someone talking.

The nine-hour flight went faster than he thought it would. They arrived there just after one o'clock in the afternoon North Carolina time, but it was seven o'clock in the evening in Germany. He reset his watch as they waited to get off the plane for the short layover.

The Marines went into the airport to take a break and grab some food. The first thing H.D. did was call Brittney. He knew he wouldn't get another chance for a long while. When Brittney answered her cell phone, H.D. said, "Hi, Babe! I made it to Germany. They are refueling the plane and then we will leave to Kurdistan."

"I'm glad you made it there, Hunter, but I have some bad news for you," replied Brittney. H.D. could tell from the sound of her voice he wouldn't like what she was going to say.

"I just got back from the emergency room," she informed him.

"You did? Are you okay?" asked H.D., really worried now.

"Yes, I'm okay, but I …. lost...the baby," she told him, sobbing into the phone.

"Oh no, not the baby!" H.D. began crying himself. He was devastated by the news. The two cried together for a minute. H.D. gathered his composure just long enough to say, "It will be alright. We can try again when I get home. I love you, Babe!"

"I love you, too," replied Brittney. *Click!* H.D. had to hang up. He couldn't talk any longer and had to catch up with the rest of his squad to board the plane. The men in his unit could tell something was wrong. He told them about the baby and they tried their best to console him. Nothing they said could take away the pain. He just sat and cried silently on the plane to let it out.

H.D. finally focused on the mission and told himself, *Get this job done and I can go home to Brittney to begin our family and life!* Brittney knew he would be gone for at least six months, so she focused on starting her wedding coordinating career in New Bern. Staying busy helped her keep her mind off missing her husband and the loss of their baby.

For Valentine's Day, she had a book with questions on each page. One of the questions was: How did you meet? She wrote the story on the page. Another question was: If you wanted me to have one more thing that you remembered about my life toward the end of it, what would that be? She wrote her favorite line from the Edgar Allen Poe poem "Annabel Lee": *We loved with a love that was more than love.* The last question was: If there was one last thing you could say to me what would that be. She wrote: Meet me in Montauk. It was a line from their favorite movie, *Eternal Sunshine of the Spotless Mind.*

19 KNOCKING ON HEAVEN'S DOOR

After the Marines loaded back up onto the plane to fly into Kurdistan, the men dozed on and off some more, trying to get their last moments of rest in. The men knew there would be very little sleep once they get to Afghanistan. The plane traveled another four hours to Kurdistan. After it landed, they departed the plane and took a bus to the Air Force base. It was a super nice place. *Life is fuckin' dandy for these people!* thought H.D. as he looked around and saw they had a nice chow hall, dance club, and bar.

They were there for two days and boarded a Boeing C-17 cargo plane to fly into Camp Leatherneck, Afghanistan. It is a huge Afghan Armed Forces base with air fields located in the Helmand Province. For this flight, they put on their Kevlar and were given one full magazine with 10 rounds of ammunition.

The flight felt very different this time: there was no sleeping, their adrenaline was pumping, and they were filled with the excitement of fighting with their brother Marines and the thrill of danger. All their training had led up to this point. There could be no doubts now. As they were approaching their landing, their lieutenant, M.T. Hart, yelled out to the men, "Make sure you're strapped in! We're fixing to do a combat landing!" *What the hell is a combat landing? They never told us about that shit!*

Suddenly, they heard *poof, poof, poof!* The pilots of the C-17 shot out flares to deflect any missile attacks. They did a hard bank to the left and dropped suddenly. H.D. could feel his stomach come up and drop along with the plane. He was glad he didn't eat much or it would have come right back up. Then, they did a hard bank to the right and dropped again. The Marines were bounced up and down in their seats like puppets. *Oh man, this is the real deal!* thought H.D. as he realized they were targets and could be shot down at any minute.

The plane flew downward and leveled out. *Whump, whump!* went the wheels as they hit the small landing strip. Then, there was a commotion of noise. The men were hustled out the side as military crew unloaded equipment out of the back of the plane. They sprinted into the hanger. Just as they got inside, H.D. heard *whoomph, whoomph!* as mortars were being fired outside.

The hanger was a concrete building with a steel roof. It was reinforced with thick steel beams. It wasn't until then that they were given information needed about the mission: their area of operations, the last unit that was there, significant enemy encounters, what kind of IEDs they were running into, and what kind of enemy actions are in the area. They were handed maps, locating where they had taken contact and where they were running into the insurgents on patrol.

H.D.'s platoon stayed at Camp Leatherneck for two days to get acclimated to the altitude. The military installation was so big; it had a movie theater, chow hall, bus routes, stores, and fast food restaurants. The perimeter fence was so far removed from where the men were, they almost couldn't see it.

There were forty men in the platoon with three squads. They sent out a leader's reconnaissance first. Six of the leathernecks went out first in a helicopter (helo) to their designated area of operations to bond with the unit already out there and start running patrols with them.

The squad was given light body armor called plate carriers. Some of them still had blood stains on them, parts were torn off, and had bullet holes. When H.D. was handed one, he was surprised at the shoddy equipment. *Really? I can't wait to use this shit!* Then, he was handed a machine gun. After he looked it over, he went up to one of the squad leaders, Corporal K.T. Liture, and said, "Cpl. Liture, they want to give me this SAW, but it doesn't have feed paws."

Cpl. Liture was a tall, handsome man with thick, dark-brown hair when it wasn't buzzed off. He had a chiseled jawline with a five o'clock shadow from not shaving for two days. His pearly white smile and bright blue eyes melted many girls' hearts. Not only were the women impressed with his muscular body, but so were his fellow Marines. Because he was extremely intelligent, H.D. looked up to him and valued his opinion.

Liture told him, "You turn that fucking weapon back into that goddamn armory and tell them I am not fucking having you carry it! Have them issue you a rifle." Boy was he pissed! H.D. went to the armory to return the machine gun, but was told, "No, you have to carry that weapon. It's serialized to you. We'll give you an extra rifle and mail you the feed paws for you to fix it." H.D. thought, *What the hell? You want me to carry this broken twenty-pound hunk of steal? For what?*

Poor guy had no choice! He carried the useless SAW *and* his rifle for days. The part finally did come for him to fix it. Cpl. Liture's M203 Grenade Launcher didn't close and the safety didn't work. He had to fix it part way through the deployment, too. Despite those frustrations, the squad was still like, "Hell yeah, it doesn't matter!"

Cpl. Liture left to lead the reconnaissance team. After a few days, H.D. and his squad of nine other men loaded up into a MV-22 Osprey helicopter. A picture was taken of them before they climbed into the bird. *Whup, whup, whup!* The helicopter lifted up and shot forward as the men listened to the deafening sound of the rotors whirling in the air. It was too loud inside for voices to be heard, so they sat quietly.

The helicopter flew low to avoid missile attack and had two door gunners holding M240 Bravos (belt fed machine guns that can fire to over a thousand yards). H.D. thought to himself, *Now those are some badass dudes!* He turned and saw one Marine nudge another and mouth the words, "You ready?" The second Marine gave him the "rock on" sign. H.D. glanced down at where they were going to land. *Shit, here I am. Here we come!* Everything became crystal clear.

As soon as the helicopter landed, dust and rock flew everywhere. The men pulled down their goggles to cover their eyes and ran out of the helicopter with their equipment into the compound where the leader team was located. The cloud of dust helped to conceal them for a minute from enemy fire.

Along with their day pack and rifles, two of the leathernecks were carrying SAWs (M249 light machine guns). Others carried radios, pyrotechnics, metal detectors, radio jammers, and IED sticks. They were told to use the little ten-foot pole to hook onto an IED if they find a wire and tell everyone to stand back. *Sure...I'll do that!* thought H.D. sarcastically.

They spent the first day ripping with the unit there and reconnecting with their own men from their squad. They weren't there long before someone yelled out, "Incoming! Incoming!" *Whoosh.... BOOM!* Everyone ducked and took cover as a rocket propelled grenade (RPG) hit just a few inches from the wall they were behind. Rock and dirt flew everywhere. The unit returned fire and then there was silence.

The men got back up to survey the damage. There wasn't any this time. While H.D. stood, looking at the barren place and mountains surrounding it, a strong feeling swept over him. He felt as if the hand of God was over them, watching them. The place was ancient and full of history going back to biblical days. There were some new buildings mixed with the old. The ground was mostly dirt with a few patches of green here and there. H.D. wondered, *How do these people live here?*

It was like a maze of buildings. Each compound was surrounded by walls with archways that led to the next compound. It would be very easy to get lost in there. The compounds were made of mud. They are all different. Some were small one room huts with no window or one window, and some of them had multiple stories or a basement. They learned to be cautious of the latter, because something is special about the person who owns them.

The steps that led to the roof were more like blocks of mud. Very rarely did they have stairs. If they did, they were made for hobbits. They would be loaded down with their pack trying to turn to go up and get on the roof. It was a very tight squeeze.

One day, they were on patrol and saw a wall of a long building with doors that were two feet tall. They were exact replicas of normal sized doors, but much smaller. H.D. wondered, *Why are there so many little doors? There's not a massive midget population here, is there? Do all the little people live on this street?* That's not the case. Those doors were probably never used.

The first compound H.D.'s team took over had a few small buildings and a massive walled courtyard, a well, and a hole blown through the wall leading into the compound next to it. They fortified the inner alley, so they could own it. There was another walled-in area in the middle with towers on either corner where they slept in tents.

They took turns rotating between three shifts: who was on guard at the towers or on the roofs, who went on patrol looking for the enemy and IEDs and talking to locals, and QRF (quick reaction force on standby cleaning items and fortifying the compound). There never was a designated rest time on deployment, *ever*. They would go days without sleep sometimes. They always varied the amounts of time they were on duty to keep the enemy from knowing their whereabouts.

Later in deployment, everyone was getting dysentery. They shit themselves, pissed themselves, and vomited uncontrollably. It was acceptable. When they were on patrol and it happened, they would cut a hole in their pants, so they could squat and shit without having to let go of their rifle. They survived off caffeine and hate. Everyone was in sync.

Instead of blaming anyone, they would adapt. "We just hit an IED. Can we still move the vehicle? How many casualties are there? Can we do this? We have to do this!" are things they would say instead of blaming the driver.

The first few days took major adjusting for the new team. They went on patrols with the unit already there and began to familiarize themselves with the area. They taught them about the Afghan people still living in the homes, where the insurgents were located last, and introduced them to the Afghan soldiers (ANA) there to interpret and support them in combat. The unit told them what area they needed to push to and left a few days later in a returning helicopter.

H.D.'s squad began pushing into the new area, kicking in doors, and searching for the insurgents. The enemy would hide in some of the homes and use bunkers or an intricate karez system, consisting of tunnels and wells, to attack them. They would make the family get out and tactfully question all men, women, and children. They relied on their interpreter to interrogate the locals and try to get information from them.

Most were reluctant to talk or gave very little information. They would search the whole compound for IEDs and boobie traps. Then, they would make the decision to let the family go or let them stay and essentially keep them prisoner for a while. Most of the time, they let them go unless they had a significant reason to hold them or didn't want them to know how many guys they were bringing into the compound to know their troop strength.

Sometimes, they encountered children playing in the street during the day or inside one of the homes. They had to be careful, because the children would be used as a distraction before an attack or armed with an IED. For H.D., that was the hardest part- the fear he would have to kill a child to protect himself and his men.

The heat was another thing they had to get used to. It would reach up to 120 degrees during the day. Combined with their heavy clothing, they were carrying anywhere from seventy to one hundred pounds of gear. Staying hydrated was a priority. Water had to be resupplied daily.

During infantry training, they were taught how to survive with less: less food and less sleep. They were taught how to clear rooms and use various weapons systems. They learned how to dig a fighting hole. The height is to the armpit of the tallest man who is going to be in the hole. It is two Kevlars deep and two rifles across with a water sump on the bottom to keep water off your feet when it rains. No matter how deep the water sump was, they still ended up with wet feet. Sandbags are placed around the top of the fighting hole for extra protection.

Beside the fighting hole, they dug a grenade sump. The grenade sump is a small hole about the width of a hand. You dig it down and as far as you can at an angle. If a grenade comes into your fighting position, you can funnel it into the hole, so it goes down. Behind the fighting hole, they dug a ranger grave where they stowed their gear. It is shallow enough that when you lie down, it can hide your body.

Using the restroom was a whole different ball game there. There were no restrooms, so they had to dig a hole, put sandbags around to sit on, and go into the hole. Trash went into another hole, which they would burn and bury when they were done. The leathernecks were constantly busy making holes, filling in holes, digging new holes, and filling sandbags every time they moved. They couldn't leave anything behind showing they were there. Anything a Marine does to reveal his position present or past is a target indicator.

The first time H.D. went on patrol, it was an eye-opening experience. Practicing for enemy fire during training was much different than the real thing. Cpl. Liture was the leader of the team with H.D. and four other men. They left the compound and headed out into the surrounding fields and compounds searching for the insurgents and IEDs. They all carried their day pack with ammunition and their M16A4 rifles. Just as they came upon a five-foot wall of a compound, they heard the *pew-pew-pew!* of bullets flying by them. H.D. and two others stood there for a second, looking to see where it was coming from.

"GET THE FUCK DOWN!" yelled Cpl. Liture at them as he

ducked behind the wall.

"OH, SHIT!" yelled H.D., suddenly realizing they were shooting at him, trying to kill *him!* Then, his warrior instinct kicked in. He raised his rifle and fired away in a matter of seconds, taking one down immediately. As the enemy was reloading their weapons, he sprinted around a corner to the left into the next compound. No one could see where he went. The insurgents began firing on them again. They fired back.

Suddenly, they heard the *pew-pew-pew!* of a rifle and saw two of the insurgents fall to the ground dead. The rest of the insurgents ran off to regroup and have tea time with their families. H.D. popped his head up out of nowhere like a squirrel and asked, "Everyone okay?"

"We're all fine, H.D., thanks!" answered Cpl. Liture. "We'd better head back to base before they attack again and get some more ammo."

"Aye, aye, corporal," the men replied.

They hustled back to their compound and told everyone where they found the insurgents, how many they saw, and took out. Then, they grabbed an MRE and water to refuel and rested a few minutes before they cleaned their weapons and restocked supplies. This was a daily occurrence for the platoon. At any moment they were attacked at their compound or while they were on patrol for the entire six months.

The next day, Liture's squad went on patrol again. The enemy was quiet. Everyone was on edge waiting for something to happen. One of the men fell into a river stream and dropped the metal detector. That's a serious no-no! Lt. Hart was with them and ordered all of them to hop into the stream and look for the detector. Liture and the rest got into the flowing stream with the water reaching up to their chest.

Lt. Hart ordered them to fan out up and down the riverbank to find the metal detector, never mind this was an area they were taking 360-degree fire nonstop. There was a significant IED threat to the men and it was now dark outside. They would need to use white lights to see and that would make them easy targets. Finally, Hart said, "It's okay. Let's go. We'll mark it up as a loss." They returned back to the compound without a metal detector.

Every once in a while, H.D. had access to the internet. He would get online and email Brittney to get on Skype at such and such time. She would stay up all night just to get a chance to talk to him. They would get an hour to talk.

While H.D. was gone, other wives were getting flowers and presents from their husbands. Brittney wasn't getting anything and began to get sad about it. She kept sending him hints, "Hey, you can go on this website and send me something." He would reply, "Oh yeah. Okay."

One day, she got a whole bunch of cookies in the mail and it didn't say who sent it. She was so excited thinking it was from Hunter, but she found out it was from her aunt. When she talked to him the next day, she decided to test him and said, "Honey, you are so sweet. I cannot believe you sent me those cookies. Did you send those to me?"

"Yesss!... I *did*!" bragged H.D.

"Oh my God! You are so sweet!" she said in her loveliest voice.

"Yeah, you're welcome!"

"How did you know they were my favorite cookies?"

"I just knew."

"Hunter, you are such a liar! I cannot believe you!" she yelled at him. He started laughing so hard. She told him, "My aunt sent those."

"I thought if I could get away with it, it was worth a try!" he confessed, giggling.

"You are so busted. Now, you'll really need to make it up to me!" she laughed. They spent the rest of the time talking about how things were going for both of them and told each other how much they loved the other.

One day, H.D. called Brittney on a satellite phone. He said, "How are you doing?" In the background, she could hear someone calling out numbers and loud pops and booms.

"What's that noise?" she asked him.

"Oh, it's nothing. Just someone dropping something," he replied. She had no idea he was calling in airstrikes and thought he was just being sweet.

On June 4th, H.D. called Brittney on Skype. Shelley and the kids were connected with her and so was Steve. They were telling him what was going on in the states and he told them some of the things they were doing to entertain themselves. The last thing he said to his dad was, "Wouldn't you like a glass of Sangria wine?"

Steve picked up on the signal informing him that H.D. was going to Sangin. He nodded and said, "Yes, Son." Then, H.D. told everyone he needed to speak to Brittney alone. They each said goodbye and told him they loved him. Once everyone else disconnected, he said, "Babe, I have one last mission to go on before I come home."

"You do?" she asked.

"I'm going to be going to Sangin," he informed her with a serious tone. She had no idea what Sangin meant. So, she said, "Okay?"

"So, yeah!" H.D. replied, sighing heavily.

"What does that mean?" she asked.

"You don't know what that means?" His eyebrows raised, surprised she didn't know.

"No!" she shook her head.

"Okay, well just don't worry about it!" he told her.

"No, you brought it up for a reason. Either it's super dangerous or there's going to be a bunch of prostitutes and you're going to have a great time. So, tell me which one is it?" she asked frankly.

He didn't say anything. He didn't sound like himself. He sounded really scared and she was beginning to get extremely worried. "I'll call you as soon as I get back," he promised.

"Okay."

"You know I love you." he said softly, looking at her face.

"Everything's going to be okay. You're going to come home. When you get here, you can tell me anything," she consoled him.

"No. You can't handle this and I won't be able to tell you this stuff. It's fine. Don't worry about it. I just won't be able to talk about it," he said honestly.

"Okay." she said, knowing it had gotten pretty bad and it was affecting him. That really worried her. Then, he told her, "I love you. I'll call you when I go."

"I love you, too!" she replied, just before he hung up.

He tried calling her again on her cell phone before he left to Sangin. She was driving her car when the phone rang. All she got was a voicemail from an unavailable number. She listened to it and it was H.D. saying, "I love you. I'm leaving right now. I'll call you when I get home. Love you, bye." She received a letter from him the very next day. At the end of the letter, he wrote: Meet me in Montauk.

H.D.'s platoon went to Sangin and dug in. The compound was big. There was a two-story house with a front entrance and a moat running along the front of the house. The house had a rooftop and a massive courtyard with a garden and a well. There was a steep staircase archway they had to climb up to get to the roof.

There was a horse stall with a brown horse inside. H.D. was shocked to see a horse in that desolate place. He went up to pat the horse on the nose. It was friendly and let him touch it. H.D. had one of the other men take a picture of himself and the horse. They used the horse stall to store their supplies and used the compound next to it as a center building. A staircase led up onto that roof, also. Underneath the staircase is where most of them slept.

Every night they faced gunfire and would fire so many rounds they'd almost be empty by morning. A helo would come in and drop off pallets full of ammunition, grenade launchers, fresh water bottles, and MREs. They'd drop it right into their compound, luckily. The men would go and cannibalize it- strip it down and distribute it.

Keeping the water cool was a challenge in the 120-degree heat. If it was left out, the plastic would melt and warp. They still had to drink it if it was hot. To combat the problem, they would use sock water. They would take a bottle of water, put it in a sock, take another bottle of water, soak the sock, hang it in the shade, and let the air get to it so it cools. It was amazing to go on patrol and come back to water that was room temperature instead of 120 degrees. They could drink from wells if they wanted to risk dysentery.

To take showers, they used baby wipes and foot powder to keep their feet clean and dry. Someone mailed them a shower bag to use as a shower. They learned their feet were the most important things. They changed their socks as often as they could and washed their clothes with well water once a month or two if they had a chance.

Some of the men had playing cards or portable electronic devices to entertain themselves. One of H.D.'s friends, Eugene "Gino" Mills, let them watch "Jersey Shore" on his portable DVD player every night. It helped to cheer the men up and get their mind off the fighting. Gino often told the men, "Stay frosty!" Everyone liked Gino, and H.D. was glad he was there with him.

Occasionally, they would get packages mailed to them from home. One time, people from Nebraska mailed sixty cans of Copenhagen for H.D. and his platoon. The men were elated when they opened that package! H.D. told them the story of when he and Chase had snuck the chew into school and the time he swallowed it. They all laughed heartily at that and loved hearing H.D.'s stories.

To have a little fun with his squad, H.D. gave himself the handle "Catshit 1" when he checked into base. He always found it humorous when he would radio in and say, "This is Catshit 1 to Litter Box. I'm coming in for a landing!" Liture would get so annoyed at him but would laugh at the same time at H.D.'s humor. The men would find ways to laugh and tease each other whenever they had the opportunity.

On June 22, 2012, H.D. and Gino were on adjoining rooftops. They started taking enemy fire from all around. *Rat-a-tat-tat!* They heard a machine gun firing at them. The men were excited. "It'll be a cold day in hell, Taliban," Gino yelled out into the countryside as he fired back at them. The rest of the squad came up on the roof to help them fight. Gino fired a grenade launcher at the enemy. *BUH-LAM!* He killed one of the insurgents and injured two others. After that, things calmed down for a few hours.

Cpl. Liture's squad was on QRF and one squad was getting ready to go on patrol; when out of the blue, Gino was hit in the neck near the collarbone by a bullet. H.D. saw him drop to his hands and knees, blood squirting from his neck. H.D. screamed for help. The bullet hit an artery and he was bleeding into his lungs. Cpl. Liture and the medic ran up the stairs to get Gino off the roof. They worked on him trying to stop the bleeding. Liture radioed in for a medivac.

H.D. remained on the roof and stood up shooting at the enemy. One of the other Marines grabbed him by his sleeve and pulled him down, shouting, "Get down, H.D.! You're going to get yourself killed!" H.D. hunkered down behind the wall but kept firing away. Nobody was stopping him from retaliating for Gino.

Liture, the medic, and two others pushed out into the courtyard and ran out into the field outside of the compound, trying to get the helo to land. The enemy began firing at them again. The men in the compound fired back, trying to cover them. It took an hour to get the bird to land. They were huddled over Gino, working on him the entire hour. Liture put pressure on the wound and packed gauze into it. The other two were shooting back at the enemy.

Gino quit breathing and his heart stopped, so they began CPR on him. They brought his pulse back four times. The medic knew he had to make a tough decision and his hands began trembling. "You know what you have to do!" shouted Liture.

"I don't know if I can do it. I don't know if I can do it," he stammered.

Liture grabbed him with one hand while his other was on Gino's neck and said, "Look, calm down. Focus on one thing at a time. You've done this a thousand times. You've done it in training. You've got this. Walk me through it as if you are teaching me how to do it."

The medic focused on criking Gino and inserting an artificial airway. He was doing everything perfectly. The helo finally landed as Liture was giving one last chest compression and the medic gave mouth-to-mouth. *Pew-pew-pew-ping!* went the sound of bullets flying past them and hitting the helo. They put him on the bird and the medics on board began working on him as they flew back to Camp Leatherneck.

Liture requested another helicopter to do a close gun run on the enemy. The helo crew chief was willing to do a run on the strafing line near them to relieve some pressure. Within minutes, out of nowhere, the helo came in like a hurricane and fired at the enemy as the Marines in the compound watched in awe of its power. The bird, just as quickly, turned around and headed back to Camp Leatherneck.

Lieutenant Hart grabbed all of them that were working on Gino and pulled them aside. He said, "Look, I know Gino didn't make it, but don't tell anyone, yet." The men nodded. They all figured everyone already knew and just didn't talk about it.

H.D. and Liture climbed back onto the roof to find enemy to shoot at. A few minutes later, the lieutenant yelled up to Liture, "There are way too many guys on the rooftop. We need to get some of them down!"

"Hey, get the fuck off the roof!" Liture yelled at two of the men. He tried to get the nonessential people down. He saw H.D. and yelled at him, "Hogan, you need to get down. There are too many bodies on the roof!" Liture turned and kept firing at the enemy. H.D. just went back to shooting as others moved off the roof. Liture looked back over in his direction, saw him, and yelled "You're still on this fucking roof?"

"I want to stay!" He yelled back as he hit one of the insurgents in the forehead.

Liture let him stay and they kept firing away. After they managed to suppress enemy fire enough, they began fortifying again. Liture went into a little garden area and started filling sandbags to put on the top of the compound and give them more cover from sniper fire. H.D. and the medic came to help him.

The medic was mentally and physically exhausted from working on Gino. Liture told the medic to go relax and come back when he felt better. The medic said, "No, it's cool. We all do our part, right?"

H.D. said, "Fuck it. I'll take care of your bags, too!" He grabbed the shovel from him, smiled, and pushed him away. The medic walked away and H.D. helped Liture and two other men finish filling the sandbags. They had packed dozens of bags and carried them up onto the roof.

They all took off their helmets. Those that had worked on Gino for the last hour were shocked and dazed. They just went through the motion of the tasks they needed to do that evening without thinking about it. All they could think of was Gino.

Before dawn the next morning, Cpl. Liture was talking to another Marine about how much it sucked they lost Gino. They never expected anything like that. All the medical training they had (and they had been through some awesome medical courses), they couldn't save him. For them to have the one injury they couldn't do anything about in the field was devastating. They had no way to drain his lungs. If it was any other injury, Gino would have found a way to seem like he wasn't even injured. He would have patched himself up and started returning fire.

They began talking about when they get to go off post. The sun started to come up. The two men took off their gear and sat down to eat a MRE. H.D. leaned into the room they were in and said, "Corporal Liture?"

He used to yell at H.D. for calling him corporal. He would tell him, "I have been a lance corporal the whole time I've been here. I have the exact same job as you do and the exact same responsibilities. Just because I have a higher pay, you don't need to call me any different or stand at parade." H.D. loved to salute him and call him Corporal Liture. Liture would yell, "Stop calling me that!" and would punish him. But, he would punish himself, too.

"Every time you call me corporal, we are going to drop and do push-ups," he warned H.D. Liture would just come back from patrol and H.D. would say, "Good afternoon, Corporal Liture!"

"Goddamn it!" Liture would yell, drop his gear, and order H.D. to drop and give him ten push-ups. He didn't want H.D. doing any more than he was willing to do. After H.D. popped his head in and said his name, Liture shouted, "What Hogan?"

"Would you like to go on patrol with us?" he asked.

Liture perked up and said, "Absolutely, I'd love to. What job do you guys need filled?"

"I need you to be my team leader," he replied, frowning.

Liture realized he was taking Gino's spot. He grabbed his gear and starting planning the patrol. One of the team members suddenly got violently ill. He was the initial squad leader. They chose another member and the five Marines with five ANA soldiers went out on patrol.

They headed east, the opposite direction where Gino was hit. They decided to check out a compound nearby. When they got about halfway to the compound, they were strung out in a big line. As they were walking through a tilled field, the battery died in one of the radios. One of the men radioed back that they needed new radios.

Liture ran back to the compound, grabbed two new radios, and gave one to the other Marine. By that time, they had been in this open area for ten minutes. They began pushing closer to a new building. They got to the building and decided who was the breaching team. They wanted an ANA guy to do the breaching of the compound. Liture told H.D., "If anything happens to me on the inside, you are in charge of the team." He was assuming the worst would happen inside that compound.

"Go take post near that tree," he ordered H.D., pointing to a tall shade tree. H.D. left the group and stood on guard at the tree. Cpl. Liture and the others entered the building and found a man with a family inside. He started asking him questions as an ANA interpreted for him. The man was smirking the whole time he was questioned.

Liture noticed he had a callus on his finger- right where it would be against a trigger guard. He looked at him and thought, *I know this guy is no good. Something is up. I want to arrest him!* He took a retina scan, took a mouth swab to collect DNA, and got his picture and fingerprints. The whole time he is doing this, he told the ANA, "I know this guy is bad. He's a smartass. He's happy we are in this compound."

"No, he's a good guy. Just because he has a callus isn't enough reason to bring him in," they replied. Their assurances weren't enough for Liture. He couldn't help thinking, *Then, why is he laughing while his whole family is cowered down and crying?*

All of a sudden, they heard a loud *POP!* Then, it was quiet for a second. *Oh shit! Is this about to start up?* Liture wondered. Then, they heard one of their men scream, "Corpsman Up!" That meant a comrade was down and the medic was needed.

They hauled ass out of there as fast as they could. Before they got through the middle of the compound, the enemy fires picked up. They were being hit by medium machine guns, small arms, and barrel-launched grenades. They came outside with rounds snapping all around them. They could see them hitting off the walls. They knew they had to figure out who the casualties were and get the hell out of there.

There was a ditch by a low wall. They went out the door and over the wall. The men sprang into the ditch and began running for a few meters inside it, trying to put as much distance as they could from enemy fire. Their medic was hit in the helmet, so they helped him to the ditch. One of them saw H.D. lying on the ground, jumped over the wall, ran more than 100 meters, slung him over his shoulder, and came back over the wall into the ditch. Then, they saw that one of their ANA guys was hit, also. They realized the one shot they heard was actually three simultaneous sniper shots!

Liture started coordinating enemy fires from the ditch. That was where it was passed down the line that H.D. Hogan was gone. He had been shot in the head and died instantly. They didn't have time to process their loss, because they started taking fire from the south, too.

Now, they really had to hunker down in the ditch. The ANA guys stayed inside the compound. They didn't want to come out into the line of fire. They looked at the Marines through the doorway. "Get the fuck out here!" yelled Cpl. Liture. "You need to get your buddy here while I'm trying to get a bird to land to get our own buddy to the fucking bird!" The ANA didn't want to leave.

Liture was furious! He jumped back over the wall, grabbed two of them by the arm, and drug them over the wall into the ditch. They didn't want to return fire, because they didn't want to pop their head over the wall. Liture had one of them fire an RPG. The blast just threw dirt everywhere. It knocked Cpl. Liture over and he felt like he had been punched on the side of his face.

He thought an enemy round had just killed the Marine next to him. He looked over and the man began to move, shaking off the pile of dirt on top of him. He realized the ANA guy didn't check the back blast of the RPG before he fired it, which is very dangerous. That just pissed Liture off even more!

They got the helo to come around the compound and Liture joined the carry team. They threw smoke grenades out and fired at the enemy. The pilot saw the smoke and landed. They got the two casualties on the bird and it lifted up into the air. As they ran about twenty meters away, they heard *ping, ping, ping!* as rounds were ricocheting off the bird. There they were in the middle of the field and open targets. It's a tilled field, so they couldn't move very quickly.

They threw another smoke grenade, hauled ass back to the ditch, and hunkered down. Trying to fight off the enemy, they waited for the second helo to come for H.D. They felt like they were in the "Twilight Zone". Time slowed down to a crawl- five minutes felt like an hour in battle. The Marines at the compound were trying to suppress the enemy from the south from murder holes (small holes they made into the walls to shoot the enemy). They threw another smoke grenade out and carried H.D. to the bird. The parajumpers hopped off and yelled, "Hurry the fuck up!"

They passed H.D. to them and the helo took off. They hauled ass back to the ditch and were there for another two hours. Lt. Hart called in a HIMARS (GPS guided rocket) and a couple more gun runs. They were running low on ammo when one of their weapons went down. Liture ran over to grab H.D.'s gun for him to use. Most of them were down to one magazine, and he had thrown all of his grenades.

When he ran back to the ditch, it was quiet enough, they thought they could make a run for it. Lt. Hart said, "Hey, I think I had my notebook out and the helo picked it up and threw it. I need to find it real quick. It has coordinates in it." He paused a minute and suggested to Liture, "If we cover you, can you see if it is out on the other side of the ditch or wall?"

Liture, still in shock from the events of the last two days, thought he meant to physically go over the wall and run around looking for it. Everyone hopped up and began shooting. Liture jumped over the wall and started running around like a chicken with his head cut off. Hart yelled back at him, "Goddamn it, Liture, get the fuck back over here! What the fuck are you doing?

"I thought you said to look for your notebook?" he replied, thoroughly puzzled.

"Get the fuck back here. Forget the notebook!" Hart yelled to him.

Liture ran back over, jumped over the wall back into the ditch. No enemy fire came while he was out there. He was waiting for accurate shots, but nothing happened. They picked up their gear and H.D.'s gear and ran back to the compound.

As they were running back, the enemy fire picked up again. A round flew right in front of Cpl. Liture's face. It burned his lips. He could actually taste the lead. That was the closest a round had ever come to him. It felt like they had literally done nothing to stop the enemy.

Suddenly, they heard *FUH-WHOOM!* from behind them as the

rocket directly hit the insurgents- killing and injuring several of them. The Marines stopped a moment and turned around to see the insurgents' dazed faces. They shook their fists in the air and yelled, "HELL YEAH! THAT'S FOR GINO AND H.D.!"

When they got back to the compound, everyone was distraught over losing H.D. It was as if the one ray of sunshine in that godforsaken place had gone out. He was the one who pushed them to do their absolute best. He was the one who made them laugh when they didn't think there was anything to laugh about.

Cpl. Liture was heartbroken and blamed himself for what happened to H.D. There was no way he could have known they were walking into an ambush. No one was to blame, except the evil being who fired that fateful shot. Completely exhausted from three brutal days with no sleep, he went into a room and lay down to rest. Shortly after he closed his eyes, he had a dream.

He saw H.D. and Gino surrounded by clouds dressed in their Marine blues, holding hands with uncertainty on their faces. They looked at each other, nodded, simultaneously turned, and began knocking on Heaven's door.

When the humongous golden door opened, Jesus was standing before them in his white tunic. They could see the holes in his palms and scars on his forehead from the crown of thorns. He smiled warmly at them and said, "Come on in, Marines. You have fought valiantly for your country. You are home now and will never have to suffer again!"

H.D. and Gino grinned, put their arms around each other's shoulders, and walked through the door together- their faces shining brilliantly with pride and eternal peace. As they entered Valhalla, they were greeted by Marines who came before them and their ancestors. Now, the two knew they were truly home.

When Liture woke up, it was early in the morning. He remembered the dream vividly and shared it with the others in his squad. The men found comfort in the dream, but still wanted revenge. They began pushing out larger patrols for the next three days they were to be there. They found some IEDs, and the insurgents had boobie trapped their escape route.

Everything was stricter. They never moved across an open field without some kind of cover. They asked for a shit load of ammo. Smoke grenades were thrown to use as concealment to sprint across danger areas. A new squad came out to rip with them and they began handing over the patrols to the new Marines. A helo came to pick them up in groups as another squad came in to relieve them from their duty.

Later at the debriefing station at Camp Leatherneck, officers questioned Liture about the missing metal detector. They had a lawyer with them. They said, "You have to write a statement about the loss of this serialized equipment. We will decide if we are pressing charges."

They got back less than twelve hours ago and were still mourning the loss of two of their men. Liture couldn't believe they were going to charge the Marine and anyone in the squad who may have been part of losing that metal detector. He yelled at all of them, "This is a bunch of bullshit! We just lost two great Marines, Gino Mills and Hunter Hogan, out there and all you care about is a goddamn metal detector!"

Liture stormed out of the room and didn't care if they threw him in the brigade. No charges were filed and the platoon was sent back home to the United States to try to resume a "normal" life. Some remained in the Marine Corps. Some got out when their four-year contract was up. Liture got out of the Marines and later enrolled in college to begin a whole new career. He never forgot about Gino and H.D.

20 MY BOY IS HOME

Late afternoon on June 23, 2012, Steve was in his barn cleaning up and preparing the yard for the fourth of July. He heard a vehicle coming down the dirt driveway and glanced outside the door to see who was coming. He stood in his blue nylon shorts, cowboy hat and boots, noticing a minivan pull into the driveway. Watching the dust cloud slowly dissipate, he wondered, *What are they doing here? They're obviously lost!*

As the minivan turned, he saw the government license plate and two men wearing the familiar Marine campaign covers. The feeling of dread hit him like a lightning bolt. The Marines got out of the vehicle and turned toward him. He shot through the door of the barn, approaching them in long strides, yelling, "IS HE DEAD OR INJURED?"

"Sir," began the first sergeant.

"You know I'm a Marine. Give it to me straight! IS HE DEAD?" he screamed at them.

Both the gunnery sergeant and the first sergeant nodded their heads. Steve turned without saying a word and walked back into the barn. He began throwing equipment he could not possibly lift under normal conditions. He was lost in his anger when suddenly he thought of Brittney. *You need to get your shit together and deal with these men, then call Brittney.*

He took a deep breath, went back outside, and saw the two Marines standing where he left them. He calmly said, "You two may as well come inside, so we can get this over."

"Yes, Mr. Hogan," the first sergeant replied.

The two men followed Steve into the house. When they entered the front door into the dining room, they saw a boat load of guns spread out on the table and rifles leaning against the wall. *Holy shit!* thought the gunnery sergeant.

"Would you like a drink of water?" asked Steve, with an eerie calmness.

"Sure, Mr. Hogan," answered the first sergeant with a bead of sweat trickling down his forehead.

"You can call me Steve, gentlemen," he replied and walked around the table through the door of the kitchen. They heard him opening the refrigerator door and rummaging in the drawers.

"Should we be worried?" whispered the gunny to the first sergeant.

"I think he's okay, but be ready in case he decides to take our heads off when he comes back," suggested the first sergeant.

The gunny let out a nervous chuckle and was relieved when Steve came back *only* carrying two bottles of water. He handed each one a bottle and moved the guns off the dining room table, taking them into the adjacent living room. Then, they all sat down at the table.

They had him sign papers and read the incident report, stating H.D. was killed in action in the Helmand Province at 8:00 a.m. by a single gunshot to the head by small arms fire. They told him what the arrangements were to fly his body into the Dover Air Force Base. Just as they were they were to wrap up, Steve's cell phone rang. It was Brittney. Steve said, "Excuse me, I need to answer this call." He stepped outside on his front deck and could hear Brittney screaming on the other end....

That same morning, Brittany woke up in the morning excited. Her husband had been deployed for just a little over six months now. He was close to finishing his last mission in Sangin and would be home soon. She had spent the last week preparing for his homecoming. His favorite beer was stocked in the mini fridge in his new 'man cave'. She even saved all the weekend newspapers for him to read up on everything he missed in town while he was gone.

Brittney left home to meet with a client to plan a wedding. That was the fifth wedding she had booked that morning. She couldn't wait to tell Hunter how her career was taking off. He would be so proud of her. She knew the news would have to wait two or three more days, because he couldn't contact her on this last mission. She was scared for him, but hopeful. He had made it this far and it would only be a few more days before he would be coming home.

After she booked the wedding, she called Tara to see if she wanted to go celebrate. They decided to drive to Raleigh. The two-and-a-half-hour drive was spent talking instead of listening to music. They were planning for when Hunter came home and finally having a genuine wedding. Brittney told her sister they wanted to try for another baby.

She checked her phone every two seconds, just to make sure she didn't miss his call. When she looked on Facebook, she saw that his platoon was in "River City". It is a military term they use when there has been a casualty and all communication has been cut off. They don't want families finding out about the casualty from social media before hearing about it from the military first. She didn't think a whole lot about it and continued her conversation with her sister.

Brittney and Tara finally got to Raleigh and decided to eat at the Cheesecake Factory. She ordered her favorite- chicken and biscuits. After she took a couple of bites of food, her cell phone rang. She didn't recognize the number and thought for a second it might be Hunter. Then, she remembered the satellite phone always had a Hawaii area code. This one didn't.

She had so many thoughts racing through her mind: *Maybe it's*

Hunter and the area code is just different? No, he's on a mission and said he wouldn't be in contact for two or three days. Maybe he got done early? Then it hit her.

She remembered something a fellow military wife told her a few months ago. She said, "When your loved one is killed in battle, Marines go to your house to tell you. If you're not home or at the address listed on your paperwork, they call you." From that moment, even before she answered the phone, she knew.

Brittney glanced at Tara with a concerned look as she answered her phone. "Hello, is Mrs. Hogan there?" asked the man, who was not Hunter. He said his name, but she couldn't hear it. All she heard was "lieutenant" and that's all it took. She leaped out of the booth and ran outside.

The man asked her where she was. Brittney couldn't talk at that point. Her brain wasn't working right; she was in shock. She didn't know where she was. She fell to the ground, crying hysterically. The lieutenant kept asking her where she was, because he was coming to her. He told her to stay where she was and he would be there.

Brittney hung up on him and didn't even remember doing it. Tara ran outside to find her. There were several strangers around her trying to figure out why she was screaming, but no words could come out of her mouth.

She had always heard about people having strange feelings or premonitions when someone close to them passes away. Even though she hadn't heard the words come out of anyone's mouth yet, she knew her husband had been killed. Tara helped pull her up off the ground as she tried to explain what the man on the phone was saying to her.

A very nice man at the mall came up to them and tried to calm her down. He told her, "Don't worry. He could just be injured. Even if he's just injured, they can't tell you over the phone. They have to tell you in person."

Instinctively, Brittney hit the speed dial for Steve's cell phone number. He said, "Brittney?" and she could hear him crying.

"TELL ME WHAT HAPPENED!" she screamed into the phone. "They didn't tell you?" he asked and there was silence for a second. "BABY, HE'S DEAD!" he managed to get out as he sobbed into the phone. Those words hit her like a ton of bricks and would echo in her mind for as long as she lived. She collapsed to the ground like a rag doll. All of the life was sucked right out of her. Everyone outside the restaurant was staring at them.

Tara grabbed Brittney's phone and told Steve she was with Brittney. He told Tara to go to their mom's house and he would call them there later. Tara was crying but found the strength to pick Brittney up off the ground, get them both to the car, and drive to their mother's house an hour and a half away. It was the longest car ride of their lives.

Brittney called her mom to tell her the news. Kristie couldn't understand a word she was saying. She thought she was laughing, because she was so hysterical. "What, Brittney? I can't understand you," she said.

She finally was able to say the words clearly for the first time, "Hunter is dead!" Kristie burst into uncontrollable tears and denied it, "No. They're mistaken. He's not dead!" It was even more heartbreaking to hear her mom's reaction. Hunter was her mom's first son. She had three girls; so, when Hunter came along, she took to him like he was her own. She loved him more than Brittney could explain. He confided in her when they fought and shared so many unforgettable memories with her. Her mom's disbelief tore her in half.

"I'm on my way to your house," she told her mom, sobbing again and hung up the phone. Next, she called her dad. When he answered the phone, he was already crying. "Dad, Hunter's dead!" she screamed into the phone.

"I know, honey. Steve just called us," her dad replied. He was sobbing and she was sobbing on the phone. Her dad told her he loved her and would see her soon. Then, she called her best friends who lived near them. They both also thought she was laughing, until they realized what she was saying. "Tell me where you are," they pleaded. She told them she was going to her mom's house and they said they'd meet her there...

Meanwhile in Nebraska, Steve put down his phone on the deck table and stormed through the front door. His eyes were burning with rage. "YOU GUYS FUCKED UP!" he yelled at the two Marines.

"WHAT?" they both replied in unison, shocked at the outburst.

"That was Brittney. I just had to tell my son's wife he's dead!"

The first sergeant immediately pulled out his cell phone and bolted out the door to find out what happened. The family members were supposed to have been given the news at the exact same time to avoid this very thing. The sergeant was furious and could be heard yelling into the phone.

"I'm so sorry, Steve," apologized the gunny as he grabbed the papers off the table, stuffed them into a briefcase, and walked out the door. Steve sat down in a chair and went completely numb. A feeling that would last for a very long time.

When Tara pulled up to her mom's house, Brittney opened the door to the car, took two short steps, and fell to her knees. Her family ran out to her and wrapped their arms around her. They were all huddled on the ground, crying and screaming in the parking lot. Everyone in the neighborhood came out of their houses to see what the commotion was all about.

They didn't care one bit. Nothing else existed but them and the incredible, undeniable void they all felt. Steve called his parents and told them to go to Brittney's mom's house. When Brittney saw them, her heart hurt ten times worse, knowing they'd just lost their grandson.

Right after they got there, the Marines showed up. Several were there, including a chaplain and the lieutenant that called her on the phone. Everyone stood up when they saw them get out of the sedan. The lieutenant walked up to them and asked, "Which one of you is Mrs. Hunter Hogan?"

Brittney stepped forward and said, "I am." He told her what she already knew, but she couldn't figure out how they got her mom's address. "Mrs. Hogan, we regret to inform you that your husband, Hunter Hogan, was killed in action this morning at 8:00 a.m. in Helmand Province, Afghanistan." They told her that she had some paperwork to go through and asked if they could come in.

The Marines came in and they went over the legalities of what was going to happen. Brittney signed several papers but couldn't tell you what they were afterward. They told her the next step was to go to Dover, Delaware and that's where they would receive his body. The plane would be there on the evening of June 26th.

Her friends, Rebekah and Jordyn, pulled up in a car. Brittney saw them through the window and went outside to greet them. Rebekah got out of the car and said, "Brittney, I'm so sorry, but you have to get in my car and listen to this song."

"I don't want to listen to a song!" Brittney was screaming and crying at the same time.

"No, you have to. I've never heard it before, but it's on my iPod on shuffle and it played four times on my way over here. I think Hunter wants you to hear it!" So, Brittney got in the car and Rebekah played the song:

> *"But I will see you again*
> *I will see you again a long time from now*
> *And there goes my life*
> *Passing by with every departing flight*
> *And it's been so hard*
> *So much time so far apart*
> *And she walks the night*
> *How many hearts will die tonight*
> *And when things have changed*
> *I guess I'll find out in seventeen days*
> *But I will see you again*
> *I will see you again a long time from now"*

Both Brittney and Rebekah were crying hysterically. Brittney asked her what the name of the song was. She said, "Hello, I'm in Delaware by Dallas Green." Brittney began crying even harder and Rebekah couldn't understand why. "Are you sure that's the name?" asked Brittney.

"Yes, that's the name," she assured her.

Brittney couldn't believe her ears. It was definitely Hunter trying to speak to her. Seventeen was their number and so was twenty-three. When she and Hunter got married, Brittney tattooed a 17 on her foot for his birthday, and he tattooed a 23 on his arm for her birthday.

Brittney went back inside and told the family about the song and what the song said. Suddenly, she stopped talking and was standing there frozen. Everyone looked at her extremely concerned. It wasn't until then that she thought about that day's date. *Oh my God, Hunter died on the 23rd!* she realized and burst into more tears. The chaplain tried to comfort her, but it was no use. The Marines gave the family their condolences, took their papers, and left.

Rebekah handed her a bottle of Jack Daniels that they had picked up on the way for her. It was Brittney and Hunter's drink. Brittney opened it and started drinking. She thought about the words of the song she just heard. It was 100% Hunter immediately trying to connect with her. It gave her the smallest semblance of comfort. But, at the same time, she couldn't feel much of anything except deep pain in her stomach that wouldn't go away. It didn't go away for months.

In a blink of an eye, her whole life had changed. Everyone's lives changed. He was an amazing man. Even though he was only twenty-one, he had the oldest soul you'd ever meet. He was everyone's best friend. He was the toughest, meanest cowboy, besides his dad.

But, those who knew him well knew a different side to him. He was the most loving, caring, honest man there was. He touched so many people's lives. He lived a life fuller than most fifty-year-old's have. It just didn't make sense. She never thought in a million years that he wouldn't come back home. She wasn't prepared to be a widow at twenty-one.

After Hunter died, Brittney didn't know how to go on living without him there. She woke up every morning with a bottle of Jack Daniels next to her. She drank to numb the pain and make it through the day. It took her a long time to see what Hunter did for her, her family, and his country. It was hard for her not to be selfish and have him with her. All he wanted to do was join the Marine Corps and fight for his country. That's what he did.

He is a hero. It's because of people like him who are willing to lay down their life for our country that we are able to live free and safe. Brittney never truly knew what it meant to be patriotic until she met him.

She didn't go back to their house in New Bern for a long time. The idea of being in the place she had spent the last year making so many unforgettable memories with Hunter was unbearable. So, instead she sent her sister to get Hank and a bag of clothes for her. Tara brought them back to their mom's house and the next morning they were off to Dover to receive Hunter's body. They got a hotel room to spend the night and wait for Steve to arrive.

Brittney stayed up all night waiting for him on the couch in the lobby of the hotel. She wasn't sure what kind of shape he would be in. She couldn't imagine the heartache he was feeling losing his only son. She wished she could make it all better but couldn't do anything.

Steve finally arrived at the hotel around midnight. She heard him call out her name and got up off the couch. When they saw one another, they ran to each other, hugged, and cried for a good ten minutes. As awful as it was, there was a sense of relief knowing they had each other to go through this. He was so strong. A true Marine.

The next morning, they met Gino Mills' family. They had received Gino's body the night before. Brittney never met Gino before Hunter deployed, but hearing the stories about him, she got the sense they were friends. It was so hard to meet them. She couldn't do it without the help of four Jack and Cokes.

That night, they went to the landing strip at the Dover Air Force Base to receive his body. Brittney had more alcohol to deal with that. When the plane landed at 1:15 a.m. on June 27th, a couple of Marines walked them out to the tarmac and they stood and waited. Hunter's mom, Tracy, was there, too. Brittney walked over to her and thanked her for giving birth to her husband. She thanked Brittney for loving her son. That was the only time she had spoken to her.

She walked back over and stood next to Steve and her family. The plane's cargo hold door slowly opened and came to the ground. Draped over the casket was the American flag. Inside the plane three other caskets could be seen. Other families were waiting outside the airport to receive loved ones.

A group of eight Marines marched up to the plane. In a series of slow, formal motions they approached the casket at the bottom of the ramp. They stopped to salute their comrade and boarded the plane to lift up the casket. Then, the Marines slowly carried it down the ramp and headed toward a white truck resembling a bread truck. They passed between two more rows of Marines who saluted the fallen Marine.

It was something you had only seen in movies and wished you'd never see in real life. For Brittney, it was like a dream. Steve looked up in the sky and could see three more planes circling the airport full of coffins- flag-draped coffins, one after the other. He turned to Brittney and said, "You know, he turned down four full-ride scholarships to college for rodeo. When we get back to Nebraska, let's see about setting up a scholarship. In lieu of flowers, people could donate to the scholarship. Someone else's kid is going to get a chance to go to college for the rodeo."

Brittney nodded in agreement. All she could think of was the words from the song, *There goes my life, passing by with every departing flight.* She was holding a new bottle of Jack Daniels, took a sip out of it, and wiped her mouth with the back of her hand. She thought she must have looked insane- she didn't have any makeup on and was walking around like a zombie, carrying a bottle of whiskey.

She didn't give a shit what other people thought. She couldn't look at herself in the mirror and felt completely empty inside. Seeing the casket made her feel ten times worse, because now it was real. She took another gulp from the bottle.

"If we only get a hundred bucks, I'll throw in another four hundred or nine hundred to give $1,000 scholarships in his name," Steve added. He looked at Brittney and saw her pale face. His heart ached for her, and he knew he was completely helpless to take her pain away. He was barely holding on himself.

It took every ounce of willpower he had left to keep from grabbing that whiskey from Brittney and drinking the whole damn bottle himself. Instead, he just reached out and grabbed her hand. His touch helped snap her out of her daze. She said, "I think the scholarship is a great idea, Pap!"

As they watched the Marines slowly and meticulously approach them, Brittney ran out to them and draped herself over the top of the casket. Tears fell onto the crisp, clean flag. The Marines carrying the casket stood motionless, eyes facing forward. Even though you couldn't see it from their faces, inside they felt the sadness of the young widow and the loss of one of their own.

Brittney didn't want to let go. Steve walked up to her and peeled her off. "Honey, they need to take him now," he said softly. Brittney let go and stood up, wiping the tears from her eyes.

As she watched the men put the casket in the truck and close the doors, Steve sent a simple text to all of his close friends saying "*My boy is home.*" For those who received it, it broke their hearts. They would never forget reading those words on their phone.

The next morning, one of his coworkers with Diamond E Bucking Bulls, Echo Sharkey, wrote a poem using that title. She included a picture of H.D. on it. The poem would later be used in a packet for other families receiving their beloved at the Dover Air Force Base.

When Brittney got back to her mom's house, she made arrangements to sell the house and move to Nebraska for a little while. Being around Steve gave her comfort. Besides herself, Hunter was closest to his dad. Father and son were so much alike. By being near Steve, it was like having Hunter there with her. They needed each other to deal with their loss.

On the last day of packing, Tara was cleaning out the freezer while Brittney was putting dishes in a box. She remembered what Hunter put in there. "Oh my gosh, don't forget our wishes!" she shouted to Tara. She wanted to read them. She grabbed the baggie out of the freezer, opened the first one, unfolded it, and saw what she wrote: *to get pregnant*. Then, she opened Hunter's. It took her breath away. He wrote *to have a baby*. She couldn't believe it! Tara smiled and hugged her sister. Brittney smiled with tears running down her cheeks. They did get their wish, but she lost them both.

Life is hard. We all go through pain and suffering. It took a long time, but Brittney learned pain isn't what defines a person; it is how we deal with it that defines us and builds our character. Even though she felt life was over at the time, she would discover in a few short years that life was just beginning for her. She was capable of accomplishing incredible things that would end up having a positive impact on many other people's lives.

21 AT LAST

Steve woke up well before dawn on the morning of July 6th. He barely slept that night, dreading the day ahead of him and anticipating the longest and worst day of his life. Burying his son was not what he should be doing today, but that was exactly what he had to do.

After a quick shower to wake himself up and a shave, he put on a white long-sleeved dress shirt and his Wrangler jeans. He slid H.D.'s Marine Corps ring on his finger and a silver chain with H.D.'s dog tag on it around his neck and glanced in the mirror. He barely recognized the man staring back- he had lost weight and looked like he'd aged ten years. *Good enough!* he thought and went quietly downstairs to the kitchen.

In the dining room, he saw Hank lying on the floor with his chin on H.D.'s cowboy boot. He didn't think it was possible for his heart to hurt anymore, but it did. Steve walked into the kitchen and poured himself a cup of hot, black coffee. He sipped it, listening to the rest of his company begin to stir upstairs. He had a full house with his girlfriend, Shelley, her three kids, and Brittney there for the funeral.

He peeked into the refrigerator to see if there was something to eat- more out of habit than want. Deciding he wasn't hungry, he closed the door. Not ready to talk to anyone just yet, he went outside and sat on the deck, watching the sun come up over the cornfield. It was going to be a hot, sunny Nebraska day.

Brittney came outside to check on him, wearing black lounge pants and one of H.D.'s olive Marine Corps t-shirts. She was also dreading the day. Without saying a word, she sat on a stool beside him and watched the sunrise with him.

The funeral was already planned out. Brittney had a difficult time making the final decisions; but with the help of Steve and their Casualty Assistance Calls Officer, Jesse, she was able to get through the legal process and preparations. It took her a week and a half to decide whether or not they would have an open casket or closed casket. There was a chance they couldn't have an open casket because of the way he was killed. She and Steve decided he would go in first and look at H.D. at the funeral home. If he thought he was viewable, he would come and get her.

After the sun rose further above the horizon and began streaming warm rays onto the countryside, Brittney announced, "Well, I guess I'll go get dressed, so we can do this, Pap!" Steve just nodded as she patted his back gently, stood up, and walked back inside the house.

He got up from his stool, strolled out to his truck, and took a drive down the gravel road. He didn't know where he was going or what he was doing. He kept driving down one road, then another, and another. Completely void of all feeling, he wasn't paying any attention to the road. Suddenly, an image of H.D. appeared out of nowhere right in front of him.

Steve slammed on the brakes and blinked his eyes to be sure he was awake and hadn't fallen asleep at the wheel. H.D. was standing before him in his military combat gear looking straight at him. He stared at his son, speechless. H.D. flashed him one of his notorious grins, waved, walked across the road, and disappeared into the cornfield to the right.

He couldn't believe what he saw, but he knew it was H.D. It was his son's way of saying, "It's going to be okay, Dad. I'm okay."

Steve sat a moment in his truck in the middle of the road and let a feeling of peace come over him. Then, he pushed his foot on the accelerator and drove back home. By the time he arrived to the house, Brittney was dressed. The sight of her took his breath away.

She was wearing a black dress with her black hair piled up into a 1960's-style beehive, because Hunter loved that on her. Brittney resembled the beauty and elegance of Jackie Kennedy Onassis. There was no doubt why his son fell in love with her. Steve smiled and gave her a big hug.

"Don't mess up my hair. I worked hard on this!" Brittney scolded him, pouting her lips teasingly.

"Are you ready to go?" Steve asked her.

"As ready as I'm going to be," she replied with a slight frown and grabbed her purse off the dining room table.

"Shell, we're leaving to the airport!" Steve shouted upstairs to Shelley.

"Okay. We're almost ready. We'll meet you there!" she yelled back down to him.

Steve and Brittney got into his truck and drove to the York Municipal Airport. They were the first ones to arrive. The airplane was due to land in half an hour. The two stood outside on the tarmac and watched as their family and friends came, along with the hearse from the mortuary and several Marines from the Engineer Maintenance Company of Omaha.

The Marines were to be used as casket bearers and escorts. They were dressed in their formal blue jacket and white or red-striped, blue pants, wearing a white belt and white cap. Moments after the Marines came, Steve heard the loud rumble of motorcycles approaching from the highway. Soon, they came into view and rolled into the parking lot of the airport- one right after another as far as he could see.

Steve was astonished at the sheer number of them. The Nebraska Patriot Guard had arrived in full force. At final count, there were 188 male and female riders wearing blue jeans and leather vests. Steve walked to where they were parked, greeted them, and shook every one of their hands. He was overwhelmed at their show of support and words of encouragement.

While the Patriot Guard was getting into place, the hum of an airplane could be heard above them. A small charter plane came into view in the sky, circled around, landed, taxied down the runway, and skidded to a stop before them. The cargo door rose up on the left side of the plane, and the two pilots became visible inside the doorway. They lowered a stand onto the ground and moved a flag-draped oak coffin into sight.

After departing the plane, the pilots stood on either side of the door holding their right hand over their heart. Seven of the Marines marched up to the plane and saluted their fallen comrade as the coffin was lowered by a lift to the stand. Then, the pilots stepped out of the way as the other Marines escorted family members up to the coffin.

After several minutes of tears and hugs, the family walked back to join the line of people by the hearse. The Patriot Guard members formed a long line, holding full-sized American flags on posts. The remainder of the Marines stood on the other side of the hearse, holding the Marine Corps flag and American flags with H.D.'s family and friends.

The seven Marines lifted the coffin off the stand and slowly marched it to the hearse. After the coffin was loaded and the door closed, Steve and Brittney got into his truck and followed it to the Metz Mortuary in York. They rode in silence amazed at the outpouring of patriotism from the people of York. Most of them didn't even know H.D., because he didn't grow up there. But, they were compelled to honor the young hero anyway.

They passed countless American flags flying from the lampposts for miles down the highway. They saw numerous utility trucks with their aerial lift extended displaying flags. When they approached downtown York, there were hundreds of people lining the streets everywhere they turned holding flags and saluting the fallen Marine.

After the hearse parked in front of the mortuary, the seven

Marines lifted it from the back and carried it inside to the viewing room. Steve and Brittney went inside to join them. "I'll go in first, Brittney. Then, I'll come get you," Steve told her in the hallway.

"Okay," she whispered softly. Despite the makeup she put on that morning, she was as white as a sheet afraid for what she might see. On one hand, she didn't want to regret not seeing Hunter; but on the other hand, she didn't want how he looked now be the way she remembered him for the rest of her life. The minutes Steve was inside the room felt like hours. All she had that morning was a breakfast of whiskey to get her through the day and had to fight the urge to throw it up.

Steve went in and closed the door behind him. After the Marines checked H.D.'s body over to make sure everything was straightened up from the flight and the morticians inspected him, they left the room so he could be alone with his son. The casket was open and Steve stepped up to it, prepared for whatever he was about to see.

When he saw his son, he let out a sigh of relief. The morticians in Dover did a fantastic job on him. He looked like the boy he remembered. However, despite the concealing makeup, Steve knew immediately where the wound was. He knew where the exit hole was, also. The bullet missed the edge of H.D.'s helmet by less than an inch.

Steve stood quietly staring at his son as a tear snuck from his right eye. He blinked it back, not about to let his wall down yet. "You were the best son a father could ask for. I am so proud of you, H.D. I love you," he whispered even though he was the only one in the room. He wished he could hear his boy say those three little words back to him one more time.

With a heavy heart, he walked back out of the room to get Brittney. "It's okay. You can see him," he promised her. Brittney was still scared, but trusted Steve's instinct. He held her hand as he walked her up to the casket. She approached the side and the first thing she saw was his long, black eyelashes sticking out over the casket. Her legs instantly gave way and she fell to her knees sobbing, "I can't do it! I can't look at him!"

"Yes, you can!" Steve replied as he grabbed her elbows and picked her up off the floor. She stood up and slowly walked over to H.D. She let out a sigh of relief and put her hand on her heart when she saw him. He still looked like the man she fell in love with. He was extremely handsome in his dress blues and cap. The image of him kissing her at the Marine Corps ball flashed in her mind.

Brittney reached into her purse, took out a love letter she wrote for Hunter, and stuffed it in his uniform pocket. She felt like she had been kicked in the stomach and her heart shattered in a million pieces. Tears flowed endlessly from her eyes. It was her worst fear. It wasn't reality until that moment. Seeing him made it true. There was no coming back from this. Her husband was gone forever!

Steve stepped back out into the hallway to get his parents and brought them in to say their goodbyes. After they had a few moments alone, he went back out to escort close friends and family, a few at a time, to see H.D. Only selective family and friends were allowed to see the open casket. After a while, Brittney couldn't withstand the unbearable sadness anymore and collapsed onto the floor.

Steve ordered the Marines to keep people away from the room. They stood firm outside the door in a tall, impressive line forming a barricade. They were the first thing you saw when you entered the building. No one could get past them without Steve's okay.

Everything was happening so fast, Steve kept his composure and comforted Brittney. He decided they had enough and went to his sister's house to stay for a few hours until the funeral at the church. More people poured into the funeral home and paid their respects with the casket closed and the Marines there to greet them. After the viewing was over, the hearse took the coffin to the church with the help of the Marines.

When it was time to leave his sister's house for the church, Steve rode in the car with his parents and Brittney. The rest of the family followed in their cars. They arrived at the St. Joseph's Catholic

Church and saw the sidewalk all around it completely lined with the Patriot Guard holding the full-sized American flags. The Marines stood along the other side of the sidewalk.

The family was escorted into two classrooms in the school section to have some privacy. Steve wandered through the church, greeting people and thanking them for coming. There were so many faces, he couldn't remember talking to most of them afterward. It was all a blur of commotion.

Steve told the Marines to keep the reporters away from the family, which they did. He was taken to the basement and walked through a door. There were numerous people lined up all the way down the hall. He met with dignitaries who came to pay their respects and gave a short interview to the reporters. Talking to so many people was the last thing he wanted to do. He really wished he could go somewhere in the middle of a field, scream at the top of his lungs, and shoot off a shitload of ammo, but he couldn't. He had to keep it together for a little while longer for his family and for Brittney.

When it was getting close to the time of the funeral service to begin, Steve went back to the classrooms to gather his family. They walked through the long hallway and into the atrium. They passed by the oak coffin with H.D.'s cowboy hat resting on top and walked into the sanctuary. Steve and Brittney sat in the front pew along with his sister, brother, and parents.

The reverend greeted the audience, read scripture from the Bible, said a prayer for the family, and read H.D.'s obituary statement. Afterward, Brittney was planning on singing a song, but Steve wasn't sure she could do it. He had a signal arranged with the mortician. When it was time for her to sing, the mortician nodded to Steve. "It's time for your song," he whispered to Brittney. She started crying. "It's up to you. You don't have to do this," he told her.

"No, I'm going to do it!" she asserted. She dried the tears from her eyes and stood up. A Marine friend of H.D.'s led her up to the altar. You could have heard a pin drop when she opened her mouth and sang, "*At last. My love has come along. My lonely days are over. And life is like a song...*" It was the song Hunter loved for Brittney to sing. Everyone was amazed at the grace of Brittney as she sang. Her voice rang out with the richness and beauty matched by none other than Etta James herself. Not a dry eye remained in the church by the time she finished the song.

Brittney sat back down on the pew and put her head on Steve's shoulder. He squeezed her shoulder tightly and said, "You were amazing. H.D. would've been so proud!" Her tears resumed their flow once again as she listened to Rachel sing "The Dance". The reverend stepped back up to the altar and read a final piece of scripture, concluding the service. Then, everyone went outside to watch the Marines load the casket into a horse-drawn wagon.

A police car escorted the funeral procession to the cemetery. Leading the front was Taylor Rudd on a white horse from Lubbock, Texas with twenty-nine other cowboys on horses. One lone Marine rode in the back of the wagon with the casket along with the two drivers in front. Following the wagon, was a man walking a horse with H.D.'s cowboy hat resting on the saddle.

Steve and his family led the rest of the vehicles and motorcycles down East Avenue to East 2nd Street and down Blackburn Avenue. He watched with pride as the people of York, young and old, were standing holding flags down each road and turn. It seemed as if every single resident of York was present on the sidewalk that day. Children were innocently smiling and waving proudly at the procession. Veterans, wearing their caps, stood with tears in their eyes saluting the wagon passing by, knowing far too well the sacrifice laid before them.

When the car turned left on Nobes Road, a fire truck was stationed on the other side with its tall ladder extended, displaying an enormous American flag. More people stood on the sidewalk for almost the entire half mile to the cemetery. Once the procession parked and the congregation stood in place, the seven Marines lifted the casket from the wagon and placed it on the platform over the grave.

Steve sat in the front row under the canopy providing shade for the immediate family. Shelley was on his left and Brittney was on his right side. His parents sat on the other side of Brittney. Brittney sat silently, recalling the day she and Hunter were standing in the yard of his Aunt Stacy's house a little over a year ago. He put his arm around her, pointed across the field, and said, "See those little dots over there in that field?"

"Yeah," Brittney answered, looking at the dots he was referring to.

"That's the family cemetery. I want us to be buried there," he informed her.

She didn't think it would happen this soon. More tears came as she listened to the reverend read scripture from the Bible and watched him sprinkle holy water over the ground. A hymnal was sung with those in the crowd who knew the words.

Next, Taylor Rudd got off his white horse, grabbed the saddle horn and rein, and pulled it downward. The horse knelt on its front legs and quickly lay on its left side on the ground. Taylor knelt beside it on one knee, took off his cowboy hat, and said a prayer as the horse remained completely still. After the prayer, Taylor pulled up on the rein and climbed upon the saddle as the animal rose. It was an unforgettable sight.

Then, the Marines lifted the American flag off the coffin and stood holding it as the 21-gun salute was performed. The gunshots rang out, startling the white horse slightly. It neighed and turned in circles but remained calm. Following the salute, "Taps" was played on a bugle with a second bugler providing an echo. The haunting sound sent chills down Steve's spine.

While the flag was being folded slowly and methodically, the *nneeaoowww!* of a small airplane could be heard above. Steve and Brittney looked up and watched a P-51 Mustang from WWII pass over from the south, turn around, came back toward the north, complete a barrel roll over the cemetery, and disappear as quickly as it came. The Marines finished folding the flag and one stood in front of Brittney with it. He knelt down on one knee and handed it to her simultaneously with the other Marines who presented a flag to Steve, his parents, and siblings. Lastly, the reverend said his final words to complete the funeral. After the family said their last farewell to H.D., they left the cemetery.

A reception for family and friends was held at the Elks Lodge. Chance's R, H.D.'s favorite restaurant in town, catered it. An anonymous donor who attended the funeral picked up the entire tab out of the kindness of his or her heart. Some of H.D.'s Marine friends came, except the ones he was deployed with, because they were still in Afghanistan. They listened to H.D.'s favorite songs. Brittney sang some of them with his buddies at the top of their lungs and they cried all night.

The following day, everyone had gone home. Brittney settled into Hunter's room at Steve's house. She was glad everyone left, because she was beyond exhausted. She had never felt so tired and alone in her life. A horrible feeling rushed over her and she almost passed out.

It was the first time in her life she had considered suicide. She didn't care whether she lived or died. Then, she thought about her family and Steve. She couldn't bear to cause them anymore pain and knew she would get through this somehow. The thought of how long it would take scared her; and she didn't know how to handle it, so she drank... a lot.

A couple of nights later, she had a dream. Hunter called her from Heaven. The phone rang with his ringtone. When she picked it up, his picture popped up and the phone displayed "Husband calling." She answered the phone in complete disbelief and said, "Hunter?"

"Hi, Baby! I'm so sorry I had to go. I love you so much!" he replied.

"Hunter, how are you calling me?" she asked. "How are you using the phone?"

"Baby, I'm Hunter. I do whatever I want!" Brittney laughed and said, "I love you and miss you so much!"

"Baby, it's so beautiful here. I can't wait for you to see it!" he told her. She could hear the pure joy in his voice. She woke up crying uncontrollably. The phone call sounded distorted, as if it really did come from Heaven. She loved the dream. Somehow, it made her feel much better. She just needed to know he could see her and that he wasn't completely gone.

After H.D.'s headstone was finished, Steve, Brittney, and Hank went to the gravesite. Steve parked on the gravel drive in front of the grave. He opened the truck door, and Hank hopped out. Hank went ahead of them and began sniffing around the gravestones. When he came to H.D.'s headstone, he made a complete circle around it and lay down on top of the newly grown grass.

Somehow, Hank knew his master was beneath him. Steve and Brittney walked around to the back of the headstone to look at it. He pulled out a bottle of Jack Daniels and they drank a toast to H.D. as they read his final words to them and those who come to visit. His epitaph said:

"To all you friends, As you pass by
What you are now, So once was I
What I am now, So you must be
Prepare for death, And follow me."

"My Boy Is Home" *by Echo Sharkey*

The pride you must have felt, when you saw him in his dress blues
He'd followed in your footsteps and wanted to be just like you.
The war was still a world away, it was comforting to know
You could sleep in peace at night and say,
"My boy is home."

The fear you must have felt, the day that he deployed
After all this man going into battle was still your little boy.
Praying day and night for the moment to finally come
When you could see him face to face and say,
"My boy is home."

The pain you must have felt, when they came to you that day
No words could bring you comfort, there was nothing left to say.
Your heart was shattered and empty, in a hell you'd never known
When you realized the chance would never come to say,
"My boy is home."

The confusion you must have felt when his body arrived that night
Back on American soil, and far away from the fight.
A bittersweet reunion between a father and his son;
This wasn't how you wanted to say at last,
"My boy is home."

The peace you must have felt when he was laid to rest
A fallen hero who gave his all, he died the most honorable death.
Knowing he sits at the right hand of God, and will never again be alone
You can rest easy at night again and say,
"My boy is home."

In loving memory of LCpl Hunter "HD" Hogan

POSTFACE

Hunter Hogan was awarded the Purple Heart. His father, Steve, still lives in Nebraska with his family. He and Brittney did establish the HD Hogan Memorial Rodeo Scholarship Fund renamed The Hunter HD Hogan Foundation to give out rodeo scholarships and money to nonprofit organizations that support Veterans. The nonprofit foundation conducts an annual rifle sale, bull ride, golf scramble, or other events to raise money. Every year, they have been able to give five to seven $1,000 scholarships to students seeking a rodeo scholarship for college.

Hank passed away this year in April, shortly after this story was completed. Gary Plumer, sadly and unexpectedly, passed away in 2014. The Jackson County Rodeo held one more rodeo that year to honor H.D. and Gary. Chase tore down the arena shortly after and continues to farm in Jackson County today. H.D.'s hometown, Brownstown, added the honorary name HD Hogan Way to Walnut Street, located by the middle school.

Brittney and her family moved back to California. She went through a difficult two years struggling with depression. Then, in early 2014, she began running with her cousin. Even though she was never really athletic or liked running, it helped calm her down and reduced her anxiety. Running gave her a time to think. She realized, "Chasing my problems away with alcohol only made them worse. I had to reflect on everything that had happened to move on and heal."

She started trying different workouts and stayed moving every day. Fitness inspired her to start her own company, Virago Fitness, and she was able to fulfill her lifelong dream of owning her own business. She went to college and earned her bachelor's degree in business, focusing on small business and entrepreneurship from the University of Phoenix. Brittney runs the company herself, selling online clothing produced at a facility in Los Angeles straight to the customer. She donates part of her proceeds to the Hunter HD Hogan Foundation and other organizations.

A portion of the sales of this book will be given to the scholarship fund. For more information on the scholarship, the website is www.circlehdrodeo.org and for information on Virago Fitness, visit www.virago-fitness.com. (June 2018)

www.patsovernllc.com

Hunter riding his horse

Showing off his "Lane Frost" outfit

Giving his serious cowboy look!

Hunter by name was truly a hunter!

Chase Plumer and Hunter Hogan as teenagers

Hunter and Chase on the Plumer farm

Hunter on saddle bronc ride 2008

H.D. with his horse Wrangler   Man could he ride!

H.D. riding at an IHSRA event in 2007

Steve and Hunter Hogan

H.D. shortly after he joined the Marines

Exchanging Marine Corps rings   What a beast!

Hunter and his wife, Brittney

They loved with a love that was more than love!

H.D. could find a horse anywhere!

LCpl. Hunter Hogan and
LCpl. Eugene "Gino"
Mills, Jr.   (June 2012)

Hunter "HD" Hogan was proud to be a Marine!

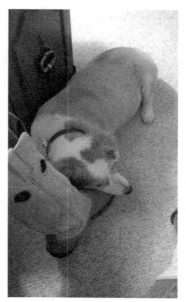

Hank lying on H.D.'s boot

I took this picture of Hank for the cover June 2017

363 7984

39403514R00146

Made in the USA
Middletown, DE
17 March 2019